A Plain Vanilla Murder

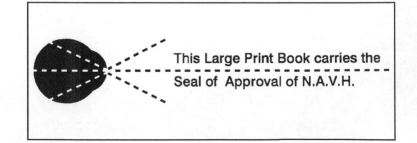

This Large Print Book carries the
Seal of Approval of N.A.V.H.

A PLAIN VANILLA MURDER

SUSAN WITTIG ALBERT

THORNDIKE PRESS
A part of Gale, a Cengage Company

Farmington Hills, Mich • San Francisco • New York • Waterville, Maine
Meriden, Conn • Mason, Ohio • Chicago

LIBRARY OF CONGRESS CIP DATA ON FILE.
CATALOGUING IN PUBLICATION FOR THIS BOOK
IS AVAILABLE FROM THE LIBRARY OF CONGRESS

ISBN-13: 978-1-4328-6529-0 (hardcover alk. paper)

Published in 2019 by arrangement with Levine/Greenberg Literary Agency, Inc.

Printed in Mexico
1 2 3 4 5 6 7 23 22 21 20 19

For vanilla lovers everywhere.
You have *extraordinarily* good taste.

Plain vanilla is an adjective describing the simplest version of something, without any optional extras, basic or ordinary. In analogy with the common ice cream flavor vanilla, which became widely and cheaply available with the development of artificial vanillin flavor.

Wikipedia

PROLOGUE

For the love of vanilla as a flavoring and as a perfume, and for its qualities as an aphrodisiac, medicinal herb, and healing aromatic, vanilla has been sought after and fought over ever since its discovery perhaps a millennium ago, in the rain forests of the Americas.

Patricia Rain
Vanilla: The Cultural History of the World's Favorite Flavor and Fragrance

The nightmare happens on a bright, warm December midday, in a lush tropical forest. The red Ford van carrying the guide, the professor, and six students is following a rickety old truck piled high with burlap bags of green vanilla pods, down a steep, zigzagging mountain road.

It is the third day of the field trip, and the group from Central Texas State University is on its way through the Sierra Madre

Mountains. In the van: the professor, two male students (Logan Gardner and Archie Adcock), three female students (Beth Craig, Patty Harris, and Shelley Harmon), and their guide, Juan Aguado. The class has been studying the vanilla orchid (*Vanilla planifolia*), the most widely used and — after saffron — the second most expensive spice in the world. They have come to Mexico to see the mountain rainforest where the vanilla orchid was cultivated for centuries before Cortez arrived and took it back to Europe, along with chocolate and boatloads of gold and silver. Mexican vanilla farmers are aiming for a comeback into the market it had once completely dominated, and the students have come to learn about their new production methods.

The group drove from Pecan Springs to San Antonio and caught an Aeromexico flight to Veracruz. From there, sardined into a rented van, they headed for the town of Papantla. Uneasily sandwiched between the modern tourist meccas of the Costa Esmeralda and the ancient Totonac ruins of El Tajin and deep in the heart of the Mexican vanilla-growing region, Papantla was for centuries the hub of vanilla's lucrative international trade and is still remembered as the "city that perfumed the world."

10

The group reaches the bustling market town in early evening. After they check in at the Hotel Provincia, the six of them go to the much recommended Plaza Pardo restaurant. They find a table on the balcony where they can watch the ornately costumed *voladores* perform their ancient flying ritual on the tall pole across the *zócalo*. At the professor's suggestion, they order *pulpo en su tinta* (octopus in its ink), *camarones a la plancha* (grilled shrimp), and *enchilada con mole rojo con cecina* (pan-fried tortillas with red mole sauce and thin-sliced spiced pork). The professor insists on banana cake with vanilla cream frosting for dessert. When it arrives, it is topped with twenty candles for Shelley's birthday. The party is splendid, a celebration to remember always, and the margaritas flow freely.

After dinner, they wander out onto the shadowy square. On this warm and muggy evening, the town is celebrating Día del Niño Perdido, the Day of the Lost Child. From the old stone church that dominates the plaza comes the sound of children's voices, singing familiar carols in an unfamiliar tongue, while thousands of candles flicker in the dark streets. Stalls offer intriguing souvenir crafts made from vanilla:

incense cones, soap and fragrance oils, lip balm and skin creams and perfumes, candles of all sizes and shapes, intricately woven baskets and toys, and raffia-tied bundles of vanilla pods. Shawled women in colorful dress call out to one another as they dart in and out of shops, *vendedores* sing out their wares, children laugh, donkeys' bells clang. As the group separates into couples to wander slowly back to the hotel, the night air is rich with the fragrance of chocolate and sweet with the cinnamon-flavored scent of *conchas* and *polvorones.* Laced over and under and through it all is the romantic, seductive scent of vanilla, the scent of a city's culture. If any of the couples disappear into the warm, fragrant dark, no one asks where they are going. Or why. It is, after all, a night for pleasure, and they are far from home.

The next morning, the students gather in the hotel lobby under an enormous painting of a vanilla orchid blossom, five celadon petals gracefully encircling a daffodil-yellow ruffled flute. The professor introduces them to Juan Aguado, a small, slender man with a bushy black mustache, thin dark brows, and the practiced patter of a carnival barker. Señor Aguado is an official with the Consejo Veracruzano de la Vainilla, the Veracruz Vanilla Council. A passionate supporter of Mexican vanilla ("The *suprema vainilla* in all the world!"), he will be their guide for the next two days.

Armed with cameras, everyone climbs into the van. With the professor at the wheel, they follow a winding road into the foothills of the Sierra Madre, passing barefoot farmers in traditional white cotton tunics and trousers, dark-haired boys bearing baskets of corn on their backs, and patient, plodding donkeys pulling carts heavy with sugar cane and bundled sticks. Large black vultures — *zopilotes* — circle in a dark cloud overhead, and on both sides of the road lie pastures of goats and fat cattle and plantations of papayas, bananas, and mangos. The warm, sunny morning gives way to a warmer afternoon, and the van's air conditioning doesn't work. But the students are dressed for the climate in shorts and T-shirts. If anybody is uncomfortable, nobody speaks of it. If anybody feels a sense of foreboding, perhaps heightened by the circling vultures, they keep it to themselves.

They stop first at a ten-acre modern vanilla plantation experimenting with dense planting techniques — five to eight thousand vines per acre, planted in amended soil and carefully irrigated. In some plots, the vines clamber up the traditional *pichoco* trees, whose light foliage affords just the right amount of shade. In others, they are disciplined like grapevines on bamboo supports and sheltered by shade cloth. In still others, shade cloth is wrapped around the perimeter to turn plots into hothouses. In a few plots, the vines share the sunshine with coffee and orange trees.

At this latitude, the vanilla orchid begins blooming in March. In the jungle, native *Melipona* bees and shiny green orchid bees pollinate the wild vanilla blossoms. But natural pollination is hit-and-miss — and mostly miss. In the plantation, bees are replaced by trained workers who can pollinate up to two thousand blossoms during the few hours the flowers are fertile. The fruit — long, green pods — ripens nine months later, in December.

According to Aguado, these pampered vines are delivering their first harvest a year earlier than traditionally grown plants, and the pods are longer and heavier. "We aim to produce more and better vanilla in a shorter period and at a lower cost," Señor Aguado tells the students. "Mexico is about to reclaim its rightful place in the world market."

The professor, who has done a great deal

14

of research on this subject, clears his throat. "That might be difficult," he remarks drily. "Last year, both Indonesia and Madagascar produced well over three thousand tons of vanilla pods each. Mexico produced — what? Four hundred tons? A small fraction of the global crop."

"Almost five hundred tons, *Señor Profesor,*" Aguado corrects him, but deferentially. With an expansive gesture, he declares, "This year, we expect to double that amount. We have the soil and the climate — and eager workers. Is it not better for them to earn pesos at home than to cross the border to earn American dollars?"

"It is indeed," agrees the professor. "But there are other things to worry about, especially in intensive plantings. Disease, for instance. Are the vanilla cultivars here resistant to *Fusarium oxysporum?*" He turns to the class. "Which is what, guys?"

Shelley Harmon, a pixie-like girl with boy-cut brown hair and large brown eyes, puts up her hand. "It's a pathogenic fungus, isn't it?" she offers tentatively. "It produces root rot."

"And don't forget *Fusarium* wilt," Logan Gardner adds. A tall, muscular graduate student in his thirties, he is working with the professor on a plant breeding project —

15

something rather secret, it seems, for it is never discussed in class. He also helps by making the arrangements for the field trips. "In fact, *Fusarium* poses a grave threat to the world vanilla crop. Which is why we are attempting to develop —"

"Which is why," the professor interrupts abruptly, "disease-resistant cultivars are sorely needed." He gives Logan a sharp, cautioning glance.

Puzzled by the exchange but attempting to ignore it, Aguado smiles at Shelley. "The señorita is indeed correct. Farmers must be on continuous guard against the threat of *Fusarium oxysporum,* especially in dense plantings."

Another of the girls, Beth Craig, points to a uniformed guard. "Is that why you've got him?" They all turn to look. The guard wears a holstered gun on his hip and cradles an assault rifle in his arms. "To protect against *Fusarium* wilt?"

The students laugh, but Aguado has lost his smile. "Disease is not the only threat our vanilla farmers face, *señorita.* Sadly, there are many thieves. Last week, on the mountain, two workers were shot and wounded by robbers. The week before, a farmer was murdered."

"Murdered?" squeaks Archie, a short,

16

round-faced young man who never takes his hands out of his pockets. "You're saying that people actually *kill* for vanilla?"

"*Sí,*" Aguado answers gravely. "Vanilla farming can be a dangerous occupation." His smile flickers, then returns full strength. "But enough. Come with me, and I will show you how we cure these precious pods."

The group follows Aguado to a metal-roofed, open-walled structure, where the just-harvested pods are blanched in tubs of hot water, then drained, wrapped in burlap, and placed in large wooden boxes to "sweat" for a day or two. They will then be rack-dried in alternating sun and shade, all the while darkening to a rich brown-black, becoming supple and oily, and smelling ever more richly of vanilla. It will be five or six months before the pods can be sold to the big international companies that will process it. And all the while, the curing crop must be guarded against thieves.

"Vanilla is an obsession," Aguado adds, almost mournfully. "To raise it, you must love it. To profit from it, you must protect it, or it may be taken from you." The students exchange raised-eyebrow glances, but they are beginning to understand that this is not an exaggeration. Sadly, they will understand it even more clearly on the very

17

next day.

The group spends the night — their second — at a nearby hotel, old and ramshackle. There are no showers or bathtubs, but they have individual rooms, the beds are made up with fresh linens, and the veranda offers a stunning view of the lush green valley below. Gathered at a large round table, all enjoy a simple but satisfying meal of *tostados* and *chalupas* topped with chorizo, sliced avocados, tomatillo salsa, and *queso fresco,* with mugs of a fragrant locally brewed vanilla-pod beer. For dessert, there is vanilla flan with caramel sauce. Around them echo the calls of jungle birds and the occasional squeals of monkeys, against the haunting strains of Ravel's "Rhapsodie Espagnole." At this higher altitude, the night is cooler and more comfortable, and there is time after dinner to wander through the romantic, torch-lit gardens.

The next morning, early, they are back in the van and headed higher into the mountains, where they will meet a traditional farmer and then go on to the mountain village of Coxquihui. Mist is draped like a gauzy shawl over the emerald forest canopy, and the morning is cool and gray. The road corkscrews as it climbs the steep mountain, until Aguado tells the professor to stop. They get out of the van to meet a gnarled, bent-over old man, Hector Hernandez, who is dressed in the traditional white peasant garb.

Several years before, Señor Hernandez and his son Ignacio cleared and planted a few steep forest acres, retaining coral trees to shade the young vanilla vines and laurel and *cojón de gato* as support. When the vanilla plants bloomed, the old man and his son and his son's wife and their four children pollinated the blossoms by hand. This week, they have just finished gathering their small forest-grown crop. The burlap bags of ripe pods are piled by the side of the road under the wary eye of Ignacio, who carries his shotgun. Ignacio is waiting for the *coleccionista,* the collector who will pick up the bags and take them to the local *beneficio.* The owner of this *beneficio* pays the farmer for his crop, then cures the collected pods before selling them to a buyer from one of the international vanilla companies.

The old man speaks in a swift, high-pitched Spanish, and Aguado translates. "Señor Hernandez will be especially glad for the *coleccionista* to take his pods today, for thieves have been active in the area. It is an *escándalo,* a scandal, how many robbers

19

there are this year!" The old man's voice grows sour and bitter. "And the bandit at the *beneficio* pays us poor farmers only a few pesos for our crop, no matter how much the gringos pay him. *Ay-ay-ay!* How are we to feed our families? We cannot eat *vainilla!*"

"What about Fair Trade vanilla? Doesn't that help?" Shelley asks, and the other students nod. They have been studying the Fair Trade movement, a cooperative arrangement that guarantees farmers a competitive price for their products, whether vanilla, coffee, or chocolate.

Aguado purses his lips. He does not want to criticize Fair Trade, but he does not want to praise it, either. He understands its limitations. "There are many barriers to such practices," he replies judiciously, without naming all the local politicians who stand in the way, each with a greedy hand out for his *soborno.* "It may be a while before Fair Trade comes to these mountains."

The group is nearly ready to leave when the *coleccionista* appears, driving a rusty old truck with wood-slat sides. The Hernandez family's bags are tossed on top of the load, documents change hands, and Ignacio prepares to climb into the front seat beside the driver. He will accompany the load of pods to the *beneficio* and collect the pesos due to his father. The Hernandez family hopes there will be many pesos, for they have worked hard and their vanilla crop provides their only cash income.

"We will follow you to Coxquihui," the professor says.

Ignacio hesitates. "Are you sure that is wise? My father is right when he says that there have been many robberies on this road." He frowns. "*We* have no choice but to take this route. You would be better advised to go back down the mountain and take the southern route to Coxquihui."

Later, some would wonder if Ignacio spoke out of a certain foreknowledge and say that his warning should have been heeded. But the professor was a stubborn man who liked to make his own decisions. "The southern route would take hours longer," he says. "I intend to stick to our schedule."

Señor Aguado frowns, agreeing with Ignacio. "In the circumstance, I recommend taking the other road, especially since we will be following a truck that is loaded with vanilla — an easy target, exactly what the thieves are looking for. The lower road is somewhat longer but more heavily traveled

21

and hence safer."

"Forget it, Aguado," the professor says roughly. "I have already told you. We can't spare the time."

The old man looks perplexed. Señor Aguado sighs. Ignacio shrugs his shoulders as if to say, "It's on your head."

"Get in," the professor says to the students, and obediently, they climb into the van. They will follow the *coleccionista* to the village, where the pods will be unloaded and they can interview the manager at the *beneficio.* Then they will drive on to a larger town where they are to spend the night in a hacienda belonging to a colleague of the professor, who has arranged a warm welcome for them.

But they don't make it that far. The old truck leads the van down the narrow, twisting road, no wider than a track. The tropical jungle looms darkly on either side and eerie tendrils of mist drift like pale ghosts through the trees. From somewhere in the forest comes the raucous shriek of a parrot.

"I will be glad to get to that hacienda," Beth is saying to Shelley, at the back of the van. "Do you suppose there'll be showers?"

"Oh, I hope so," Shelley replies, running her hands through her pixie cut. "A cool shower would be wonderful, wouldn't it? And I can wash my hair. This humidity makes it feel so sticky."

"What is that?" the professor says, slowing the van. "Looks like a road block."

"I suppose it is a check point," Aguado replies, as several men in camouflage gear and armed with assault rifles step out of the jungle in front of the *coleccionista*'s truck. "As you know, during harvest, the police inspect the papers of anybody who is carrying vanilla." He pauses, frowning. "But these fellows do not look like —"

"It's an ambush," the professor says abruptly. "Let's get the hell out of here!"

"No!" Aguado puts a hand on his arm. "No, it is better to wait. The thieves will take the beans they want or the bribe they are looking for. Then we will be free to —"

But the professor is wrestling the van into a tight U-turn on the narrow road, twisting the steering wheel hard to the left and accelerating with a spray of gravel. The vehicle is pulling away fast when the vanilla thieves see what is happening. One raises his rifle and fires a sharp burst through the rear window. The van lurches off the road, careens down a steep embankment, and smashes hard against a tree.

23

For seven people, the nightmare has just begun.

For one, it has just ended.

CHAPTER ONE

The vanilla vine grew out of a murder — two murders, in fact. That's the story, anyway.

The Totonacs, the first people to cultivate vanilla, lived on the eastern coast of Mexico in what is now the state of Veracruz. Their king had a daughter who (naturally) was so beautiful that she was consecrated to the goddess of fertility. The royal princess made the unfortunate and very human mistake of falling in love with a handsome commoner. Forbidden to marry (naturally), the lovers fled to the forest, where the priests caught up with them and killed them. From the blood of the murdered lovers grew a tall, strong tree, embraced by a beautiful orchid vine. When the orchid flowered, the air was filled with an intoxicating aroma. Nine months later, the fruit was ripe. Observant Totonacs

25

drew the natural conclusion.

China Bayles
"Vanilla: The Ice Cream Orchid"
Pecan Springs Enterprise

Novelist Mary McCarthy once wrote, "We all live in suspense, from day to day, from hour to hour; in other words, we are the hero of our own story." I've given a lot of thought to this, and I think it's true. The trouble is that we never really know when a new chapter of our story begins. Most of the time, in fact, we don't even know it's a story — that is, with a cast of characters, in a setting, with a plot and several subplots — until we're in it up to our necks.

For example, does this story (the one I'm about to tell you) begin with the mythic murder of a princess and her handsome commoner, somewhere in the jungles of Central America? Does it start with a passionate desire for an exotic flower and its delectable fruit? Or perhaps it begins in unspeakable loss, unbearable pain, and a corrosive desire for revenge. The roots of some stories go deep into the past, and I can't be sure what sort of seed was the genesis of this one. I only know how and when I came into it and what happened after that.

So, since I'm not sure where to begin, I'll start with the workshop that Ruby and I taught that fateful Monday in September, which was a kind of beginning.

For me, anyway.

I was standing in front of a group of women in the Gathering Room of Thyme Cottage, about to begin a PowerPoint presentation on vanilla, the world's most popular flavoring. I would be talking about how the plant is grown, harvested, cured, and marketed, illustrating my narrative with photographs from a recent field trip I'd taken to Veracruz, Mexico. But I began the workshop by telling the mythic tale of the beautiful Totonac princess who was murdered, with her lover, because of their forbidden love affair.

"And *that*," I added, "explains why the vanilla orchid likes to wrap itself around a tree — although it might take a little imagination to see the vine as a beautiful princess."

I turned the pot on the table in front of me, so everyone could have a good look at the two-foot vine, which was fastened to a cedar post that I'd wrapped with sphagnum moss. "As you can see, this one is clinging to the cedar support. When it's mature, it will produce a lovely yellow orchid-like flower. If it's successfully pollinated, there'll be a ripe vanilla pod nine months later." A titter fluttered around the room when I added, "No wonder the myth is told as a 'birds-and-bees' story."

I picked up the pot and stepped in front of the table so that the people in our "Not Just Plain Vanilla" workshop could see the plant more easily. "Like other members of the orchid family," I said, "the vanilla orchid has aerial roots that cling to its support, help it grow upward, and take in water and nutrients. It also sends roots down into the soil. In its native tropical habitat, this vine can grow to two hundred feet. In a greenhouse, it'll probably top out at fifteen or twenty." I paused. "Questions?"

Mrs. Birkett — the oldest member of our local herb guild and a longtime Crockett Street neighbor — put up her hand. "I've heard vanilla called a spice, but I've never understood that. At the grocery store, it comes as a liquid in that little brown bottle. So why is it a spice?"

"That puzzles a lot of people," I said. "But the answer is pretty simple, really. Herbs and spices come from different parts of a useful plant. *Herb* refers to the leaves, flowers, or stems. *Spice* refers to the seed, fruit, root, or bark. Vanilla extract is made from the fruit of the vanilla orchid — its pod, or bean — so we call vanilla a spice."

Mrs. Birkett nodded, satisfied. "Thank you. Now I know."

The woman sitting beside her spoke up. "I'm an ER nurse. I've read that vanilla is used medicinally. Is that right?"

I squinted to see her name tag. Karen Taylor — someone I didn't know. She looked like a nurse, though. Brown hair cut sensibly short, no makeup, simple skirt and blouse, a brisk, no-nonsense manner. I replied, "There's been some laboratory research on vanillin — the active plant chemical in vanilla. It's been shown to reduce free radicals, slow cell mutations, and restrict the blood supply to tumors. So it may be useful in treating some cancers."

"And the scent has a calming effect," my partner Ruby Wilcox added. "Researchers doing mood mapping say that just a whiff of vanilla can make people feel relaxed and happy." There was a general whisper of *yesses* around the room, and somebody said, "To me, vanilla smells like home. Like my mother. Whenever I smell it, I think of her."

Another hand went up. "How much sun does a vanilla plant need?" The questioner, Edith Barlow, wore her auburn hair in a loose cloud around her shoulders. "Can I grow it in my living room?"

"Good questions, Edith," I said. "You may see vanilla advertised as a house plant, but growing it is tricky. It needs warm temperatures — nothing lower than fifty-five — bright light, and a super-sticky humidity level, around eighty-five percent. *Vanilla planifolia — planifolia* just means 'flat-leaved' — is a tropical vine that grows best in a greenhouse." I smiled at the auburn-haired woman. "But don't give up hope. If you don't have your very own personal greenhouse, check with Sonora Garden Center. Maggie Walker, the owner, offers an orchid boarding service. She'll be glad to board your vanilla plant, keep it healthy, and give it everything it needs. When it's ready to bloom — when it's three years old and about ten feet tall — you can take it home and enjoy the blossoms. You can even try your hand at pollinating it."

"A boarding service for *orchids*?" the nurse asked disbelievingly. "You've got to be kidding."

"Nope." I hoisted the pot I was holding. "This little lady is still a baby, just eighteen months old. She lives at Sonora, where Maggie takes good care of her." Conveniently, Maggie and I have arranged a little quid pro quo. She keeps my vanilla plant in exchange for a free ad for Sonora in my email newsletter.

"Maggie really knows her stuff when it comes to orchids," another woman said. Her salt-and-pepper hair was clipped close to her head, and her expression was alert and sprightly. "Boarding is cheaper than having your own greenhouse. A lot less trouble, too, if you're into orchids. They aren't very pretty when they're not blooming, so Maggie takes care of mine until they're ready to bloom again."

"Do you have visiting privileges?" someone asked in a snarky tone, and laughter rippled through the group.

"Absolutely." The gray-haired woman took the question seriously. "I drop in every few weeks to see how my babies are doing. I don't want them to forget me, you know." More laughter.

"Is Maggie boarding a vanilla orchid for you?" I asked.

The woman nodded eagerly. "It's four years old and already about fifteen feet tall. It should bloom in the next few months, and Maggie says she'll show me how to pollinate it."

"Good luck," I said. "If you get any pods, maybe you'd be willing to share." Everybody laughed, and I looked around. "Any more questions?"

When I didn't see any hands in the air, I put the vanilla plant on the table and picked up my laptop's remote. "If you'll turn out the lights, Ruby, we'll be on our way. I took these photos on a trip I made last year with a college botany class that was studying vanilla. We'll be visiting the Mexican town of Papantla, which clings to its history as the vanilla capital of the world. Then it's on to a commercial vanilla plantation and a traditional vanilla farm in the jungle, to see how vanilla is grown, harvested, and cured. At the end, we'll visit a small manufacturer in Veracruz, to see how vanilla extract is produced."

When my talk was finished, Ruby and I would demonstrate some uses for vanilla powder and paste, compare real vanilla extract to the less-expensive artificial vanilla flavoring, and share bowls of vanilla custard and several vanilla-flavored treats. The following week, the group would meet again for some hands-on work with vanilla pods. I would focus on the culinary side of things, while Ruby would demonstrate how to make vanilla-infused body oils, a vanilla sugar facial scrub, and a fragrant incense made from vanilla powder. At the end, we would hand out recipes and tips for storing and using vanilla pods. Everybody loves recipes.

But before I start my PowerPoint photos, a quick introduction may be in order for those who haven't visited us before. My name is China Bayles. Some years ago, I left the practice of criminal law in Houston and opened an herb shop — Thyme and Seasons — in Pecan Springs, Texas, a small, friendly Hill Country community halfway between Austin and San Antonio. A few years later, I married Mike McQuaid, a former homicide detective, currently a private investigator and part-time faculty member in the Criminal Justice department at Central Texas State University. McQuaid and I are parents to two great kids: his son Brian, who is majoring in environmental sciences at the University of Texas at Austin; and my thirteen-year-old niece Caitlin, who plays the violin and runs a small chicken-and-egg business in our backyard.

Ruby Wilcox (the tall redhead standing at the back of the room) owns the Crystal Cave, the only New Age shop in Pecan Springs. The Cave is located in the same building as my herb shop, and Ruby is my partner and best friend. She sells incense and rune stones and tarot cards and books;

33

teaches classes in astrology and meditation and the tarot; and offers birth chart readings and Ouija board sessions. She's also psychic, which occasionally manifests itself in some pretty interesting ways. You might ask her about our recent ghost, who taught us a few things about the century-old building where our shops are located.

Some people may think Ruby is a bit of a flake, but in all the years we've worked together, I have rarely known her to have a bad idea. In fact, I will admit that while I have the stamina and dogged persistence it takes to run a small business, Ruby is the one with the creativity, originality, and imagination it takes to run an *innovative* small business. You might say that her right brain makes up for what my left brain lacks and vice versa. Which makes us excellent business partners and the very, very, *very* best of besties.

To look at us, though, you'd have to say that we're an odd couple. Ruby is slender and tall — six feet in her flats — with fair skin, freckles, and remarkable carrot-colored hair that tends to frizz no matter what she does to it. She loves clothes that will make you blink, like the bright purple tunic top and purple-and-blue paisley yoga leggings she was wearing today.

I, on the other hand, am short and stocky, with a widening gray streak in my unremarkable brown hair. My work uniform is invariably jeans, tennies, and a forest green Thyme and Seasons T-shirt. Call me unglamorous, but not having to figure out what to wear every morning gives me time to figure out a few really important things, like how to get a decent breakfast into my husband and daughter, get the dog and cat fed, and get to the shop before the customers do.

But while Ruby and I are admittedly an odd couple, there is nothing odd or offbeat about our partnership. Together, we own and manage Thyme for Tea (a tea room, in the same building as our shops) and Party Thyme (a catering service). With Cass Wilde, we have the Thymely Gourmet, a meals-to-go food delivery service. Cass also manages the tea room kitchen and helps with the catering. In this always-hectic three-ring circus of ours, the three of us consider ourselves lucky if we can keep from dropping too many balls or missing a trapeze or getting bitten by an irritated tiger. Do not for a single moment think that running your own business is a piece of cake.

And there's Thyme Cottage, once a stone stable, now a lovely remodeled cottage on the alley at the back of the gardens that surround the shops. I rent it by the week as a bed-and-breakfast for tourists who visit Pecan Springs. (If you're in the neighborhood and looking for a place to stay, let me know.) When it's not rented, Ruby and I use it for workshops and classes. We like it because it has a kitchen and adjacent large living room that we call the Gathering Room.

And that's where we were holding our September "Not Just Plain Vanilla" workshop, one of the most popular events on our entire class schedule. It never fails to fill, with a waiting list, on the very same day we post it. Everybody loves vanilla.

It took about thirty minutes for me to show the photographs and answer questions about vanilla farming in Mexico. I had taken the photos on a field trip for a class I audited the previous year. It was taught at CTSU — Central Texas State University — by Professor Carl Fairlee, who is known for his studies of *Vanilla planifolia.* During the winter break, Dr. Fairlee always leads a field trip to the Mexican state of Veracruz so his class can see how vanilla is grown, harvested, and processed. I didn't tell the group that he is also Maggie Walker's ex-husband

— my friend Maggie, who owns the garden center we were talking about earlier — but we'll get into that later.

And I didn't mention the most disturbing part of the story. A couple of years before I took the trip, the van Dr. Fairlee was driving had gone off a steep cliff on a narrow mountain road. One of the girls, Shelley, was killed, and two other students were seriously injured. Details were hard to come by, and there was a great deal of confusion about the facts. In one version, Dr. Fairlee swerved off the road to avoid hitting a monkey. In a more dramatic version, the van was fired on by a gang of men intent on robbery and rape. The more times the story got told, the darker and uglier it became. If the Mexican police investigated the crash and determined what actually occurred, their version of the story didn't make it back to campus.

But whatever the murky truth of what happened on that mountain, it was especially sad for Ruby and me. Shelley Harmon, the student who was killed, had worked in our tea room the previous summer, and (with her friend Beth Craig) had rented a little house from Mrs. Birkett, just down the block. Shelley Harmon was lively, energetic, and always cheerful. Our customers missed her. *We* missed her.

Because the trip had been university-sponsored, CTSU authorities launched what they called a "thorough investigation." Some people wanted to pin the blame on Dr. Fairlee, if only for putting his students into a dangerous situation. But if he was held to be at fault, we never knew, for the results of the investigation were not released. They were kept secret.

A few people questioned this, and there was a persistent rumor that Shelley's mother, who lived out in West Texas somewhere, had hired a lawyer and intended to sue both Dr. Fairlee and CTSU for wrongful death. But the two-year statute of limitations came and went and the talk eventually died down. By the time the next academic year began, the tragedy was all but forgotten, and it was back to business as usual. Except in the tea room, of course, where Ruby and I often spoke about Shelley and wished we could turn the clock back.

When I went on the vanilla class field trip, there were no accidents, bad or otherwise. The weather was wonderful, the Mexican food exceptional, the vanilla farms interesting. The vanilla bandits (if there were any) left us in peace. Everything went as planned, and I came back with a much better understanding of the where, who, and why of vanilla — and more photos than I knew what to do with. I was using quite a few of them in today's workshop.

"And that's what goes into that little brown bottle you buy at the grocery," I said to the group as I turned off the computer and signaled to Ruby to turn on the lights. "As you can see, growing and processing the stuff takes a lot of time and labor. As Señor Aguado says, 'Vanilla is an obsession. To raise it, you must love it.' I think that's true — and it may be more true of vanilla than any other spice or herb." I paused and looked around. "Okay, who has a question?"

A woman — heavyset, with dark curly hair and apple-red cheeks — put up her hand. In an aggrieved voice, she said, "I'm Donna Gibbons. I've been planning to start a small artisanal business making vanilla extract. But the price of vanilla pods has gone through the roof. Is it ever going to level off?"

"Your guess is as good as mine," I said with a shrug. "As long as the supply is limited and the demand is high, the price will stay high. Every time the vanilla plantations are hit by a destructive cyclone or a vine-killing drought, the price will go higher. The last time I looked, a pound of Grade A

39

pods was selling for about two hundred seventy-five dollars. A pound of pods will make about a gallon of liquid extract. However, you don't need —"

Donna broke in. "Two hundred seventy-five dollars! But that means I'd have to charge seven dollars for a four-ounce bottle of extract, just to break even. And that doesn't count my time and equipment!"

"Or the vodka you'd have to use to make the extract," said the woman sitting beside her.

"Or the bottles and labels," Edith Barlow added. "Or advertising."

"Makes you appreciate imitation vanilla," the nurse remarked, and everyone laughed.

"Hey, people," I said. "Hold on a minute. If you're making extract, you don't need gourmet-grade pods. As long as the vanillin content is high, you can use short pods, mis-shapen pods, even split pods."

"Does that lower the cost?" Donna asked hopefully.

"Sure does," I replied. "At the current price, three dollars will buy enough Grade B pods to produce a four-ounce bottle of extract. If you can sell that bottle for seven dollars — and if you don't spend a bundle on other supplies — you might make two or three dollars a bottle."

There was a murmur around the room, and Donna said, "That sounds a lot more reasonable."

"If we're ready, then," I said, "Ruby and I will show you how to make real vanilla extract and vanilla paste at home — without pawning the family jewels. And it will be cheaper than if you'd bought it at the store. Guaranteed."

"Well, that was fun," Ruby said, as we said goodbye to the last workshopper and began folding up the chairs. "I thought the discussion about the cost of making vanilla extract was interesting. It opened a few eyes, I'll bet."

"Homemade vanilla is wonderful, to keep or to give away," I said, stacking chairs against the wall. "But at the current prices, it might be tough to make it for sale. I talked to Donna for a few minutes afterward and suggested that if she was serious about turning the craft into a business, she ought to consider producing other flavorings, too. Orange, lime, lemon, chocolate — they all cost less to produce. They'd broaden her market. And give her a cushion in case the price of vanilla goes even higher, which it could."

"You could carry them in the shop,

couldn't you?" Ruby got a broom and began to chase cookie crumbs.

"I could, on consignment. I told her to give me some samples and prices." I went into the kitchen and started putting our workshop supplies into a cardboard box. "Oh, I've been meaning to ask — is Grace feeling better?"

Grace, who just turned four, is Ruby's granddaughter. She's been sick with tonsillitis and her mother, Amy, is thinking about having her tonsils taken out — a big event in the life of a little girl.

"Much better, yes," Ruby said. "Looks like Grace is keeping her tonsils, for now, anyway." She put the broom away and came over to stand at the counter, a smile tugging at her mouth. "And there's news. Baby news, I mean."

"Oh, really?" I arched my eyebrows. "Do tell, Ruby! Is Amy going to have another baby?"

Ruby's daughter Amy and her partner Kate have been together for several years now, and when same-sex marriage became legal, they were among the first in Pecan Springs to wed. As you might guess, this liaison hasn't won the approval of all Amy's relatives. Amy's grandmother, Doris, has been heard to snort "lesbians." And Shannon, Amy's sister, pretends that Kate is just a roommate. But Ruby loves Amy, respects and appreciates Kate, and adores Grace, an enchanting little girl who lives up to her name in every way. She would love it if her mother gave her a baby brother or sister.

"No, not Amy." Ruby leaned her elbows on the counter. "This one is going to be Kate's baby. They just told me last night. They are over the moon, both of them."

"Wow. Kate." I blinked. "Well, *that's* interesting."

Kate Rodriguez is a take-charge woman who owns her own accounting firm. She is very good at what she does and is genuinely helpful to her clients (I know, because she is our accountant), so her small business has grown. She now has a couple of junior accountants — both young women — working for her, so she has a lot of responsibility. But she's the kind of woman who could manage all that, plus a baby, without turning a hair.

"So Kate's going to be a mother," I said reflectively.

Was there some envy in my voice? Well, maybe a little. Putting my legal career at the top of my priority list for all of my twenties and part of my thirties took me out of the motherhood queue. At least, that's what I'd thought. But Brian (McQuaid's son) and Caitlin, my niece, our adopted daughter, have filled any empty mother-spaces in my heart. I'm not really sorry I passed up the chance to have a baby of my own, although sometimes I'm a little wistful.

And if I'm looking for a big dose of baby excitement, I can always drop in on my friend Sheila Dawson, who is due to have her first, a boy, in another couple of months. Sheila — Smart Cookie to her friends — is also Pecan Springs' police chief, so there is quite a lot of local interest in her pregnancy. People are wondering how she's going to fit a baby into her very demanding job.

Ruby pulled me back to the conversation. "They drew straws," she said. "Kate won."

"Excuse me?" I was missing something here. "They drew straws for what?"

"For who was going to get pregnant." Ruby gave me a look that said I should have been smart enough to figure that out for myself. "They've been discussing it for quite a while, but the question was always *who*. Amy gave birth to Grace, so Kate figured the next one ought to be hers. But Amy is younger and had a really easy time with Grace, plus her work schedule at the vet clinic is pretty flexible. Kate is older and has her hands full with her accounting business." Ruby waggled her gingery eyebrows. "They talked and talked but they couldn't agree."

I got it. "So they left it to chance."

"Exactly. Logical, don't you think? Kate drew the longer straw, so she won. It took several cycles, but she's preggie."

Several cycles. "Where did they — ?" I stopped. "Who is the —" I shook my head. "I hardly know what to ask."

Ruby giggled. "It's all pretty new to me, too. They started out with a clinic in San Antonio that works with same-sex couples. They were going to use an anonymous donor via the clinic. But they talked about it with some of the family, and Kate's sister's husband said he would be honored to be the father. Remember Ron? Kate's brother-in-law?"

I did. Ron and I met at a barbeque at Amy's and Kate's early in the summer. "Nice guy," I remarked. "Lives in Houston?"

Ruby nodded. "He's a computer systems analyst and so smart. He's in good health and he and Kate's sister, Gail, have two bright, active kids, both boys. Kate and Amy agreed that he would be perfect, and Gail thought it made sense."

"I see." I finished putting stuff in the box

45

and began wiping the counter. "So did they do it?"

"Yes." She hesitated. "But if you're asking, did Kate and Ron actually *do* it — in the old-fashioned way, I mean — the answer is no. They didn't."

I was actually okay with living in the dark about the details, but Ruby was going on. "According to Amy, Ron volunteered for active duty. His wife wasn't exactly in favor, though, and Kate said a definite *no.* They did it with a turkey baster. Artificial insemination," she added, making sure I understood.

I understood, all right. I wrinkled my nose. "I hope they got a lawyer."

"A lawyer?" Ruby asked blankly. "They've got a doctor. What do they need a *lawyer* for?"

"Well, gosh, Ruby," I said. "Think about it. An anonymous donor is one thing, and the clinic will already have worked out the legal complications. A family member is something else altogether. What are the father's rights? Does Kate's brother-in-law expect to be involved in his child's life? What will Kate and Amy tell their child about him? They'll see one another often, won't they? Will the little one call him *Daddy* or *Uncle Ron* or what? And what about his responsibilities? Is he off the hook or will it be share-and-share-alike? Will he help pay for braces on his kid's teeth? Ballet lessons? College?"

"Wow." Ruby's eyes were wide. "I'm not sure they thought about any of that."

"Well, they should," I replied. "As time goes on, how is Kate's sister going to feel about her husband's child? And what if they do some tests before the baby is born and find out that there are abnormalities? It happens, you know. Who gets to decide whether the pregnancy ought to be terminated?" There was plenty more, including an interesting Texas appellate court ruling that had come down on this very subject recently. But I was running out of breath.

"Those are good questions," Ruby said, pursing her lips. "Still, knowing Kate, I expect she's already worked out most of the answers. She's pretty good with stuff like that." She reached across the counter and patted my hand. "It's sweet of you to offer your legal expertise, China, but I really don't think they need you."

"I wasn't *offering*," I said stiffly. "I was just pointing out some real world stuff. Having kids is complicated enough. In a situation like this, there could be a lot more complications. *Legal* complications. At the

47

very least, I hope they have a contract that sets out everybody's expectations."

"I think you're exaggerating the problems," Ruby replied. "But they're coming over to my house for supper tonight, and I'll tell them what you said." She straightened up. "Why don't you and Caitie join us, so you can tell them yourself? McQuaid's still out of town, isn't he?"

I shook my head. "He's getting back today." My husband's investigative work takes him on the road frequently. He and his partner Blackie Blackwell — Sheila's husband — were working in Dallas, on an investigation of corporate fraud. "We'd better take a rain check. But thanks anyway. Caitie loves to play with Grace."

In fact, Caitie is now old enough to babysit Grace, so she's added that little income stream — seven-fifty an hour — to what she earns from her egg business. At heart, Caitie is an entrepreneur.

"Another time, then," Ruby said. She looked up at the clock and sighed. "Oh, gosh, nearly four. If we're done here, I need to get back to the shop. I have a couple of orders that have to go out today." It was Monday, so our shops were closed — which doesn't mean, of course, that we hadn't been working all day. We were. We were

48

workshopping, although that tends to feel more like fun than work.

"We're done here." I picked up the box. "Could you bring the vanilla orchid? We can put it in my car, and I'll take it back to Sonora before I go home."

Ruby picked up the plant. "That bit about Maggie Walker boarding people's orchids — I'd never heard that before. Does she do a lot of it?"

"She's got a whole greenhouse filled with them," I said as we went out, locking the door behind us. "It's apparently a big part of her business these days. People buy orchids at the supermarket, then they discover they don't have the right place to raise them." Over my shoulder, I added, "Sorry to miss out on supper. Please tell Amy and Kate what I said about getting some legal advice. I'm sure Charlie Lipman can help them." Charlie is an able Pecan Springs attorney who is known as the town fixer, everybody's go-to guy in times of trouble. Even mine, on occasion.

"Okay," Ruby said. "But I still think you're being a worrywart."

I fished my car keys out of my bag. "That's what lawyers get paid to do, Ruby. They worry. So their clients don't have to."

But that isn't always true. Sometimes the clients *do* have to worry.

CHAPTER TWO

According to the digital clock on the desk, it is 3:40 on a Monday afternoon, but Sheila Dawson — well into her eighth month of pregnancy now — longs to pull out a drawer and put her feet up. Her normally trim ankles have swelled to the size of small tree trunks, and elevating her feet usually helps.

She quashes the impulse, however, and leans back in her swivel chair, the enormous black leather desk chair that had belonged to Bubba Harris, the previous chief of the Pecan Springs Police Department. This chair has always been several sizes too large for her — just another of the many things about her job that don't fit but are difficult to change. It's the chief's chair. It cost as much as new ballistics vests for three of her patrol officers, and replacing it is out of the question. She's stuck with it.

But now that she is bigger than a blue whale, the damned chair almost fits. In fact, it's just about the only chair she can sit in comfortably these days. If she didn't have to walk the length of a football field to use the ladies' — she has to pee a couple of times an hour, more often if she drinks coffee — she and her chair would be all set. (The men's, of course, is right around the corner. Handy for Bubba, not so handy for her.)

Somehow, her pregnancy — her first — has not been what Sheila thought it would be. She has read that being pregnant is a naturally happy time, or at least a time of serenity and contentment — which is good because everybody says that a mom's emotional well-being affects her baby's neurological and psychological development. A serene and happy mom-to-be spends the months of her pregnancy planning, dreaming, and imagining what life will be like once she's a mom for real. Right?

Wrong. Sheila's pregnancy hasn't exactly been happy or even halfway serene, and she hasn't had much time for planning, let alone dreaming and imagining. Persistent nausea plagued her through the early months, landing her in the hospital twice. That's past, but now she's bothered by her ankles and her back and her bulk and having to pee so often. And especially the *waiting,* the uncertain feeling of being betwixt and between, neither here nor there, as if she were a non-person living in a perplexing, disorienting nowhere-ville.

But she isn't. She is living in Pecan Springs and dealing with the constant pressures of a tough job. Being a female police chief in a small Texas town is hard. Being a *pregnant* female police chief (especially now that she is so unambiguously, unmistakably pregnant) has proved harder by several orders of magnitude. She will be very glad when this neither-nor time is over and she is simply a female chief of police who happens to be a mother, too.

And she hasn't even started to think what *that* means. Oh, she and Blackie are doing what they need to do, as far as the essentials are concerned. They have bought a crib and a baby box to go *in* the crib, a baby carrier that doubles as a car seat, a breast pump, a half-dozen bottles with newborn nipples, and a supply of ecologically viable biodegradable newborn diapers (to save the planet). Blackie — a wonderfully supportive husband who will be a fabulous dad — is planning to work from home as much as he can for the first few months, and they have found a licensed and experienced child care provider for times when they both have to

53

be gone. They are methodically ticking things off their mile-long to-do list. They are very well organized.

That's on the outside. On the inside, it's a different story. Sheila is finding it hard to remember the yearning she felt for a child, *her* child, as if it were the single missing piece in the puzzle of her life. Worse, she can't begin to imagine what her life will be like after the baby — Noah, he's named — is born. Will she be able to breastfeed, or will that be a disaster, the way it was for her sister? Will she know what to do when Noah is colicky, or has diaper rash, or won't go to sleep? Will she love him desperately and want nothing more than to hold him in her arms, or will she be continually imagining what is happening at the office? Will there be time in the day to do everything that has to be done?

So, no. She doesn't have a clue what her new life will be like. All she knows is that it will be different from the life she has been living. She will be different. Blackie will be different. The fourth of November (the day Noah is due) will mark the end of her independent, self-regulating, separate self and the beginning of another self, different, new, unknown, with a whole set of unfamiliar responsibilities. That's the sum of what she knows, and it isn't enough. Not nearly enough.

She is thinking bleakly about all this when there is a quick rap at the office door. She picks up a pen, pulls a paper toward her, and pretends to be studying it. "Come in," she calls.

It's Connie Page, her civilian assistant. A competent woman, not quite middle-aged and recently divorced, Connie is perfectly capable of handling most of the department's paperwork herself — of running the department, come to that. She's been the chief's right-hand woman for better than a decade and knows the community of Pecan Springs as well as she knows the inside of her kitchen. She also knows what the chief needs to see and what she doesn't, and Sheila is grateful for every piece of paper that Connie keeps off her desk. Her assistant is one of a kind. Irreplaceable.

This afternoon, Connie looks as efficient as always in her white blouse, dark skirt, and low-heeled shoes, her dark hair cut short and neatly curled. But she is empty-handed and there is a distinctly troubled expression on her normally calm face. She says, "I need a couple of minutes on a personal matter, Chief."

One look tells Sheila that whatever-it-is is

something she does not want to hear. But she pushes the paper away, summons a smile, and points with the pen at the chair in front of the desk. "Sit, Con. What's up?"

Connie sits, settles herself in her chair, and opens in her usual straightforward way with the bad news. No prologue, no explanation, no excuses.

"What's up is that I need to take a leave. A couple of months. Maybe more. I can't tell you right now how long I'll be gone." Her voice is taut, her hands are clasped tightly in her lap. "I'm sorry, Chief. Really sorry."

Oh, bloody *hell,* Sheila thinks. Not this. Not now. Not until after I deliver — and not then, either. I can't get along without you, Con. I can't!

But she somehow manages to wipe the apprehension off her face and smooth the kinks out of her voice. "Sounds like you're dealing with a big problem. How can I help? Besides giving you whatever time you need, I mean."

Connie's carefully expressionless expression crumples. "Thank you." She fumbles in her skirt pocket and pulls out a tissue. "I don't think anybody can help. It's my sister. Lillian just found out that it's cancer. Uterine cancer, stage three. Surgery next week — a hysterectomy — and then what they call 'sandwich' therapy, alternating chemo and radiation. The docs don't know yet how long this will go on, but it sounds like a while." Her voice drops. "And then there's whatever happens after, of course. So I can't tell you how long I'll be gone."

"Uh-oh," Sheila says softly. *Uterine cancer.* She shudders and touches her belly. Her cousin died of uterine cancer five years ago, and the loss is still fresh.

But that's not the only bad news. Sheila knows that Connie's sister is their mother's resident caregiver. Their mom, who lives in Dallas, has Alzheimer's. This could be a long absence. Worst case, it could be permanent.

"I am *so* sorry, Con."

As if in sympathy, the baby stirs — Noah, named for Blackie's father, a famous local lawman, Adams County sheriff for many years. Blackie had followed in his father's footsteps until he and Sheila were married. They waffled over that decision for months, because both of them felt it was too risky to have two cops in the family. Finally, they'd agreed that Sheila would stay with the PSPD while Blackie retired as sheriff and joined Mike McQuaid as a private investigator. Sheila worries that he might miss his job as sheriff, but he seems happy.

"Less paperwork," he says when she prods him. "More interesting cases, a greater variety, and I don't have to worry about getting elected — or getting shot." He frowns. "But I still have to worry about you getting shot, wife. Don't take any chances. You hear me now? You *hear*?"

Noah kicks again and Sheila puts a calming hand on her belly. "Will you be staying with your mom while you're in Dallas?" she asks, trying to sound matter-of-fact.

"Yes." Connie blows her nose. "My sister and I want to keep Mom at home as long as we can. And somebody has to help Lillie after her surgery." She lifts her shoulders and lets them fall in a weary shrug. "That's me, of course. And of course I'm glad to do it. I'm just sorry it has to happen right now."

By "right now," Connie means the final six or seven weeks of her boss' pregnancy. Sheila flinches at the reminder. Life without Con? Jeez. What will she *do*?

But she puts a brave face on it. "Don't worry, Con. We'll manage."

It won't be easy, though. When Sheila came to the Pecan Springs Police Department from campus security at CTSU, the department didn't have a pregnancy policy — for the simple reason that they had only one female officer, a former meter maid who was past menopause. Now, there are a half-dozen women on the force and a new policy covers both pregnant officers and new mothers. Modified assignments, maternity uniforms, paid leave, even paid breaks for pumping breast-milk — what the boys in the cop shop snarkily call "paid boob breaks." Sheila intends to set a strong precedent by taking full advantage of the policy. But she's been counting on Connie's help to manage the paperwork that floods through the office in a constantly rising tide. With Connie gone, she'll be on her own. How will she *do* it all?

"I know you'll manage." Connie is trying to look on the bright side. She wrinkles her nose and adds, with her usual blunt realism, "I just don't quite see how."

Neither does Sheila. But she says, with exaggerated firmness, "You're not to worry about it. That's an order." She lightens this with a half-smile, the best she can manage. "When do you need to go?"

"Lillie checks into the hospital on Monday, a week from today. I'd like to drive up there on Saturday. That will give me the rest of this week to find a person to take over my desk and see that she gets settled."

"Do you have somebody in mind?" Sheila

asks hollowly. The thought of breaking in a new person at Connie's desk is chilling. She'll never be able to find anything. She won't know how to answer the phone. She'll be unhappy about working late. She —

"Billie Jo Hooper is a possibility," Sheila says. "There are one or two others who might work out, but Billie Jo is a smart kid, eager to get ahead in the department. I'd like to give her a chance."

Billie Jo is young, very pretty, and (in Sheila's opinion) too flighty. But Connie is right, she's smart. She works in Personnel, which gives her some insight into scheduling and workforce issues. "How about if you make a list of three possibilities," Sheila says, "including Billie Jo. Both of us can interview all three before we make a final decision on your replacement."

"*Temporary* replacement," Connie corrects her, with a bleak smile. She is blinking back tears. "I'm not trying to guilt you, but I don't want you giving my job away."

"Watch your mouth," Sheila says and adds, "I wouldn't think of it," as if there is no question of Connie's not returning, although of course there is. "If it's Billie Jo, you'd better have a word with her about those see-through blouses she wears. They're fine for two-steppin' at the Broken

Spoke but not in the chief's office. And her nails." Billie Jo wears inch-long false nails, usually painted a dark, intense red. "Her fingers look like they've been dipped in blood."

"I'll let her know," Connie says. She straightens her shoulders and goes on in a firm, mother-hen voice, "And I want you to take care of yourself, Chief. No bouncing around, no pushups, no jogging." Diplomatically, she adds, "And maybe start watching the calories just a little?"

"I'll try," Sheila says, understanding that Connie is trying to strengthen the connection between them and feeling, with some chagrin, that the caution about calories is justified. After months of persistent nausea, her appetite has become turbocharged. She's hungry all the time so she eats all the time and she's gaining more weight than she should. She's always been slim and she can't quite get used to this bulky, out-front belly. Her back hurts because her center of gravity has shifted. She's pulled off-balance, so she's continually bumping into things, raising bruises on herself and startling the baby. The extra weight slows her down and adds to an exhausted frustration. And she hasn't been able to wear her duty belt for weeks, which makes her feel that she's out of uniform. Which in turn makes her feel that she's not part of the team. Funny how that works.

Of course, Sheila knows she is no shirker. She's on the job and will be, right up to the minute she goes into labor. There's no special reason she *has* to wear her duty belt. The chief's work mostly involves going to meetings, confronting and/or placating the city council, and signing forms — no gunfights at the O.K. Corral. And while her maternity uniform may get raised-eyebrow glances from the other officers (male, of course), nobody has suggested that she's not doing her bit. Still . . .

She sighs. She would love to get out in the field for one last investigation before the now inevitable moment when Noah changes her life forever. But it would have to be a real investigation, not a car theft or a burglary or a domestic violence call. Something challenging. Something interesting and out of the ordinary. Something that reminds her that she is not just a paper-shuffler, personnel manager, and budget-cutter, but a law enforcement officer with a duty to serve and protect the citizens of her community.

But Sheila knows that this is about as likely as Mayor Browning's enthusiastic endorsement of her departmental funding request for the next fiscal year, which stands a snowball's chance in hell of surviving next week's budget hearing. And if by some astonishing luck a challenging, interesting investigation did come along, it would be handled by the detective unit — now down to three full-time detectives. *Another round of personnel cuts,* Sheila thinks, *and we won't have any investigators at all. Just street cops.*

She turns her attention back to Connie. "Please stay in touch," she says, "so I know how things are going. I'll miss you." She repeats it emphatically, fervently, for it is God's truth. "I will *miss* you, Con."

"Thank you." In control again, Connie pushes her chair back and stands. "I'll get the paperwork for my leave started. And I'll tell Billie Jo that we want to see her."

Sheila stands, too, using the chair arms as leverage to push herself up. She has to go to the bathroom. "Make sure you talk to her about the blouses. Be stern. I don't want the guys coming in here and looking down her —"

She is interrupted by the phone on her desk. Connie waggles her fingers, turns, and leaves as Sheila picks it up. It is Dylan Miller, PSPD's lead detective. "Just got a call from Denise Maxwell, security chief on the CTSU campus. They've got a body."

"Not an active shooter situation?" Sheila asks quickly.

"No. A corpse. A professor. Been dead a while, she says."

A professor. Sheila's pulse quickens. She knows Denise Maxwell, her second-in-command when she held the campus security chief's job. She had been on campus long enough — three-plus years — to learn to love CTSU and the academic life that flourished there. Students came not just from Texas but from everywhere and from all walks of life and age groups: teens and young adults, single parents aiming for a better job, dream-chasers from foreign countries, military veterans, midlife adults looking for new directions, retirees determined to keep their minds sharp. And these days, everybody was talking about guarding the campus community, keeping it safe from terrorists with bombs and AR-15s. Or even a psycho with a couple of handguns and the will to use them, like that guy at Virginia Tech. All he'd had was a Glock 19 and a Walther P22. In some ways, there were more challenges in the job she left than in the one she had now. Sheila sometimes wonders if she has made a mistake.

"Actually," Miller says, "it appears to be a suicide, which means that Maxwell doesn't have to report it to us. She can call in a justice of the peace for a ruling and let it go at that. But she apparently has a couple of questions about the scene. She wants us to come up and take a look before she brings in the JP. Sounds pretty routine to me."

"Yeah," Sheila says regretfully. It sounds pretty routine to her, too — until Miller pauses and clears his throat. She can hear him being careful with his words.

"Thing is, Chief, Maxwell is asking for you, particularly. I told her you're on light duty and mostly piloting the desk these days. But she's pretty insistent. Says she wants *you*."

He seems apologetic and perhaps even a little condescending — or maybe Sheila is more sensitive to patronizing males than she used to be. But he sounds even more arrogant when he says, "It would be good if you called her and let her know why you won't be coming. Tell her I'll be there as soon as I can get away. I'll take Connors with me, on the off-chance that this might turn into something we need to be involved in."

Light duty? Piloting the desk? Sheila straightens her shoulders, frowning. Just where does Miller get off telling his chief what to do, especially on something as potentially big as a faculty suicide? And if Maxwell has questions, maybe this isn't a suicide.

The campus is part of Pecan Springs and there are established procedures for the division of responsibilities. Campus security officers are trained as police officers and licensed by the State of Texas. They deal mostly with traffic violations and drug and liquor problems, of course, and to a lesser degree with burglaries, robberies, sexual assaults, and criminal mischief. But they have direct telephone and radio contact with the PSPD, the Pecan Springs fire department, and emergency medical services. When they need backup, they know who to call. There have been telephone and email threats that get everybody's attention, but there's never been a faculty suicide. This is out of the ordinary.

Out of the ordinary.

"Did you get the name of the victim?" she asks. "Location?"

"Not yet." Miller sounds surprised. "I was planning to get all that when I —"

"How quick can you be ready to go?"

"Why, five minutes, I guess. But if you could just call her and —"

Sheila speaks briskly. "Detective Connors is off the hook on this one. Call Maxwell and get the location of the body. Tell her that you and I will meet her there in twenty. Pick me up in the parking lot in five."

Without waiting for his muttered "Yes, ma'am," she hangs up the phone and goes to the door. "Connie, Denise Maxwell called. There's been a suicide on campus. I'm going up there and taking Miller with me."

"Yes, ma'am," Connie says. She looks up. "I've added Paula Mason and Lucia Fernandez to the interview list. I just talked to Billie Jo, and she's on her way. But you don't have to see her today. You go do what you have to do. I'll schedule all three for tomorrow."

Sheila nods. "Don't forget to mention those blouses. And her nails."

Feeling better than she has for several weeks, she heads for the bathroom.

CHAPTER THREE

The clock on the dash says 4:18 when Sheila settles herself awkwardly in the unmarked Chevy Impala Dylan Miller is driving. It has been parked in the hot September sun — September is still summer in the Hill Country — and is as steamy and stifling as the sauna at the gym. She slides the seat back as far as it will go and pulls out the seat belt, lifting up the baby in her belly and fastening the lap belt across the top of her thighs (she lacks a lap) and the shoulder belt between her breasts (no lack of these, and they're tender). The belt is stubborn and Miller pretends not to notice that she's struggling with it.

His casual pretense makes her even more conscious of the ungainliness of this maneuver, and her face colors as she pulls her rumpled maternity top down. She hates the damn thing. It's like a circus tent, and she's the elephant. She grew up knowing that she is attractive (the luck of the gene pool), and she has always had the reflexes of an athlete and the stamina of the Energizer bunny. Now, her weight and her shape make it difficult to move without calculation, she's exhausted by lunchtime, and as for feeling attractive, forget it. Her blond hair is like coarse straw, her face is splotchy, and while *radiant* or *glowing* may describe some soon-to-be-moms, it definitely does not apply to her. The washed-out baggy-eyed woman in her bathroom mirror is a stranger whom she does not want to meet.

Miller starts the car and turns on the air conditioner, which blows a stream of hot air across Sheila's face. He cocks his head. "All set?" he asks, with a snarkily solicitous half-smile.

Sheila turns the AC setting to cold and pushes the vent to direct the air onto her face. She resists the impulse to growl. "Let's go."

"Yes, ma'am," he says, and pulls away.

In contrast to Sheila's wrinkled uniform, Miller is in neat plainclothes — pressed jeans, blue shirt and darker blue tie, tan jacket with leather elbow patches, and polished cowboy boots that boost his height, so that he tops Sheila by several inches. Sheila knows that he's wearing a Sig Sauer

P320 in his shoulder holster, and that he's an expert marksman, one of the best in the department. Crisp dark hair, deeply tanned face, lean and wiry build. Single, never married, which may account for his evident discomfort around her now. (Did the poor man never have a mother? A sister?) His features are too irregular to be good-looking; his dark eyes are wary, watchful. He has a way of anticipating others' mistakes, and he's impatient with the shortcomings of human beings in general. He likes the headwork but lacks empathy, which makes him a better detective than a cop.

"You called Maxwell?" she asks, bracing her feet against the floor as the Impala makes a hard left out of the lot.

"Yes. She's expecting us." Driving with one hand, Miller adds, "She said she was glad you could come, since you know your way around the campus." He arches an eyebrow. "I got the idea she wasn't talking about the physical layout."

"I was chief of security there for three-plus years," Sheila says. "It's a small campus, so you get to know a lot of people." The lap belt is tight in the wrong places and she readjusts it. "Did Maxwell give you a cause of death?"

"Shot himself. In his lab — his greenhouse, that is — sometime last night. That's what it *looks* like, anyway." Judiciously, he adds, "She said."

"Ah," Sheila says. *That's what it* looks *like, anyway.* Which suggests that Denise, who is a bright young woman with a sharply critical eye, is wondering whether what it *looks like* is different from what it *is.*

Which was smart, Sheila thinks. If you go into an investigation assuming that it's a suicide because that's how somebody called it in, you're likely to miss important information or contaminate the scene. It was also smart to call the PSPD up front. If this turns out to be a homicide, the university won't want to handle the investigation and will be anxious for PSPD to take the case. And since the campus was once her turf, it would make sense for her to partner Miller on this. The thought of it perks her up, makes her feel like a cop again. Almost.

She tries to keep her voice flat. "Did you get the name of the deceased?"

Left hand on the wheel, Dylan fishes in his right jacket pocket and pulls out a small notebook. He flips it open with a thumb. "Fairlee," he says. "Carl Fairlee. Botany prof."

"That'll be the Plant Sciences building," Sheila says. "Take Lampasas all the way up

71

the hill. The building is just past Bandera, on the left."

She frowns, remembering Fairlee, but not in much detail. Late forties, maybe early fifties. Balding, a bit of a paunch. Full professor, tenured, a researcher in, *what*? Tropical plants, maybe. She thinks he's the one who stuck that greenhouse on the roof of the Plant Sciences building — the cause of some unhappiness on the campus, although she can't remember exactly why. Funding, or the source of it, something like that. She does remember that Fairlee liked to work late, and when she drives up Lampasas at night she often sees lights in that rooftop greenhouse. The whole building will be dark as the grave, but there's Fairlee's greenhouse, lit up like the party deck on a cruise ship.

Sheila turns her head away from Miller, looking out of the window and allowing herself a small smile. Strangely (or perhaps it isn't strange at all), the farther she gets from her office, the lighter and more energetic she feels. While she loves policing, she doesn't love sitting behind her desk, which is what she does, now that she's chief — and especially now that she's pregnant. She didn't go into police work because she wanted to be stuck at a computer keyboard, or slogging her way through an endless landscape of meetings and memos and budgets. She became a cop because she has a tremendous respect for the law — not for *laws,* necessarily, but for the Law with a capital L. Being a police officer means helping to preserve order in an otherwise disorderly and chaotic world. Helping to enforce the laws that bind people together, preserve their rights and uphold their obligations — although experience has taught her that justice is never as clear and simple out in the world as it is on the pages of the Texas Penal Code. She doesn't deny that the administrative job she's doing is important. Without all those stacks of paper, the constant memos and emails and meetings, the cops on the street can't do what they do. But none of that yields the deeper satisfaction of hands-on police work. Deep down and enduringly, she misses it.

Ironic, she thinks. She had wanted the PSPD chief's job, and she got it. She wanted a baby and she got that, too. Now what? What she has is a tedious desk job and a baby coming in forty-nine days, on top of which she is losing her super-competent assistant and gaining an inexperienced young thing who has to be told to wear blouses that the guys can't see through.

73

Miller is driving fast, heading north up Lampasas on the east side of the CTSU campus, above the river. Pecan Springs is located halfway between Austin and San Antonio, on the long-inactive Balcones Fault, where eons ago, a series of earthquakes erected a palisade of limestone cliffs. To the west of the palisade rises the rugged Texas Hill Country, famous for its upland string of spring-fed rivers and river-fed lakes, cupped like brilliant blue sapphires in the cedar-clad hills. To the east, on the other side of I-35, lies the blackland prairie: once fertile farms and pastures, now a patchy hodge-podge of small towns and sprawling subdivisions separated by shopping malls and office parks.

Pecan Springs is different things to different people. Some see it as a cozy bedroom community, a serene place to come home to after a stressful day at work in Austin or San Antonio. For others, it is a safe, comfortable enclave in which to raise kids, or a promising place to start a small business or go to college. Still others are lured by its potential for big-money commercial investment, especially along the I-35 corridor, where property doubles in value every time it changes hands.

Sheila gets that, all of it, and understands

how everybody manages to see a different piece of the same small town. There is nothing cozy or comfortable about *her* Pecan Springs, though. What she sees are the daily crime reports, with domestic violence and property crimes topping the list, and too many opioid deaths. One way or another, drugs — both supply and demand — are behind most of the crime in Pecan Springs. It wouldn't surprise Sheila to discover that the professor's death was drug-related.

They've reached the top of the hill and Miller stops for the light at Bandera, as a gaggle of students — long-legged girls in short shorts, guys in ragged jeans with heavy backpacks — crosses the street in front of them. The Plant Sciences building is on the other side of the intersection, on the left. Brick, with three wrap-around tiers of mid-century modern windows, it was built shortly after World War II, when CTSU was still a small teachers' college. Even from here, Sheila can see Fairlee's greenhouse perched like a shiny hat on the building's roof, several people clustered around it.

"Park there," she says, and points to the curb cut nearest the main entrance. Miller makes a left, swings the Impala into an empty visitor's slot, and they get out. A uniformed campus police officer — young, mid-twenties, Sheila guesses — is standing beside the main entrance. The name badge on the pocket of his uniform shirt says *Wakeland, Boyce.*

Miller flashes his PSPD badge and says, "Chief Dawson and Detective Miller, here to see Director Maxwell."

"Yessir, Chief," Wakeland says, snapping to attention.

Stone-faced, Miller corrects him. "*This* is Chief Dawson." He gestures to Sheila.

The officer colors. "Sorry," he mutters. His surprised glance goes to Sheila's belly and he pinches his lips together. Without another word, he leads them into the building and past the Plant Sciences departmental office. He is heading for the stairs when Sheila says "I know the elevator is slow as molasses, but let's take it."

"Whatever you say, ma'am," Wakeland replies, with barely muted snark. When they get out on the third floor, he points to the left. "Down that hall, up the stairs. On the roof."

"Thank you," Sheila says. She and Miller walk past a phalanx of closed office doors to the end of the hall. A sign on the wall beside the stairs says *Dr. Fairlee's Greenhouse/Lab. By permission only.* When they reach the top of the narrow stairs, the door opens into the glare of the bright afternoon sun, and Sheila blinks.

The greenhouse is some twelve or fourteen feet wide and twenty feet long. The outdoor temperature is in the upper eighties on this sunny afternoon, and the door in front of them is propped open. Inside, hoses snake across the damp gravel floor, shade cloth protects some sections from the too-bright sun, and fans are circulating the warm, moist air. The place is jam-packed with green and blossoming plants, most of them orchids, in an incredible variety of exotic colors and erotic shapes. There are also shelves lined with rows and rows of glass vials and small jars in which tiny green plants are growing.

"Helluva good place to grow pot," Miller says, *sotto voce,* and Sheila nods. Marijuana is illegal in Texas, but three or four plants might be safely concealed in this lush green forest.

An open center aisle runs the length of the greenhouse, and two people stand near the far end. Five or six feet away, a body lies on the floor.

"Director Maxwell," Sheila calls and steps forward, careful not to trip over the tangle of hoses on the gravel. The last thing she needs is to do a belly flop.

Denise Maxwell turns. Trimly uniformed in navy blue, she is a black woman, late twenties, with an erect posture and a combed-out short afro that emphasizes the sharp angles of her face, which are softened by a smile.

"Chief," she says, and holds out a hand. "Thanks for coming."

"Glad to, Denise," Sheila says. She gestures to Dylan. "Dylan Miller, our lead detective."

The man standing with Maxwell is short and portly, gray-haired with gold-rimmed glasses, in his early fifties. He is wearing a rumpled dark suit and a pained expression. Maxwell says, "This is Dr. Selms, the chairman of Plant Sciences. Carl Fairlee is — was — one of his faculty members."

"Good to see you again, Dr. Selms," Sheila says, remembering conversations with him when she was chief of security. And remembering that he had wanted the building left unlocked past midnight so students could use the Plant Sciences library on the first floor. She wonders if he still insists on that. She glances toward the body, sprawled face-down on the greenhouse gravel floor. "Sorry for the occasion."

"Chief," Selms says. His glance flicks to her maternity top and back to her face. "I'm

not sure why Ms. Maxwell thought it necessary to bring in the Pecan Springs police.
Carl's suicide is campus business. Tragic, of
course. I hope we can keep it quiet."

"I think we all just want to be sure there
are no questions," Sheila says, but Selms is
shaking his head.

"I simply don't understand," he mutters.
"How could Carl do it *here,* of all places?"
He raises his arms in frustration and lets
them drop. "And for God's sake, *why?* Was
he sick? Was he on something? Drugs, I
mean. Was he —"

He breaks off and turns to Maxwell. "I'm
acquainted with Carl's wife, Maggie — his
ex-wife, I should say. She owns that garden
center on the east side of town. Sonora, it's
called. I want to let her know about this, so
she can tell their children before word starts
getting around." His tone is peremptory. He
isn't asking permission.

Maxwell nods. "It's kind of you to offer,
Dr. Selms. No details, please. Just tell her
there'll be a full investigation. We'll be in
touch with her shortly."

"And what about the Plant Sciences
faculty?" Selms is sweating heavily. He pulls
out a large white handkerchief, takes off his
glasses, and mops his glistening face. "People can see that something is going on, and

I really must make an announcement. I've already gotten a couple of urgent calls from the dean's office."

"I understand," Maxwell says. "Go ahead and update Dean Clayton. It would be best to simply tell her that the body has been found, without going into detail, and that the PSPD is here." Tactfully, she adds, "She will likely prefer to let the provost and President Richmond know before they release the news to the faculty."

Good for you, Denise, Sheila thinks, admiring Maxwell's finesse. Bureaucracy first, faculty later. And Selms won't be making the announcement.

Selms suppresses a sigh. "I suppose you're right. Well, I'll go make the calls." He glances briefly at Sheila. "If you want me, Chief, I'll be in my office." He nods to Miller and bustles up the aisle toward the door, obviously glad to be gone.

"Glad you could come," Maxwell says to Sheila, with the slightest emphasis on "you." She casts a sidelong glance at Miller, which he pretends not to see. He reaches into his pocket and pulls out two pairs of disposable Tyvek booties, handing one pair to Sheila, who pulls them on. She considers kneeling on the gravel to get a closer look at the body, then rejects that idea. She can probably get down, but getting up would be difficult, like a rhino getting up from a nap. Anyway, she can see what she needs to see by simply stepping closer.

Fairlee is lying on his stomach, arms flung out, head turned awkwardly to the right. He is a long-limbed, lanky man, dressed in khaki pants and a blue plaid shirt, his ginger hair pulled back in a limp ponytail. A handgun with a suppressor lies a few inches from his outstretched right hand. Sheila can see the entrance wound, a small, neat hole just above the right temple. It is filled with a black bubble of dried blood and surrounded by a barely visible reddish-brown area of abraded skin. Blood has pooled under and around his head, soaking into the gravel, so there must be an exit wound on the left side of the head.

Sheila frowns, leaning closer. She is looking for the round imprint of the gun barrel, which she has seen on suicide victims in cases where the gun was pressed against the skin — and not seeing it. She is also looking for soot and stippling, the powder tattoo. She is not seeing that, either. Still, she's aware that suppressors can produce atypical entrance wounds, so that's not conclusive.

Miller has no problem getting up or down and is already squatting on his haunches on

81

the other side of the body. He pulls a hand lens out of his jacket pocket and peers through it at the entrance wound. After a moment, he glances up at Sheila and gives a slight, quick shake of his head. He's looking for — and not seeing — the same things she looked for and didn't see. But he glances at the suppressor, and she knows what he's thinking.

Sheila turns to Maxwell. "How about filling us in, Denise?"

"Fairlee's RA — Logan Gardner — found the body at three-fifteen this afternoon. The two of them were supposed to meet downstairs, in the prof's office. When Gardner found the office door locked, he came up here to the greenhouse, spotted the body, and called it in to security. Officer Wakeland was here at three-thirty-two. I was in a meeting on the west side of the campus. I arrived at three-forty-eight."

Automatically, Sheila looks at her watch. It is 4:50.

"Selms was here when I arrived," Maxwell adds. "With Gardner and Officer Wakeland. The RA is waiting downstairs. He's been cautioned not to talk to anybody."

"RA?" Miller asks. "What's an RA?" He is now looking closely at the gun, still lying on the ground.

"Research assistant," Sheila says.

Maxwell nods. "Gardner is a graduate student, working on his PhD. Says he spends a lot of time here in the greenhouse. I understand that he and Fairlee were involved in some sort of plant breeding project. Something to do with orchids."

Sheila asks, "Suicide note?"

"If there is one, I haven't found it. But I haven't checked Fairlee's office downstairs."

"You've called Judge Davidson?" Miller asks. He is taking photos with his cell phone.

In Texas counties that don't have a coroner or a medical examiner, a justice of the peace is required to rule on all unattended deaths and decide when and where an autopsy must be performed. After decades of service, Maude Porterfield finally retired — "older than God," as she herself says, "but still kicking" — and Arthur Davidson was recently elected to replace her. Davidson's chief qualifications are twenty years as Pecan Springs High School head football coach, twenty-four years as First Baptist deacon and church youth leader, and three years as director of the church choir. No legal or law enforcement experience.

"I put in a call to Davidson after I called your office." Maxwell's mouth quirked. "He took the afternoon off to go fishing. Somebody had to drive out to the lake to fetch him."

Sheila rolls her eyes. "He doesn't have a cell?"

"Apparently not." Maxwell is straight-faced.

"Let's tell Davidson to order an autopsy," Sheila says. A few years before, there had been an attempt in the Texas legislature to require autopsies in all apparent suicides. Inspired by the case of a Texas woman whose philandering husband nearly got away with staging her murder to look like a suicide, the bill had been supported by the Justice Court Judges Association. It would take the heat off local JPs, many of whom — like Davidson — have little experience with forensics or criminal investigations. But it hadn't gotten out of the Criminal Juris-prudence committee. Autopsies cost too much. Poor counties couldn't afford them.

"Good idea," Maxwell says.

"But I want it done locally," Sheila adds. "At Adams. Otherwise, we could be waiting for a week." One of the docs at the Adams County Hospital does autopsies on occa-sion, but most bodies are sent to Austin, to the Travis County Medical Examiner's Of-fice on Sabine Street, adjacent to the Uni-versity Medical Center Brackenridge. The

84

TCME has five full-time medical examiners and serves a forty-two-county region in Central Texas. It is competent and expert, but out-of-county bodies get in line behind the local traffic, which can mean that the autopsy report is delayed by several days. If you're in a hurry, or if you think it's a simple autopsy without much toxicology testing, the body should go to Adams.

"Local is good," Maxwell says. "I'm in favor."

Miller lifts Fairlee's arm, testing for rigor, then rises to his feet, straightening in an easy, graceful motion that Sheila envies. "Rigor's passed," he says. "He's been dead for more than six or seven hours."

"It's hot in here," Sheila points out. "Makes it harder to judge."

"There's that," Miller agrees. He nods at the gun. "Glock 43. Suppressor."

"Yes," Sheila says. "So it is. A little unusual, don't you think?"

Suppressors, also called silencers, are an after-market modification, legal in Texas only in the past couple of years. But if you buy one, you have to register it with the Bureau of Alcohol, Tobacco, and Firearms, pay a $200 transfer tax, and wait for eight or nine months before the paperwork clears. It's a costly and cumbersome process.

"It's one of the reasons I called you guys," Maxwell says. "I looked around and found a cartridge." She points to it, lying on the gravel several feet away. She has marked it temporarily by turning a small empty pot upside down beside it.

That's my girl, Sheila thinks approvingly. She says, "Anybody know offhand if the gun belongs to Fairlee?"

Maxwell replies, "Selms says that he's known the man for a couple of decades and is amazed that he owned a gun."

Maybe especially a gun with a suppressor, Sheila thinks. Most casual gun owners don't see the need. "So what's the other reason you called us?"

Maxwell straightens her shoulders. "Fairlee reported a break-in weekend before last, here at the greenhouse. Officer Wakeland looked into it and took a few photos. The door was jimmied, but nothing appeared to have been taken."

"You thought that was unusual?" Miller asks. He is taking photos of the spent cartridge.

"Not in itself, no," Maxwell replies. "But early the next morning, I got a phone call from Fairlee. He'd had more time to look around, he said. He discovered that whoever broke in had gotten away with a plant."

86

"A *plant*?" Miller sounds skeptical.

Maxwell nods. "An orchid. A 'demon orchid,' he called it. Apparently, part of the blossom looks like a devil and the petals look like claws. For some reason — I don't get why, exactly — it is supposed to be valuable. Unusual. Rare, even. It was from Colombia." She pauses. "It was apparently in some sort of glass case, a terrarium, according to Fairlee. He was pretty upset about the theft, and not just because the orchid was worth a lot of money. He said there were other valuable plants in the greenhouse, and he was angry because now he had to worry about security." Another pause. "He said he had a suspect in mind."

"Did he tell you who?" Sheila rests a hand on her belly. The baby is moving restlessly, pushing against her bladder. She knows she has to locate a bathroom — *How far away? On the ground floor, maybe?* — in the next few minutes.

Maxwell shakes her head. "He said it was a personal matter, and he didn't want the university involved. I got the impression that he suspected another faculty member. The theft happened on a Sunday night and the building was locked, so it had to be somebody who had a key." She hesitates. "He said he was taking care of the matter himself. I warned him it was a bad idea to get confrontational on this and asked him again to give me the name of his suspect."

"And what did he say?" Miller asks.

Maxwell looks down at Fairlee's body. "He said 'Like hell I will' and hung up on me."

Sheila has already seen and heard enough to know that a ruling on the cause of Fairlee's death ought to be delayed until after the autopsy and the preliminary investigation. And that this is a job for a detective unit, not for campus security. She says: "I can offer a crime-scene team, if you're ready to request it, Denise. Miller plus two. And me." She knows that Miller is listening.

Maxwell nods, obviously relieved. "I think there's an MOU on collaboration — I'll have to look it up."

"It's not complicated," Sheila says. She helped to write that memorandum of understanding when she was sitting at Maxwell's desk and Bubba Harris was Pecan Springs' chief of police. "Just initial the paragraphs and sign the last page. Your vice president will need to sign, and then you can fax it to me. Or scan and send a PDF."

"You'll be taking the lead?" Maxwell asks. "After all, you know your way around the campus."

Sheila glances in Miller's direction. His mouth tightens but he nods shortly, resigned.

Damn straight, she thinks. "Yes," she says. She leans toward Maxwell and lowers her voice. "Where's the nearest bathroom, Denise?"

By the time she gets back, Judge Davidson has arrived. The new JP is a rotund, jovial-looking man in his late sixties, still in his fishing clothes and moving in a cloud of *eau de catfish.* He surveys the scene uncertainly.

"What do you want me to do, Chief?" he asks.

"Order an autopsy," Sheila says, wishing (not for the first time) that Judge Porterfield had not retired. Newly elected justices are supposed to attend eighty hours of classes at the Texas Justice Court Training Center, but this one seemed to have missed several critical sessions. He has been in office for only a few months, and already there have been murmurings of discontent among police officers and people with matters before his court.

"An autopsy?" Surprised, the judge takes off his hat and wipes the sweat off his forehead with the sleeve of his blue shirt. "How come? Sure looks to me like the fella killed himself." He points. "See there? That's the gun, right where it fell out of his hand. Bet it's got his fingerprints all over it."

Sheila suppresses a sigh. "Right, Judge. But in most cases where the victim shoots himself, the barrel is pressed against the skin. There is zero evidence that this happened here — no soot, no pressure mark. In fact, the lack of any visible powder tattooing suggests that the gun was fired from a distance of thirty inches or more."

"And his arms aren't that long," Miller says. "Especially since that gun has a suppressor."

"Is that what it is?" says Davidson, peering at the weapon.

"We'll have his hands tested for powder residue," Sheila says. "The autopsy should be done quickly. If we send him to Austin, it could be a week. Maybe two. Let's get it done at the county hospital."

"Bet it's cheaper, too," the judge says, as if cost is the deciding factor. He borrows Sheila's cell to phone the order to his office answering machine, complains that he had to leave the lake when the fish were biting, and is on his way.

Miller takes more photos, then bags Fairlee's hands, the dead man's cell phone and keys, the rest of what's in his pockets, and the gun and cartridge. By this time, two EMTs have arrived to pick up the body. Wrestling the loaded gurney down the narrow stairs to the third floor isn't an easy job. But they get it done and head for the hospital. When they're on their way, Miller calls Dr. Berry — Fred Berry, the surgeon on duty that evening — who promises he'll get on it quick as he can.

Sheila looks around. To Miller, she says, "Let's get a team up here tonight to make sure we haven't missed anything. I'm going downstairs to talk to the guy who found the body. Selms, too. Maybe you can get started on Fairlee's known movements on Sunday, last contacts, et cetera. But let's keep it low-key until we have a cause of death."

"Got it." Miller nods shortly. They both know why. If it's suicide, they can hand it back to Maxwell.

Inside the greenhouse, it was hot and humid. Outside on the roof, the dry breeze feels good against Sheila's damp skin. Looking down on the street, four floors below, she can see curious passersby, students and faculty, craning their necks to look up.

"I don't see any reason to lock the building," Sheila tells Maxwell. "But for now, let's cordon off the stairs to the roof and post one of your security officers on the third floor, where he can watch the stairs and keep an eye on Fairlee's office. Better cordon that, too." The office could be considered as part of the extended crime scene — if she's right. If that's what this is. A crime scene.

"Sure thing," Maxwell says. She leans forward and lowers her voice, although there is no one nearby to hear them. "I'm glad you're taking this one, Chief. There's been bad blood in this department ever since this greenhouse thing went up here, you know."

"No, I didn't know, but I'm not surprised," Sheila says. "Tell me about it."

She can appreciate Denise's wariness. Campus politics are labyrinthine. A dispute involving faculty can be vicious, even if it looks like nothing more than a petty turf war over a few inconsequential footnotes in an insignificant publication. It can also be something bigger, dirtier, and deeper. Embezzlement, for instance, or fraud, like the time the chairman of the physics department double-billed the university for thousands of dollars of conference travel, then tried to blame it on his secretary's bad bookkeeping.

"There was one humongous stink about

that greenhouse," Maxwell replies. "Dr. Fairlee paid for it out of a research grant. He hired a contractor and had it built over the last couple of weeks of August, while almost everybody was gone. He didn't clear the construction with anybody. Not Dr. Selms or the dean or *anybody.*"

"No kidding." Sheila blinks. "Wow. That took hutzpah. Or something." When she worked on this campus, you couldn't install a bookshelf in your office without getting permission from the powers that be. That greenhouse must have been a sharp thumb in the university's collective eye — or a middle-finger salute. Perhaps it still was. A permanent and highly visible up-yours.

"Oh, you bet," Maxwell says fervently. "Everybody thought it was simply bizarre. The student newspaper called it 'Fairlee's Folly' and treated it like a friggin' joke. But of course it wasn't. I figured that the dean would order Buildings and Grounds to tear the thing down, but she didn't. Then I heard that Fairlee got reprimanded and his salary frozen. But the Plant Sciences faculty thought that wasn't good enough. One of the profs wrote an open letter to the dean saying that Fairlee should be fired and got half the faculty to sign it. There were threats, hate mail, even some vandalism."

"Vandalism?" Interesting. Rivals? Threats? Hate mail? All irrelevant or connected to the death? Sheila takes out her notebook and starts making notes.

"Twice. Shots fired from the street at night, probably from a passing car. Nobody hurt, just glass broken. Also the break-in I told you about, and the plant Fairlee claimed was stolen."

"And the threats?"

"He forwarded me three or four emails, anonymous. I've hung onto them, as well as several pieces of hate mail he got. All pretty juvenile, I thought. Could have come from a student. Or a professor pretending to be a student."

"Fax them over, please," Sheila says. She scribbles her email address on a notebook page, tears it out, and hands it to Maxwell. In her mind, she has already moved past suicide to homicide, thinking that the sooner the investigation gets underway, the better.

"Yeah. What else can I do?"

"How about compiling a list of faculty who have an office in this building. Do you have somebody who can do interviews? Pin everyone down as to their whereabouts on Sunday night and early Monday morning, through five or six a.m."

Maxwell brightens. "I can do that myself."

"Good. We need to know what times they were here, whom they might have seen in the building or the parking lot, whether they saw or spoke to Fairlee while they were here."

"Fairlee's office is on the third floor," Maxwell says. "If you want to check it out, I've got a passkey."

"And I'll need to talk to the guy who found the body," Sheila reminds her. "Selms, too."

"Both are in the department office, first floor. I would go with you, but the dean wants to see me. She'll have to hear from me why I'm involving the PSPD." Maxwell pauses at the door to the stairs, giving Sheila a sympathetic glance. "I hope this isn't too tough on you, Chief. Being on your feet, I mean. When are you due?"

Sheila flinches. Come to think of it, her feet hurt — it's the swelling in her ankles, of course. And her back, always her back. But she's not going to show it.

"Early November," she says, shifting her weight. "And no, it's not too tough." She lets a smile ghost across her lips and makes a joke of it. "As long as I'm within commuting distance of a bathroom. Put me out in the middle of the campus, and I could be

95

in serious trouble."

"Understand," Maxwell says. "Never been there myself, and to tell the truth, I don't think I want to. But my sister — she's a pediatric nurse — just had her second. Plumbing problems the whole time, seems like. She had to quit work in her eighth month." She grins. "Kinda makes you wonder why people have babies."

Fairlee's third-floor office is the standard one-window affair with a littered desk, bookcases double-stacked with books, and piles of papers and computer printouts on the floor. If there's a suicide note in this mess, it doesn't immediately jump out at her, and Sheila doesn't have a warrant. But she notes that there is a laptop. They'll want to have a good look at that. She'll also check with Selms to see if Fairlee used another computer somewhere. And she'll tell Miller that they're sealing the office until they can come back with a warrant. Ditto Fairlee's home or apartment. Assuming, of course, that she's right. That they're dealing with a homicide.

And there are other things to consider. Friends? Girlfriends? How about rivals? She'll ask Selms — he might know. The wife, too — no, ex-wife. She'll get the name from Selms and pay the woman a visit. As she mentally scrolls through the list of tasks, Sheila feels energized and invigorated, back on her A game. Lots to do, plenty to organize, a killer to find — if she's right.

But first things first. The kid who found the body.

Logan Gardner, Fairlee's research assistant, is waiting in a small conference room off the departmental office. But he is no kid. In his early thirties, he is an athletic-looking man with a square jaw, a summer tan, and sun-bleached short-clipped blond hair. Wearing jeans and a yellow shirt with the sleeves rolled up, showing golden hairs gleaming on bronzed arms, he's sitting at the conference table when Sheila comes in and introduces herself. He looks stunned. And troubled.

"It was a shock, I'll tell you." He shakes his head despairingly. "I mean, Dr. Fairlee had a hell of a lot going for him just now. Publications, grant money, a commercially promising —" He breaks off, shaking his head. "I keep asking myself why he would kill himself. Why, why, *why*? It just doesn't make any sense."

"I'm sorry," Sheila says, taking a seat on the other side of the table. She won't say anything definitive about the cause of death until she has Berry's autopsy results. "I understand you were his research assistant. Had you worked together long?"

"Since I was an undergrad. Three — no, almost four — years now. We've got this important breeding project going. I don't know what's going to happen to it." He swallows. "Now that he's dead, I mean."

"I don't know much about plants," Sheila says, opening her notebook. "But just glancing around the greenhouse, it looked to me like Dr. Fairlee was into orchids in a pretty big way. Is that right?"

"Yeah. He has some very rare orchids up there." Gardner clasps his hand on the table. "But that's a hobby, not his main research interest. *Our* main research interest. I mean, I've been working with him on it for a couple of years." He hesitates, like a little boy who has a secret and isn't sure he should be talking about it. But he's also proud and excited, and the excitement wins out. "It's . . . it's vanilla."

"Vanilla?" Sheila says blankly. She's not much of a cook, but even she knows what vanilla is. "You mean, like in ice cream?"

Gardner nods eagerly. "Yeah, right. Vanilla is an orchid."

"Really?" Sheila is surprised. "An orchid? I had no idea." Actually, she had no idea that vanilla came from a *plant*. It was just . . . vanilla. In that little brown bottle.

"Most people don't. Have any idea, I mean." Gardner leans forward, his voice earnest. "You see, what we've learned is that different vanilla species can exchange genes across species barriers, which opens up the possibility for developing a whole new generation of commercial cultivars. We've been working on a hybrid that's disease resistant and super-productive. Plus, it has a remarkably high level of vanillin — the stuff that makes vanilla smell and taste so good. That's really important right now, with the cost of vanilla so high."

"It is?" Sheila asked.

"Yeah. Sky-high and going higher. Dr. Fairlee and I were all set to file a plant patent, but —" He stops and his face seems to shut down.

"But what?" Sheila prompts.

His face hardens and he turns his head away. "But now I'll need to figure out how to keep what belongs to me," he says. "It might turn out to be a little . . . tricky."

Sheila isn't sure what he means by this, but they can go into it later, if it's relevant. Right now, she needs to pin down other details. She takes notes while Gardner describes his discovery of the body earlier that afternoon, then asks him for his movements on Sunday and doesn't answer when he wonders out loud why that's important.

"Since this is a suicide," he says. His gaze rests on her badge, then her shoulder patch. "You're a town cop, aren't you? How come you guys are involved?"

"Do you have reason to believe it *isn't* a suicide?" she asks. When he shakes his head mutely, she says, "We get involved when campus security invites us. It's all just routine." She repeats her question. "Sunday night?"

Frowning, he says, "I was home, working on my dissertation." He chuckles wryly. "I do that a lot, these days. Trying to finish, so I can start looking for a job."

"Anybody with you?"

He shakes his head. "No. My roommate was out of town."

"Thanks," she says. "We may come up with a few other questions, so let me get your contact information. Cell number? Email? Residential address?" She writes them down as he gives them to her, then closes her notebook. "I think that's it for now, unless you have some questions."

"I guess I . . ." He flexes his fingers. "There are some plants that need attention. Okay if I go upstairs and take care of that?"

"The greenhouse is off limits for a day or two." Sheila stands. "Is that going to be a problem?"

"A day or two?" He sounds doubtful. "Yeah, maybe. A problem, I mean. We have the plants on a regular watering schedule, and Dr. Fairlee would hate it if we lost something." He stands too, rubbing the back of his neck and frowning. "I guess I don't understand. How come it's off limits? Dr. Fairlee's body is . . . I mean, he's gone. I saw the EMTs taking him away."

"There's a bit more to do up there," Sheila says, going to the door of the conference room. "I'll see about letting you in tomorrow afternoon. And someone will call you to make an appointment for an interview." She smiles. "Thank you, Mr. Gardner."

"Yeah," Gardner says. "Well, thanks."

But his frown has deepened.

There's one more stop to make, in Selms' office. Sheila is wondering whether she should use the bathroom again, but this preliminary interview shouldn't take very long. She decides she can put it off.

The chairman's secretary — a plain-faced, auburn-haired woman of middle age, in a pink blouse, pink beads, and gray pleated skirt — looks up over tortoise-rimmed glasses. Her eyes are red-rimmed, her lips are pale, and her face is splotchy. She has been crying.

"Chief Dawson," she says, and her voice breaks.

The name plate on her desk says Charlaine Rudolph, but Sheila doesn't need the reminder. They had met several times when Sheila had Maxwell's job. She remembers Charlaine as a rather prissy and tight-laced but very competent secretary.

"Hello, Charlaine," she says now. "Is your boss available?"

"He's on the phone with the dean, discussing this terrible business." With an effort, Charlaine gestures toward a chair. "Please *do* sit down." She reaches for a tissue. "Forgive me," she says in a lower voice. "I've known Dr. Fairlee for many years. I considered him a . . . friend."

"I'm sure it's hard," Sheila replies sympathetically. She sits, wondering if she made a mistake about the bathroom. "Will Dr. Selms be long, do you think?"

"I don't think so. He and the dean are deciding what to do about the announcement." Charlaine dabs at her eyes. "Suicide! I simply cannot understand it. Why, I saw him on Friday afternoon, just as cheerful as could be, walking down the hall, swinging his arms and whistling. I loved to hear him whistle," she adds emotionally. "Especially 'Yankee Doodle Dandy.' He wasn't from Texas, you know."

"Where was he from?" Sheila asks.

"The northeast." Charlaine's voice is heavy. "Vermont. He always considered himself a Yankee, which set him a bit apart from most of the other faculty. That, and his greenhouse, which caused quite a lot of unhappiness. It was kind of a mess, actually, and there was some jealousy over it. Some people were . . . upset."

An observant lady, this one, Sheila thinks, remembering that departmental secretaries often know more about what's going on than anybody else. " 'Some people were upset,' " she repeats slowly. "Do you have a particular person in mind?"

Charlaine looks away. "Oh, you know faculty," she says, with a vague wave of her hand. "They're like brothers and sisters. They get along most of the time, but there are egos." Another dab at her eyes. In a different voice, she adds, "Far be it from me to criticize, but there's always more competition than you might think, both professional and . . . well, personal."

Sheila hears the subtle emphasis on the

last word and is about to ask what it means, but Charlaine is holding up one finger. Her attention has been drawn to the phone on her desk, where the light has stopped blinking.

"Dr. Selms and the dean are finished now, Chief. You can go in."

"Thanks," Sheila says, and stands. "I would appreciate it if you could give me Dr. Fairlee's home address."

Charlaine reaches for a pink phone message pad and jots it down quickly. She tears off the page and hands it to Sheila. "Here you go."

Sheila thinks it's a bit odd that Charlaine has a professor's home address at the top of her mind, but she only says, "Thanks. Will you be around tomorrow? We may have a few more questions for you."

"Of course." Charlaine lifts her head. "Eight to five, off for an hour at noon — although I usually eat at my desk."

She hesitates, sighs, and adds, "This is my life, you know. I'm always here."

It doesn't take much imagination for Sheila to hear the self-pity in her voice.

Dan Selms is leaning back in his chair, staring fixedly out the window. On the sill are several blooming orchids.

"Dr. Selms," Sheila says, and his head jerks around.

"Oh, yes, Chief Dawson." He pushes himself out of his chair. "Won't you come in and sit down?" He gives her a solicitous smile. "You must be tired, being on your feet all afternoon." He doesn't add *because you're pregnant,* but she knows he's thinking it.

"Thank you," she says. Her ankles feel stiff and her feet hurt. She wishes she could put them up. But she sits, as he does. "I need to tell you that Director Maxwell has asked the Pecan Springs Police Department to take an active role in the investigation of Dr. Fairlee's death. She will clear that formally with the dean, and there will be an interagency MOU."

Selms' mouth drops open. "I don't understand," he protests. "Carl killed himself, didn't he? Why —"

She holds up her hand. "Dr. Fairlee's body has been removed for autopsy. The stairs to the roof have been sealed, as well as the professor's office, and Ms. Maxwell is posting an officer on the third floor. We'll have an investigative team in the greenhouse this evening." She pauses. "Perhaps you can tell me whether Dr. Fairlee used a departmental computer — in addition to the laptop in his office."

Selms looks startled, then dubious. "A departmental computer? No, not that I know of, but my secretary can probably tell you. And what's this about an autopsy? I thought —" He pulls his thin brows together. "Isn't it a little unusual? In the case of a suicide, I mean. And if you don't mind my asking, why are the police involved? Surely our campus security people can handle this matter without —"

"Ms. Maxwell has several reasons for feeling it would be better if we collaborated," Sheila says firmly. She nods toward the plants on the windowsill. "They're beautiful. So you're interested in orchids, too?"

"Yes." Selms' voice is stiff. "In fact, my interest predates Dr. Fairlee's." He gestures toward a wall that is hung with a dozen or more large color photographs of orchid blooms. "I have published several important papers on orchid biology, including the status of genomics, transformation technology, and the molecular regulatory mechanisms of floral development. My most recent research was published in the journal *Plant and Cell Physiology*. It is true that I have been somewhat hampered by a lack of laboratory space, but perhaps that will now be mitigated by —" He stops.

Sheila is watching him. "Mitigated by . . ." she prompts.

"That's of no importance." He leans forward on his folded arms, adjusting his tone. "Carl's research has hit a few snags lately. I understand that he was quite disappointed in the rejection of a paper a few weeks ago. Perhaps that was one of the reasons for his suicide." He shakes his head sadly. "I simply cannot understand a man who takes his life. Surely he had a few productive years left."

Sheila doesn't react. "Have you been able to reach Dr. Fairlee's former wife?"

"I've reached *my* wife." Selms takes off his glasses and rubs the bridge of his nose. "Quite coincidentally, Beverly had planned to go out to Sonoma Garden Center this afternoon. Maggie Walker — that's Carl's ex-wife — owns the place. I have prevailed on Beverly to tell Maggie what happened." He puts his glasses back on. "Carl's parents are both dead, I'm afraid. There's nobody else. Except the children, of course. A boy in college, a girl in high school. They will be devastated."

"I'm sure," Sheila says sympathetically. She glances at the clock on the shelf. "It's late, and I'm sure you'd like to leave. What time will it be convenient to talk tomorrow?"

"I'm teaching until ten," he says. "After that, I keep office hours for my students." He frowns. "But I don't understand, Chief Dawson. The man *killed* himself. Why do you need to go to all of this —"

"Just routine," she says, rising. "Tomorrow morning at ten, then. And thanks again."

Now she really *has* to find that bathroom again.

CHAPTER FOUR

Some herbs — sage, for example, or rose-mary or thyme — are content to grow peaceably in our backyard gardens, lend-ing comfort and pleasure to our everyday lives. Other herbs and spices, like chiles, cumin, garlic, and cilantro, are deeply identified with a particular cuisine. And still others are found simply everywhere, in everything, often integrated so subtly that we don't even notice them.
Vanilla, for instance.

China Bayles
"Vanilla: The Ice Cream Orchid"
Pecan Springs Enterprise

Vanilla is a member of the orchid family, one of the oldest families of plants in the world, a family that probably evolved more than 90 million years ago. Orchids are the largest family of flowering plants, with over 25,000 species in the wild and more than

100,000 hybrids created in laboratories and hothouses. . . . Vanilla produces the only edible fruit in the entire orchid family. . . . [It] is the most labor-intensive agricultural product in the world.

Patricia Rain
Vanilla: The Cultural History of the World's Favorite Flavor and Fragrance

Pecan Springs is still a small town, but in the late afternoon traffic, it was almost five o'clock by the time I got to Sonora Garden Center, out on King Road, a couple of miles east of the interstate. When I first moved here, the place was owned by Wanda Rathbottom. Called Wanda's Wonderful Acres, it was a three-acre plant paradise hedged in by acres of green pastureland and small truck farms.

But Wanda got into financial trouble and had to sell out. Allan and Betty Conrad bought it, tripled its size, and gave it a new name, Sonora Garden Center, reflecting their interest in plants of the arid Southwest. Their business did very well until it turned out that Allan Conrad was involved in an across-the-border drug smuggling operation with roots that reached south to Matamoros. He went to prison and his wife lost the garden center in an asset forfeiture,

110

prima facie evidence for the old adage that crime doesn't pay.

Maggie Walker, Sonora's third owner, was one of the first people I met when I moved to Pecan Springs. An experienced plantswoman, she helped me put in the herb gardens that surround Thyme and Seasons. Now, most of the herbs and other plants I retail at the shop come from Sonora. Maggie doesn't have the best bedside manner — she is short-tempered and blunt-spoken. But she is always ready to suggest an interesting alternative to potted geraniums or tell you that you absolutely do *not* want that invasive Japanese honeysuckle Walmart has on sale. And she has maintained and enlarged Sonora's display gardens, which are an important part of the garden center.

During the Conrads' tenure, they specialized in xeriscape plants suited to our hot, dry Central Texas summers, and Maggie has kept that emphasis. When you come through Sonora's front gate, the first thing you see is the large circular garden, some thirty or forty feet in diameter. In the center is an eight-foot waterfall that plunges down a wall of rough limestone and into a large pool surrounded by several mature Mexican bamboo palms, showy clumps of exotic grasses, a statuesque Argentine saguaro cactus, and an acacia tree that looks like it might offer welcome shade to a pride of Serengeti lions. Scattered around are a dozen smaller gardens featuring agaves and yuccas, prickly pear bearing garnet-colored ripe *tunas,* and other species of cacti, all with an attractive gravel mulch.

But Maggie has broadened the garden center's focus with her own interests. In fact, what first attracted me was her amazing passion for orchids, which is as deep and constant as mine for parsley, sage, rosemary, and thyme. She has a master's degree in horticulture and has been in love with orchids since her student days. In fact, she married her botany professor, Carl Fairlee (whose graduate seminar on vanilla orchids I audited), at least partly because he collected orchids — which turned into a huge problem when they got a divorce. Believe me, there is nothing more fiercely acrimonious than a pair of orchid fanciers divvying up their collection. Just one example: she had to give her ex a prized *Dendrobium* in order to keep her favorite harlequin *Phalaenopsis* hybrid, which she had bred herself.

Maggie's orchid greenhouses are her major addition to Sonora. The larger one is a retail house, where she displays blooming orchids for sale. If you're looking to grow

112

your orchid collection, that's where you're likely to spend a lot of time and a fair amount of money. When you go in, you'll be struck by the sight and scents of hundreds and hundreds of orchids. Orchids in large pots sitting on the damp gravel floor, lined up in neat rows on benches, hanging overhead. Huge white orchids as big as a lady's garden hat and tiny white orchids the size of a snowdrop. Red frilly flowers and sleek, shiny yellow flowers and some that are striped, spotted, or mottled. One resembles Darth Vader, another an iridescent sea anemone, a third an exotic lavender parrot with a bright red head and a yellow beak. Some — those with monkey faces, weird wings, corkscrew spurs, bristly whiskers, and other bizarre accessories — might not even be recognizable as flowers, if you weren't looking at them in an orchid house.

And do be careful. Orchid addiction is a serious and highly contagious disease. Once you get infected, you're dead. Start with a simple little moth orchid from the supermarket, and before you know it, you're a raving orchiholic who is dying to get her greedy little hands on a Holy Ghost or a Spotted Tiger. (Did I say that orchids have quirky common names?)

The second, smaller greenhouse is where

113

Maggie boards other people's orchids and where my *Vanilla planifolia* lives when it's not strutting its stuff in one of our vanilla workshops. "The boarding greenhouse is like a combination summer camp and spa for orchids," Maggie tells potential clients. "For two dollars a month, we will pesticize your plant, fertilize it, and otherwise coddle it in a climate-controlled environment just like the misty tropical jungles of home."

And that's where I was headed when I turned a corner and ran into Ruben, one of Maggie's half-dozen garden center staff. After several years of toting and hauling pots and plants, Ruben and I have become good buddies.

"Hey, Ruben, where'll I find the boss?" I asked.

"In the boarding greenhouse." Ruben, a gangly, gossipy young man with a bad case of acne, hooked a thumb over his shoulder. In a lower voice, he added, "Just a heads-up, Ms. Bayles. Our Maggie has been on the warpath since early this morning. Something to do with her ex, I gather." I'm not saying that Ruben stoops to listening at keyholes, but he can usually be counted on to know what's happening — and he likes to share what he knows.

"Wouldn't be unusual." I chuckled, knowing Maggie's short fuse. "Is she flinging things?" I had once seen her throw a pot against a wall so hard it shattered.

"Not yet," he replied with an answering grin. "But I definitely wouldn't rule it out." Ruben has seen her bad temper, too. In fact, he's been a recipient of it, on occasions when he hasn't done his job and plants have suffered or customers have gone away unhappy. Maggie's employees have learned to be wary of her outbursts.

A moment later, I was entering the boarding greenhouse. When my *Vanilla* is at home there, it lives in a corner just inside the door, next to a tall, vining scorpion orchid with a menacing bloom that resembles an orange-and-yellow five-legged spider about to leap into your face — exactly what you would expect from an orchid in the genus *Arachnis.* The warm, humid air was full of the plaintive melody of George Gershwin's "Rhapsody in Blue," playing through a speaker high in a corner. The idea came from an Illinois botanist who claimed that exposing his greenhouse plants to Gershwin for twenty-four hours a day made them grow taller and heavier than music-deprived plants. Maggie varies the selections in her sound system, but she usually stays with gently soothing semiclassical music.

115

Whether the orchids appreciate being entertained is still an open question, but visitors and the staff certainly do.

I was settling the vanilla's pot into its usual corner when "Rhapsody" ended and I heard Maggie's voice. I straightened up, about to call to her, then prudently decided not to interrupt. She was several aisles away and talking to someone about her usual subject — orchids — in a strident voice. Maggie is like a puffer fish, which is highly toxic unless you know exactly how to handle it. If you do, it's a much-loved delicacy. If you don't, well, you're dead. Today sounded like a toxic day.

"If you want to sell me any imported orchids," Maggie was saying, "I need to see your CITES certificate." (She pronounced the word *site-eez*.) "You know what that is?"

A woman answered, doubtfully, "I'm not sure I —"

"If you don't know what CITES is, you don't have their certificate," Maggie cut in. "I won't take any imported plants without it. I've got enough problems to deal with in this business. I don't need the orchid police on my tail."

I've heard Maggie talk about CITES often enough, so I know what it is. The Conven-

116

tion on International Trade in Endangered Species, an international treaty designed to ensure that commerce in wild animals and plants doesn't threaten their survival through overharvesting and illegal trade. It protects some fifty-eight hundred species of animals (think giant pandas, elephant tusks, and rhino horns) and thirty thousand species of plants, including many medicinal herbs. CITES also includes orchids. *All* orchids. Which means that if you want to tuck a wild Madagascar orchid or a Mexican spiny jewel orchid into your luggage before you fly home, you need CITES' blessing. Like it or not.

As the sound system slid into Pachelbel's "Canon," the woman said something I couldn't hear. But Maggie, obviously impatient, cut her off again.

"I understand what you're saying. Most orchid collectors agree that CITES helps to save tigers and gorillas, and in principle, we're all against illegal trafficking. We know that people can love a plant to death and that collecting in the wild has to be done carefully, to preserve the species. But if the CITES folks really wanted to protect endangered orchids, they would do something to stop habitat destruction." Maggie's voice was climbing as she got wound up. "Where

117

orchids are concerned, CITES is a joke. But it's no laughing matter. I do not intend to end up like poor George Nathan."

"George Nathan," the woman said. "Who's he?"

"One of the most reputable orchid importers in this business, that's who." Maggie's words were clipped. "His house and his greenhouse were raided by the orchid police on an anonymous tip which proved to be *wrong.* But that didn't matter, because they conveniently found a few other little things to pick on. His plants were seized, he and his wife lost their house and their savings, and the poor guy ended up in prison for almost a year. I'm not taking a risk like that, and nobody else with half a brain will, either. Believe you me, lady, it ain't worth it."

I believed her. I also believed that if George Nathan had had a lawyer who knew his way around a courthouse without a tour guide, he wouldn't have gone to jail. CITES ought to have its feathers clipped, legally speaking.

Maggie wasn't finished yet. "So if you want to sell me orchids that you've brought back from South America or the Philippines or wherever, you make sure to bring me your CITES certificates and all the other paperwork that country requires."

"Thank you," the woman said humbly. "I will."

A moment later, I heard the greenhouse door close behind her. I somehow doubted that she would be back, which was probably Maggie's intention. It sounded like breeding orchids was a whole lot safer than collecting or buying from collectors. Maggie was protecting herself from other people's mistakes and errors in judgment.

In another moment, she was standing beside me. Her work uniform — jeans and a brown T-shirt that said "Sometimes I wet my plants" — wasn't much different from mine. But her dark hair was cut short and spiked in a punky hairstyle which is as in-your-face as Maggie herself. Its tip-ends were dyed bright green to match her green canvas half-apron, the pockets of which were filled with tools of the horticultural trade: pruning shears, plant ties and labels, soil temperature thermometer, soil moisture meter, and gloves. Her feet were bare in bright green garden clogs. She was scowling.

"I thought that was you." She wrinkled her nose. "You're probably thinking I was too hard on that lady."

"You're probably right," I said. "But I'm

119

sure she needed to hear it. People could save themselves a whole lot of grief if they would read the fine print." I paused. "Is that story about George Nathan true — or something you made up as an object lesson?"

If it was true, my lawyerly self was deeply offended. Those who commit real crimes should be prosecuted and punished appropriately. But America locks up more people than any other nation, and it's no secret that overcriminalization is a significant problem, at every level of the justice system. Texas has seventeen hundred crimes on the books, fifteen hundred of which exist outside the state's penal code — which leads to some serious inconsistencies. For example, dredging for oysters at night can be a felony, while concealing a human corpse is only a misdemeanor. Where's the justice in that?

"You bet it's true," Maggie growled, her dark eyes snapping. "George was accused of having an illegal *Phragmipedium kovachii* from Peru, which he did *not.* But while the ignorant cops were rummaging through his thousands of plants, they found a couple they thought were illegal — they *weren't* — and some paperwork he hadn't caught up on. They decided to make an example of him, to scare other orchid collectors."

"That's unfortunate," I said, meaning it. When the law is used to target scapegoats, innocent people can be hurt, guilty people can go unpunished, and the rest of us learn to distrust the justice system.

Maggie narrowed her eyes. "Believe me, I am not for a minute defending poachers. But ask the environmentalists and they'll tell you that habitat destruction is a bigger and badder threat to orchids than poaching." She pushed her lips in and out. "You know, back in the day, my ex-husband Carl and his friend Dan Selms — they were best buddies back then — used to drive south across the border on collecting trips. These days, what they did would be called smuggling, and the cops would be all over them."

"Really?" I asked, interested. Smuggling is a risky business. Coca and cannabis, for instance, two high-demand, high-value psychoactive herbs, are rich booty, but if you're caught, the consequences include a hefty fine and jail time.

"Really," Maggie said. "The guys would come back with the van absolutely loaded with stuff. Don't tell anybody, but Dan Selms put himself through graduate school that way. Selling the orchids he collected, I mean."

"Oh, orchids," I said. Not coca or cannabis. I raised an eyebrow. "Actually, I've met Dr. Selms. I would never in the world imagine him as an orchid thief."

"Well, it isn't an all-bad thing, you know," Maggie went on. "Several of the orchids Dan brought back from Central America are extinct now because their native forest has been destroyed. But he saved the species. They've been propagated in greenhouses and are available to anybody who wants one. Some of them even carry his name." She gave me a crooked smile. "Which makes my ex see red, of course. He can't tolerate other people's success. A pity. It's destroyed what used to be a very close friendship."

Interesting. I knew about the rivalry between Dr. Fairlee and Dr. Selms, the chairman of the Plant Sciences department. But I hadn't known that it had its origins in orchids. Smuggled orchids, at that.

Maggie nodded at the pot I had just set down. "I see you've brought your vanilla orchid back. How was the workshop?"

"Full, with a waiting list, and a lot of fun. Everybody loves vanilla — although there were plenty of complaints about the price of the pods." I looked around. "Anything new and interesting here?"

"Oh, lots," Maggie said, her voice warming. "Come over here and take a sniff of this gorgeous *Oncidium.* Her name is Sharry Baby and she smells just like chocolate! Her owner went off to Europe and isn't around to see her bloom, which is a pity, because she is drop-dead gorgeous. Maybe you'll be tempted to get one for yourself."

"She's beautiful," I said, when I saw the long, flowering spray thickly covered with dark orange blooms, tipped with white. I bent over and took a deep breath of the heavenly chocolate scent. Wouldn't it be wonderful to have a plant like this, of my very own? But I'm a realist. Orchids are a full-time occupation, and my days and nights are already booked. I have no business getting romantically involved with a new botanical passion, however seductive. I took one last, regretful whiff of Sharry Baby. "Plain vanilla will have to be enough orchid for me."

Maggie chuckled. "I understand. Vanilla's blossom may not look like much, compared to these exotic beauties. But it's the only useful orchid. The rest are just decorative."

"Actually, that's not true," I said. "The Turks use the tubers of a wild orchid to make a drink and a kind of ice cream. *Salep,* it's called. It's supposed to be an aphrodisiac — a kind of floral Viagra."

Maggie looked doubtful. "No kidding?"

"No kidding. And dozens of orchids are staples in many folk medicines. Like the Gold Orchid, which is currently being used to treat diabetic retinopathy. Vanilla isn't the only 'useful' orchid, by a long shot."

"Ha," Maggie said, looking pleased. "I knew if I kept after you long enough, China, I'd turn you into an orchid fan."

"Hello," a treble voice called over the last measures of the "Canon." "Maggie, where are you?"

"Hi, Beverly," Maggie said. "China and I are over here. Come and help us admire this gorgeous *Oncidium*."

"Oh, there you are." The woman coming toward us was carrying a cardboard box containing several potted plants. She was Beverly Selms, a friend from the herb guild and another orchid fancier. Tall, gray-haired, and professional in a trim khaki blazer, red blouse, and black slacks, Beverly owns one of the most successful real estate firms in Pecan Springs. She is married to Dan Selms, the man Maggie was just talking about, who put himself through grad school as an orchid thief — smuggling and selling rare orchids.

My friendship with Beverly goes back to the year we worked together to raise money

124

to renovate, repair, and refurnish the Myra Merryweather House for the Pecan Springs Herb Guild. It was a lot of work but well worth it. The old Victorian is now a showplace with a historic home designation — thanks to Beverly's expert knowledge of old homes and my acquaintance with Victorian gardens. We don't always agree on means and ends, but she is a take-charge woman and tremendously efficient. I have to admire her energy and determination.

Maggie's relationship with Beverly is a little more complicated. Yes, they share a common devotion to orchids and have other community interests as well — they both serve on the Friends of the Library board, for instance. But the professional rivalry between the men in their lives has made for a rather uneasy relationship, even after Maggie's divorce. I've noticed that they're a bit standoffish with each other.

"That's a lovely Sharry Baby," Beverly said, with an appreciative glance at the chocolate-scented orchid. She set down the box as the first bars of Gershwin's "Summertime" flowed languidly from the speaker. "I've brought three Dendrobiums for you to board."

"Nice," Maggie said, bending over to get a look at them. "When did they finish blooming?"

"Just last week." Beverly stepped back and dusted her hands. "One is yellow, the other two a deep, royal purple. They were all really pretty."

"It'll be about four months until they bloom again, then." Maggie took a black marker and a couple of white plastic plant labels out of her apron pocket, scribbled Beverly's name and today's date on the labels, and fastened them around the stems. "You know the drill, I guess. I'll email you a shelf number. You're free to drop in and check on the plants any time we're open. We'll notify you when they're in bud and ready to bloom." All business, she picked up the box. "I'll get these logged into the system now."

"Thank you," Beverly said. "I'll bring my Venus slipper in another week or ten days. It's coming to the end of its bloom." After Maggie said goodbye and made off with the orchids, she turned to me.

"Gosh, China, you're just the person I wanted to see. One of my clients bought that old Victorian a couple of doors down from Ruby Wilcox's Painted Lady. She's thinking of restoring the garden so that it has an 1890s look, but she doesn't know where to begin. Can you help?"

"Of course," I said. "Tell her I'm available and we'll work out a time." I paused. "I'm glad I ran into you, too, Beverly. I've been meaning to ask if you want to stay on the Merryweather House committee. It's my turn to chair it this year, and we need to come up with some ideas for fundraising." The Merryweather House is an old place, and something always needs repair. This summer, it was a family of raccoons in the attic. They weren't very considerate tenants, and there was quite a bit of repair and cleanup to be done after we evicted them.

"Count me in," Beverly said as we left the greenhouse and headed for our cars. "And I had an idea for —" Her cell dinged and she checked the caller. "Excuse me a minute, China. It's Dan. He's been trying to reach me, but I was in a meeting, and when it was over I forgot to call him back."

"No problem." I shoved my hands into my pockets and pretended not to listen.

Into the phone, she said, "I'm at Sonora right now, Dan. Sorry I couldn't take your —"

She broke off, listened a moment, then stopped in the middle of the gravel path, beside a display of bronze chrysanthemums. The color drained from her face.

"What?" she whispered, her eyes wide.

127

"When?" She listened some more. "With a *gun*? That is so hard to believe! Especially knowing him, I mean. He doesn't — didn't — seem like the type to —"

She shuddered and closed her eyes. I stopped pretending not to listen. Something was going on here. Something serious.

"I understand." Her voice was thin. "But do you really think I should? You're his boss — don't you think *you* should be the one to tell her?" She was chewing on her lip. "Or maybe you could call Reverend Clements, over at First Presbyterian. That's where she —" A longish pause, then a glance at me. "Well, I suppose, if you really think it's the right thing to do. China Bayles is here with me, and she's a closer friend than I am. Maybe she can help."

She said goodbye and slid her phone into her blazer pocket. "I just can't believe it," she muttered, still incredulous.

"Believe *what*?" I asked urgently. "What's going on, Beverly?"

She looked straight at me, her gray eyes wide. There was a tic at the corner of her mouth. "Maggie's ex-husband has killed himself."

"Carl Fairlee?" I gasped, horrified. "Oh, no!" My first thought was that he was the last person on earth to do such a thing. But of course you can never tell what devils live in somebody's private hell. And I had only audited that one seminar with him. I hadn't known him well at all, really.

My next thought was for the woman who had known him very well. "Oh, poor Maggie!" I said. "She'll have to tell the kids."

Maggie might not mourn her ex-husband, but the children would. There were two. Chelsea, Caitie's playmate and friend, came for frequent sleepovers at our house — in fact, she had stayed with Caitie on Saturday night. Lyle was in his first year at Texas A&M, studying horticulture. I knew him from Sonora, where he worked every summer.

"Dan wants me to tell her," Beverly said grimly. "Before she hears it on the local news." She made a face. "In my opinion, *he* ought to do it. Carl was one of his faculty members." Her shoulders slumped. "But then, he's never been very fond of Maggie. I think he's . . . well, maybe a little afraid of her."

I could understand his feelings. Maggie has a strong personality. She doesn't pull her punches — which is probably why I like her. "Who found Dr. Fairlee?" I asked. "Where?"

"One of his grad students. In his greenhouse lab, on the roof of the Plant Sciences building. Campus security came right away, Dan says. And the Pecan Springs police, as well. In fact, the chief herself came, along with a detective. Dan was surprised by that."

It wasn't a surprise that the PSPD would be brought in to help the campus police investigate a campus suicide, if only to ensure that suicide was the right call. But it was a bit of a surprise to hear that Sheila Dawson — the chief and a very good friend — had taken the call, especially since she was pregnant and on light duty. But she had once been in charge of security on the campus and probably still had connections there. Perhaps she had even known Dr. Fairlee.

"Under the circumstances," I said, "I have to agree with your husband. Hearing it from a friend will be easier for Maggie." I spoke reluctantly, knowing what was likely to come next. I was right.

"You'll go with me, then, won't you?" Beverly gave me a pleading look. "Maggie is probably a lot more comfortable with you than she is with me. You were close to her during that awful divorce, when Carl was so incredibly —"

She broke off, shaking her head. "He's dead. I shouldn't speak ill of him."

But I could finish her incomplete sentence. *When Carl was so incredibly mean and nasty.*

Because he was. He had insisted on — and got — cash for his share of the equity in their house, even though he knew that Maggie had taken out a substantial second mortgage to pay for the greenhouse construction at Sonora. Worse, she had been forced to sell the house at a time when the Pecan Springs real estate market was at rock bottom. And then she had to find an affordable house in the same school district, so the kids' activities wouldn't be disrupted.

There had been other things, too, stories about affairs with other women, younger women, students. And that awful business of dividing the orchid collection, which had hurt Maggie so deeply. Perhaps it sounds trivial, but she had propagated most of those plants. They had been like children, and he had taken the best of them.

"I *hate* him," she had cried over and over, her hands clenched into tight fists. "If that sonofabitch were here right now, I would punch him right in the mouth. I could . . . I could just *kill* him, China."

But that was then, this was now, and the man was dead. Maggie would tell herself that she no longer loved him, maybe even

131

try to remember how much she hated him. But I was sure she couldn't forget that they had once been friends and lovers and she would mourn the life they had shared. It would be a shock — and even more of a shock for the children. The fact that he had killed himself would make it just that much worse.

Beverly touched my hand. "You'll go with me, won't you?" she repeated. "Please?"

I straightened my shoulders. There was only one right answer. "Yes, of course. Hearing it from us will be easier for Maggie than hearing it from a stranger." I swallowed. "How did he . . . Maggie will have to know. Did your husband say where or how it happened?"

"He shot himself," Beverly said in a pinched voice. "Dan says it surprised him, because Carl wasn't a gun guy. But maybe he thought it would be easier that way."

In my former incarnation as a criminal lawyer, I had seen enough of the dark side to know that sudden, unexpected death is never easy, no matter how it happens. It leaves an ugly scar on the living. But this wasn't the time to say so.

"Come on, then." I sighed, resigned. "Let's get it over with."

CHAPTER FIVE

Thomas Jefferson is credited with vanilla's arrival in the United States. When he returned from his ambassadorship in France in 1789, he was dismayed to discover that no one in the States knew about vanilla, so he wrote his French attaché requesting that he send him fifty vanilla pods. Clearly Jefferson's personal passion was well received since soon it was used as a flavoring and a medicine, and — you're right — an aphrodisiac. In the 1800s Dr. John King advised in the American Dispensatory that one should use vanilla to, "stimulate the sexual propensities." He went on to give a very carefully detailed recipe for a decoction promising amorous evenings. If the good doctor was right, a hefty swig of vanilla extract before bedtime could work like a charm.

"Sex, Love, and the Vanilla Bean,"
Patricia Rain
https://vanillaqueen.com/sex-love-and-the-vanilla-bean/

I was late getting home from the garden center and relieved to discover that Mc-Quaid (who returned that afternoon from an investigation in Dallas) had taken supper into his own hands. He had put hamburgers, portobello mushrooms, and summer squash on the grill, while Caitie — at fourteen, quite a competent cook — assembled a salad with sliced avocado and fresh tomatoes. All I had to do was take some leftover vanilla pudding out of the fridge and add strawberries, a dusting of flaked coconut, and a few sprigs of mint. *Voila!* Dessert.

The evening had cooled off enough to eat on the deck behind the house, in the shade of a large live oak tree. We live in an old Victorian off Limekiln Road, in the Hill Country ten miles west of Pecan Springs — far enough from civilization that we don't have to smell auto exhaust or be pummeled by the thump-thump-*thump* of the neighbor's woofers. Instead, we're treated to the scent of honeysuckle and late-blooming roses. We can listen to the breeze brushing the papery leaves of the big sycamore tree beside the stone fence. And we can laugh at the antics of Caitie's chickens, a mixed flock that includes a prize-winning Buff Orpington hen named Dixie Chick and Extra Crispy, a Cubalaya rooster with a splendid

134

orange-red shawl of feathers and an elegant black plume of a tail. Extra Crispy is a survivor. A few weeks before, he had been rooster-napped at the Adams County Fair, along with an extremely valuable all-black Ayam Cemani rooster named Blackheart. This rooster heist produced a long string of interesting consequences, including the arrest of the chicken thief, who was engaged in tending the mother of all pot grows.

Also joining us on the deck for supper: Mr. P, Caitie's orange tabby cat, perched on the deck rail, his tail twitching. And Winchester, our basset, sprawled across the steps, one brown eye fixed on the flock (the chickens are *his* responsibility, after all, and he is devoted to them) and the other alert for possible bunnies. Should a cottontail be so bold as to venture in the direction of the parsley border along the path, Winchester would be after him in a flash. His short, stubby basset legs may make him look clumsy, but he has the heart and soul of a hunter.

As usual, there was plenty to talk about over dinner. McQuaid related the highlights of his latest forensic investigation, which had turned up enough evidence to charge the employee who had made off with hundreds of thousands of dollars of corporate

135

trade secrets. And Caitie, her dark eyes sparking with indignation, told us about the spelling bee she had lost because she put a u in the word *honor.*

"I *know* I saw it spelled that way in a book," she insisted. "H-o-n-o-u-r."

"I'm sure you did," I replied. "You've been reading *The Railway Children,* haven't you?" When she nodded, I said, "That book was published in England, Caitie. British and American spelling isn't always the same."

"Not the *same?* But it's all English, isn't it?" Caitie rolled her eyes, that gesture that every girl magically masters the day she turns thirteen. "Really! That is so *unfair!* How are we supposed to know?"

"You're not," McQuaid said. "The United States and England," he added with a grin, and paraphrased George Bernard Shaw. "Two countries forever divided by a common language."

Caitie was not mollified. "I'm going to find the word in the book and show it to my teacher."

"Excellent," McQuaid said approvingly. "I'm all for teacher education." He put another hamburger on his plate. "China, what's up with you today?"

I talked about our vanilla workshop and my trip to Sonora, but I saved the report of

Carl Fairlee's suicide until dessert was finished. I hated to tell Caitie. Her father (my half-brother), her mother, and her favorite aunt had all died in the last few years, and her friend Kevin was undergoing chemo for a brain tumor. She didn't need to hear about another horribly senseless tragedy. But Caitie and Dr. Fairlee's daughter Chelsea are best friends. I knew she would want to comfort her. And I wanted her to hear it from me before she heard it on TV or at school.

"Chelsea's father *killed* himself?" she whispered, her dark eyes large and horrified. "Oh, no!" She pushed back her chair and jumped up. "I have to call her. Right now!"

"I'm sure she would appreciate that," I said gently, confident that Caitie — out of the depths of her own losses — would find the words that would help her friend begin to live with hers.

When Beverly and I told Maggie, she had been stoic, but underneath, I could sense the emotions churning. Grief that the man she had once loved was dead. Anger that he had ended his life and left Chelsea and Lyle to deal with the loss of their father. Guilt that she no longer loved him and hadn't been there for him when he needed her.

Guilt is even more merciless than grief or anger.

But her most insistent question was *why.* "I just don't understand," she cried, shaking her head. "Carl wasn't sick. He'd found another girlfriend. And his research seemed to be going well. In fact, he told me just last week that he was applying for a plant patent for that vanilla hybrid he and Logan Gardner were working on. Why did he *do* it?"

Now, putting the last dish into the dishwasher, McQuaid whistled softly. "I can't quite get my head around Carl Fairlee shooting himself. Remember when that new campus-carry law went into effect? Fairlee was one of the couple of dozen faculty who led the protests against it. Not that it did any good," he added darkly.

An ex-cop with a strong opinion on this subject, McQuaid sides with the law enforcement professionals who have gone on record against campus carry. Which did not move the needle at the legislature one freaking iota. This is Texas, after all.

"Odd that Maggie didn't mention that." I rinsed the grease off the hamburger plate and handed it to McQuaid. "But she did say she had no idea where he might have gotten the gun. She didn't think he had ever fired one — during their marriage, at least."

"They're sure it's suicide?" McQuaid poured soap into the dishwasher dispenser cup and shut the door.

"I guess so." I finished wiping the counter. "That's what Dan Selms told Beverly, anyway."

McQuaid turned the dial to start the dishwasher. "Well, if you heard it from Dan, it should be accurate. He's chairman of Plant Sciences, and that's his building. He should have a handle on the details." He shook his head. "I'm sure he's pretty upset about it. At one time, he and Carl were really close friends. They used to go plant-hunting together in Mexico, back in the day when that was legal. *Mostly* legal," he added wryly. "I'm told they occasionally brought back some pot."

"I've heard that the two of them were rivals," I said. "Do you know the story there?" Every couple of semesters, McQuaid teaches a class in the Criminal Justice department, in the building next door to Plant Sciences. He's acquainted with many of the Plant Sciences faculty and has known Dan Selms for a long time.

Winchester had gone upstairs with Caitie. She must not have been able to connect with Chelsea, because she was starting to practice her violin. Win is a music enthusiast and raises his voice in song when she starts to play — rich, fluid basset howls, punctuated by sharp, piercing basset barks, not quite in time with the music.

Caitie put up with his performance for a few minutes, then I heard "Sorry, Winnie, but you have to leave now," followed by the sound of her door firmly shutting. There was one last, tuneful howl, and then Win began making his way down the stairs. He goes up easily, but with those short, stubby legs of his, he lives life close to the ground. He finds the view from the top of the stairs intimidating, something on the order of a descent of Mount Everest. So he comes down tail first, one step at a time, backward.

McQuaid took the half-full carafe out of the coffee maker. "I'm having a cup. Want one?"

"Please." While he poured, I pulled out a chair and sat down at the kitchen table. Winchester finished his descent and arrived at the kitchen door. Suspecting that people who are drinking coffee might also be eating cookies, he regarded us with a gloomy hopefulness. He believes that a loyal basset ought not to be left out of the general feasting.

"No, Win," I said firmly. "We've already had dessert. We are not having cookies."

But dads are more lenient than moms. "A little doggie biscuit won't hurt him," McQuaid said, pouring a mug of coffee. He took one out of the pottery canister that has Winchester's name on it, in bright red letters. "Here you go, Winnie." Winchester accepted the biscuit graciously and, with a triumphant *see there?* glance over his shoulder at me, carried it off to his doggie bed beside the pantry door, where he made short work of it.

"The rivalry?" I prompted.

"I understand that it goes back to some orchids they brought back from Mexico." McQuaid poured coffee into the mug on the table in front of me. "And then there was that disagreement about the greenhouse." He poured a cup for himself. "I don't know if you remember, but I was on the committee that reviewed the situation for the dean's office."

"I do remember, now that you mention it," I said. "There was a problem with the way that greenhouse got built, wasn't there?" Maggie had mentioned it once or twice, but I hadn't paid a lot of attention.

"Yeah. The Plant Sciences faculty members share a large greenhouse a couple of blocks away from their building, but Fairlee wanted his own. He was doing some plant

141

breeding experiments and I guess he didn't want other people looking over his shoulder." McQuaid sat down at the table across from me. "He finally got a grant with enough money in it to build a small greenhouse, so he went ahead and did it without getting permission, at the end of the summer term. When fall classes started, there it was, up on the roof. Fairlee had already filled it with hundreds of plants, a lot of them from his orchid collection."

"It was Maggie's orchid collection, too," I said. "They divided it. In the divorce."

"Really? I didn't know that." McQuaid leaned back in his chair. "Anyway, Fairlee's colleagues were jealous because he had a greenhouse all to himself, while they still had to share. Dan Selms was hopping mad because Fairlee had done it on his watch and without his permission, which made him look like an idiot who didn't know what the hell was going on with his own faculty. The dean was so pissed off about the unauthorized construction that she sent for the building inspector, hoping that a few codes had been violated so she could order it taken down. And the provost wanted to know how much it cost and where the funds came from. By the time it was over, even the university president was in on the act."

"But Dr. Fairlee got away with it." I pointed out. "That greenhouse is still up on the roof."

McQuaid rubbed his nose. "Possession is nine-tenths of the law. Our committee argued about it for a while, but we finally recommended that Fairlee keep the green-house, as long as his students could use it. But everybody was still mad. So Dan froze his salary, the dean wrote a nasty letter for his file, and the provost seized a chunk of his grant funding. He said it was to pay for extra electrical and water connections, but everybody knew it was punishment."

Hesitantly, I said, "Maggie mentioned a girlfriend. Do you know who Fairlee was seeing?"

McQuaid took a swig of his coffee. "For a while, he was dating the departmental secretary, Charlaine Rudolph. But lately, I heard something about a graduate student."

A *graduate* student? Carl Fairlee had to be almost fifty, but I supposed it wouldn't be the first time a professor got involved with a much younger woman.

"Do you think he might have killed himself because he was unhappy about his situation at the university?"

"He'd pretty much weathered that, so I doubt it," McQuaid said somberly. "But there are always things we don't know. Like maybe he was sick. Sometimes when people get a scary diagnosis . . ." He finished his thought with a shrug.

"If that's what it was, Maggie didn't know anything about it. And she thought his research was going well. He told her he was applying for a plant patent." I sighed. "She tries to appear stoic about it, but I know she must feel terrible. It's hard when something like this happens and you don't know why." I turned my cup in my fingers. "On a happier note, Ruby is having a small dinner party tonight, to celebrate a baby."

"A baby? Who do we know — ? Not Sheila, I hope," McQuaid added quickly. "She's not due for a while yet, is she?"

"Not until November. And this one's a while off, too. It's Kate and Amy's baby. Kate's baby, to be specific. She drew the long straw. Her brother-in-law, Ron, is the father."

When I explained about drawing straws, he chuckled. And asked the same question I had. "Just out of curiosity, did they do it the old-fashioned way?"

"Nope. She used a turkey baster." Seeing his raised eyebrow, I added quickly, "Artificial insemination."

"I understand." McQuaid sighed. "But

144

somehow that takes all the . . . joy out of it, don't you think?" His voice softens. "I mean, if you're going to start a baby, it ought to begin with . . . well, love. Shouldn't it?"

I was touched by his response, although I could see by the look in his eye that he was thinking about boy-girl baby-making love, which didn't exactly fit in this case. "But it *has* begun in love," I reminded him gently. "And Kate and Amy and Grace and Ruby, too — there will be plenty of love." I paused. "I do hope they took care of the legal details, though. Kate's brother-in-law is not an anonymous sperm donor. He's a member of the family. What happens if he decides he wants . . ." My voice trailed off.

"Finish your sentence," McQuaid said patiently. "What if he wants *what?*"

"Wants more," I said. "Just . . . I don't know. More. A relationship with the child, maybe."

I was thinking of the Texas appellate ruling I had read just the other day. In a donor-or-dad case, the court had found that a sperm donor (a friend of the mom) was the legal father of the child conceived by artificial insemination and that he had all the rights and responsibilities of fatherhood — including child support and custody. The ruling showcased the traps an unwary birth mother might stumble into, which could have been avoided if she had talked to a lawyer for fifteen or twenty minutes before she used that turkey baster.

There was a silence. "How about you, China?" McQuaid touched my hand. "Do you want more? Do you ever wish we'd had a baby?"

I looked at him, loving the quirk of his eyebrow, the firm corner of his jaw, the softness of his mouth. "Sometimes," I said. "Sometimes I wish I had *your* baby." I took a breath, thinking of roads not taken, journeys not begun. "But there's Brian and Caitie. They're ours. And we have each other. That's enough, don't you think?"

"Yes." He picked up my hand and raised it to his lips. "If you do."

CHAPTER SIX

It is Tuesday morning, not quite eight-thirty, and Miller comes into Sheila's office. "Hey, Chief," he says.

Sheila looks up from the stack of papers she is signing. "Good morning, Detective Miller," she says drily. "How nice of you to knock."

He doesn't notice her irony. "Fairlee's prints are on the gun," he says, "although of course they could have been faked. However, there's another, half-smudged print on the suppressor, just above where it screws into the barrel. That print is *not* his. I sent it through AFIS. Just got the results. No match."

"Too bad," Sheila says. AFIS is the FBI's national automated fingerprint identification system, which attempts to match prints submitted by law enforcement with prints acquired through arrests, employment background checks, military records, and other noncriminal sources. Whoever left that print has no FBI history, which means that their needle just got lost in a bigger haystack. A much bigger haystack.

Sheila hadn't slept well the night before, and she knows there are dark circles under her eyes. The baby was restless — is he going to be a night owl? Blackie's half of the bed was empty and will be for the rest of the week; he's in Dallas, wrapping up a case he and McQuaid have been working on. She's not afraid, and she's not even lonely; Rambo, her Rottweiler, is always on duty. (As a K-9 officer, Rambo has his own badge.) But she wished for the comfort of Blackie's warm body and his calming, steadying presence. When she couldn't sleep past five, she got up, showered, sat down to two eggs over easy with bacon and toast, and came to work early, dropping Rambo at the department's K-9 kennel on her way.

But if she hoped to finish the stack of papers Connie had left on her desk the night before, she was disappointed. She was summoned to a seven a.m. emergency meeting with Mayor Phyllis Browning, who has been fussing about the department's hiring plan. Pecan Springs is growing, and Sheila has requested three more patrol officers to relieve the overtime situation. But new hires translate to higher benefits, and Mayor Browning has her eagle-eye on the bottom line. She pointed out that it's cheaper to overload the cops you have than it is to hire and train new cops. Sheila made the opposing argument as resolutely as she could, but the discussion ended in a frustrating stalemate.

And then there was an eight a.m. interview for Connie's replacement, one of three Con has set up: Paula Mason, in her late fifties, with tight gray curls and a clipped voice. Ms. Mason, who works in the 911 Communications Center, seemed brisk and competent. But after ten minutes with her, Sheila had the feeling that she was too by-the-book to handle the oddball problems that often ended up on the chief's desk. This reminder that Friday is Connie's last day adds another layer of tension to an already stressed morning. The darker possibility — that Connie might not come back — looms like a supercell thunderstorm on the horizon.

"So. A partial on the suppressor." Sheila drops her pen on the desk and pulls her attention back to Dylan Miller. "Any prints on the cartridge you picked up in the greenhouse?"

Miller lowers himself into the chair on the

other side of the desk. He's looking crisp and cool this morning, in a blue-and-white striped shirt, blue tie, light-blue blazer, pressed chinos. His spruceness makes Sheila feel uncombed and unkempt.

"Nope. The cartridge is clean." He pauses. "And the gun was stolen."

"No surprise there," she says, scrawling her name on an order for five more armored vests. She knows that Texas leads the nation in the number of guns — almost four thousand — reported stolen over the past four years from licensed gun dealers in the state. Plus some two hundred thousand estimated to have been stolen from Texas citizens in the same period, most of them *never* reported. A tsunami of stolen guns. "I'm just surprised that you've got that information already. How did you manage that?"

A few nights before, Sheila and Blackie had watched a TV show where a cop picks up a gun used in a shooting and notes the serial number. He sits down at his computer, runs a trace, and *hey presto,* the gun owner's name, address, and other vital signs pop up on the monitor. Got him. A little legwork and cut to the chase.

But Sheila and Blackie are both law enforcement professionals and they know that's not how it works. There is no national database, no centralized record of gun owners and their weapons, and no report of how many people own guns, or how many are bought or sold, or even how many exist. There is the National Tracing Center, yes, in Martinsburg, West Virginia — but it has no searchable database of guns and gun owners. That's been the law since 1986, thanks to the gun lobby, which is worried that the government might use a national gun registry as a tool to confiscate guns.

So instead of a quick, easy computer search, weapons traces are done by humans, by hand, using whatever paper forms and microfiche are available. To make things unimaginably worse, almost two million new records arrive every month and are stashed in a rapidly multiplying squad of shipping containers in the center's parking lot. A routine trace back to the original point of sale can take a couple of weeks or more — *if* it's successful, which it isn't, thirty-five percent of the time. And even if the record is located, the cop who requested the trace still has to find out where the gun went after it was originally purchased. This is not like tracing the vehicle identification number on a stolen truck or the microchip in your neighbor's lost dog.

But there is one fortunate exception.

"Lucked out," Miller says, sounding pleased with himself. "Traced the suppressor to the original owner — guy named Harold Martin, in Las Cruces, New Mexico. Martin bought it for a Glock and registered it — properly — with the ATF. I plugged in the serial number, and his name came up."

The ATF. Alcohol, Tobacco, and Firearms. Which requires the owner of a suppressor to register it, under a law originally passed in 1934 to control exceptionally dangerous weapons like sawed-off shotguns, the machine guns used in the infamous Valentine's Day Massacre, and suppressors. (But not, inexplicably, AR-15s.)

"Good news," Sheila says. "Is Martin the most recent owner?"

Miller shakes his head. "Martin says he hadn't had it more than a couple of weeks when somebody broke into his place and walked out with three rifles and two handguns, including the Glock and the suppressor."

"Figures," Sheila says pragmatically. "The whole lot probably went to a gun show." That's where stolen weapons usually end up, meaning that the Glock is basically untraceable. Many people who sell at gun shows claim they are selling as a hobby, not

152

a business. Unlike gun-shop operators, they aren't required to have a license, keep records of sales, or do background checks.

"Right. We know where the gun came from, but bottom line, no connection to Fairlee."

Sheila signs her name on the last piece of paper, pushes the stack away, and glances at the clock on her desk. Eight thirty-three. "Okay. Let's see where we are. Anything back from Berry on the autopsy?"

"Nada. He had to deal with a couple of victims involved in the crash on the interstate last night. He said he'd get to it first thing this morning, if he could. Haven't heard anything yet." Miller looks down at his notebook. "I sent Gene Parsons and Megan Donnelly up to Fairlee's greenhouse last night to do a careful search." They are the other two detectives in Miller's small unit. "No suicide note. Nothing out of order, nothing that could be pinned to the shooting. Apparently, the greenhouse sees a fair amount of traffic. Kids from Fairlee's classes are doing projects there, his research assistant works there, and so on. So even if we'd found something, it might be hard to connect it up."

"What about Fairlee's apartment?" Sheila had given the address to Miller, along with

Maxwell's bizarre story about the building of the greenhouse. "And his car? It's probably in the parking lot behind the Plant Sciences building."

"The apartment is sealed, ditto the office. I figured we'd hold off on searches until we hear from Berry. If this is a homicide, we can get warrants from Davidson. We'll need to get Fairlee's auto registration and look for his car, too. His keys are in the evidence envelope."

"Sounds right," Sheila says. "We could be looking at homicide here, so no cutting corners. We go by the book, all the way." She adds, "Have you set up the case log?"

"Not yet. Waiting on Berry's report."

"Good." Sheila pulls out her notebook. "Maxwell is interviewing faculty with offices in the Plant Sciences building. On our list for today — yours and mine, I mean: Rudolph, Selms, and Logan Gardner, the research assistant. And the ex-wife. Maggie Walker."

Miller was taking notes. "Rudolph?"

"Selms' secretary, Charlaine. I know her from when I worked on campus. She said something yesterday that caught my attention, something about professional and *personal* competition in the department. I want to ask her what she meant."

She pauses. *We're getting ahead of ourselves,* she thinks. Both she and Miller are behaving as if homicide is a done deal. But if the autopsy shows that Fairlee killed himself, the case will be closed and they can go back to their usual jobs.

She is about to remind Miller of this when his cell phone rings. The ringtone is a classic, old-fashioned *brrring!* like the telephones in old Hollywood noir films.

"Miller," he says. He listens a moment, intently, then, "Hang on, Doc. She's right here." To Sheila he says, "It's Berry. He's finished, and it's homicide, no question. No gunpowder residue on Fairlee's hands, no tattooing around the entry wound. Also no bruising and nothing under his fingernails to suggest a struggle."

The surge of adrenaline in Sheila's system boots the baby into a somersault. "Time of death?" she asks, trying to keep her voice steady.

"Time of death?" Miller repeats into the phone, and listens. To Sheila he mouths, "That it?" When she nods, he says "Thanks, Doc, for getting on this so fast. Really appreciate it."

He clicks off the call and pockets the phone. "The greenhouse temperature probably hastened rigor, which makes it a little

155

harder to be sure. Berry is putting death between eight p.m. Sunday and midnight. He'll email the report in an hour or so."

Homicide. Sheila presses a hand against her belly. "Let's make sure the cause of death is not released until after we've completed the first round of interviews. That'll give us a little lead time."

"We can seal it," Miller says. "But there may be leaks at the hospital end. That's the price of getting it done locally."

"I know," Sheila says. "But let's do what we can. Get Parsons started on those warrants. I'll let Judge Davidson know that we need him." There's something she has to do first, though. Urgently. She pushes herself out of her chair.

On his way out the door, Miller meets Connie, on her way in. To Sheila, she says, "Lucia Fernandez from Dispatch is here, about the temporary —"

Sheila raises her hand. "Fairlee is a homicide, Con. Dr. Berry is emailing the autopsy report. Call Judge Davidson and tell him that Miller and I will be bringing search warrants. After that, we're heading up to the campus for interviews. I'll be out most of the day."

Connie nods, all business. "What do you want to do about Ms. Fernandez?"

"Let's have her come back later." *Later. Later when?* "No, how about if you go ahead and interview her. I'll see her as soon as I can."

"Got it," Connie says. "Also, Director Maxwell, up at the campus, faxed these." She hands Sheila a folder and glances toward the desk. "Did you — ?"

"All signed," Sheila says. "Every damned one of them." She smooths her rumpled maternity top, wishing she could wear her duty belt. The badge and uniform are good as far as they go, but they have never been quite enough. It's the belt — her gun, her cop gear — that makes her feel like a real police officer. She misses it.

The baby kicks hard against her bladder. "I'll be back in a minute," she says. "There's something I need to do."

Urgently.

It's 9:10 when they get to Davidson's storefront office. The JP is wearing a business suit, although several fishing rods and a large metal tackle box are sitting in a corner. He signs off on the warrants without question, and Miller phones Gene Parsons to tell him to get started on Fairlee's apartment. It's not a crime scene, but they may turn up physical evidence there that points

157

them to the killer, or to other circumstances that have to be investigated.

"You know the drill," Miller tells Parsons. "We want all computers and digital devices — Alexa if there is one. Checkbook and bank and credit card paper records. Keys to safe deposit boxes and storage units. Address book. Password list." He listens for a moment. "Yeah, right. When you're finished in the apartment, search Fairlee's campus office. Call me if you turn up anything significant. Oh, and tell Donnelly to go up to the Plant Sciences building, pick up Fairlee's laptop, and see if she can get into it. If she can, we'll want to look at his emails and files. Ditto his cell phone — it's in the evidence locker. Better do that first, in fact. It might require a passcode."

That done, Sheila and Miller drive up to the campus. The sky is cloudy and the sultry morning air smells like rain. Showers are forecast and students hurry to class carrying furled umbrellas.

Miller's DMV check of Fairlee's auto registration has turned up a blue Honda Element, a boxy van-like SUV. When they locate it in the parking lot behind the Plant Sciences building, they see that Fairlee obviously used it to haul plants. The rear seats have been removed to enlarge the cargo area, and the floor is littered with empty pots, hand-lettered plant tags (mostly for orchids, it appears), and gardening tools. There's nothing much in the glove compartment, except for a couple of dozen gas receipts. When Sheila glances through them, she sees that some are Pemex receipts from Mexico, dated in the just-past summer. *A plant collecting trip, like the one Gardner mentioned? Some fun in the sun, or something else? Alone or with a buddy? Or a girlfriend? Anything illegal in the booty he hauled home?*

She bags the receipts and tucks them into her shoulder-carry briefcase. Miller phones the station and requests a wrecker to pick up the Honda and tow it to the impound yard, where it can be dusted for prints. And then it's time to start on the interviews. But first —

"Give me five minutes for a pit stop," Sheila says to Miller, and heads for the ladies'. She's washing her hands when her cell dings.

Connie's voice is low and guarded. "Sorry to bother you, Chief. I'm using your desk phone. I have Jessica Nelson in my office. She happened to be at the hospital this morning and heard that Dr. Berry had filed the Fairlee autopsy report. She's asking to see it, and she wants to talk to you about it."

Known to her close friends as Slugger, Jessica Nelson is an alert, energetic young reporter at the *Pecan Springs Enterprise.* Sheila met her a couple of years ago when Jessie was a CTSU grad student, doing an internship at the newspaper. She proved herself by surviving a potentially deadly encounter with a kidnapper, which came to a sudden conclusion when she whacked him with a seven iron — hence Slugger. Her book on her kidnapping had a short run on the true crime best-seller lists and earned her a permanent slot on the cops-and-courts beat at the *Enterprise.*

"Put her on," Sheila says. "I'll talk to her." She scowls at her image in the mirror, thinking that the minute Connie leaves for Dallas, the office will go completely to hell. And there's not a damned thing she can do about it.

"Hey, Chief," Jessica says. Her voice is warm and friendly. There isn't that much interesting crime to report on in Pecan Springs, and Sheila knows that Jessie is always on the lookout for a breaking story. She is resourceful, creative, and infinitely nosy, which can be a royal pain. But you never can tell when you may need a media asset, so Sheila stays connected. Besides, she can't help liking Jessica.

"Hey, Jess." Deliberately, she puts a smile in her voice. "What's up with you today?"

"Oh, the usual. Listen, I happened to be at the hospital on another story this morning, and I heard that Doc Berry has submitted the autopsy report on Carl Fairlee, the Plant Sciences professor. How did he rule? And when are you releasing the report?"

Sheila doesn't ask how Jessica knows this, or what else she may have learned about Fairlee's death. With Jessie, information is a one-way street, always inbound. She crunches facts like one of those vehicle crushers you see in scrap yards, turning it out in tidy bundles of prose.

"The autopsy report will be sealed until we are further along in our investigation," she says, resigned to the fact that Jessica will hear what she isn't saying.

"So it's a *homicide*!" Jessica's voice is turbocharged with a barely suppressed excitement.

"I didn't say that," Sheila replies automatically.

"I know you didn't," Jessica says. "I had Fairlee for a class once. Not the best professor in the world, maybe — but the only one who's managed to get himself murdered lately." Brightly, she adds, "I'm sure Hark will want to run with it in the next edition. So what can you tell me?"

Hark Hibler is the editor and publisher of the *Enterprise.* When he took over the newspaper a few years ago, it was dedicated to printing the good news about Pecan Springs. Just the good news and nothing else. This made the place sound like the sweetest, coziest little town in Texas, which of course pleased the local merchants and the chamber of commerce but didn't begin to tell the true story. In fact, it was demonstrably fake.

Hark, on the other hand, is enthusiastically dedicated to printing the *real* news, which isn't always good. Sheila knows that he is even more likely to feature the Fairlee murder because it happened on the campus, to a man who has already stirred up some interesting controversy by sticking that unauthorized greenhouse on top of the Plant Sciences building, like a finger in everybody's eye. Sheila also knows that Jessica Nelson will be dogging the case. Homicide sells newspapers.

"I can't tell you much," Sheila says guardedly. "For the time being, you can say that the police are conducting interviews. We'll let you know when we're ready to release more information."

"Have you identified any persons of interest?" Jessica's voice takes on an edge. "The ex-wife? The girlfriend?"

The girlfriend. Sheila's eyes narrow. "You've got an inside track on this one?"

"No, sorry," Jessica says hurriedly. "Just thinking out loud. Could you maybe give me a quote I can use in the online edition?"

"You might say we're following several leads," Sheila says, then corrects herself. "Make that several significant leads." In the grand scheme of things, the trace on the gun is significant, even if it won't take them anywhere.

"Got it — thanks. I'll call you this afternoon, to see where you are." Without waiting for Sheila to say *No, don't bother,* Jessica adds, "In the meantime, I'll get started on interviews."

"Just don't get in our way," Sheila cautions, but in a friendly tone.

Selms is still teaching his nine o'clock class, but Charlaine Rudolph is at her desk. After Sheila introduces Dylan Miller, they take seats while Charlaine tapes a note that says "Back in a few" to the door and closes it.

"Coffee?" she asks. Her voice is brisk and precise. "There's a coffee maker in the faculty lounge. I will be glad to get you —"

Miller shakes his head. Sheila says, "No, thank you." She longs for coffee, but she has to restrict it — caffeine makes her pee. And the baby doesn't need to start life prewired.

Charlaine nods pleasantly. "Well, then," she says, smoothing her skirt under her as she sits down. "How can I help you?" Today, it's a black blouse and black beads with yesterday's gray skirt, perhaps as a token of mourning for a departed faculty member. But she's wearing the same neatly coiffed auburn hair and tortoise-rimmed glasses and looks every inch the proper secretary.

"Yesterday, you mentioned that there's always more competition among the faculty than we might think," Sheila says, taking out her notebook. "I wonder if you could say a little more about that, Charlaine. Who were Dr. Fairlee's chief competitors?"

Charlaine knitted her fingers together. "Well, I suppose you'd have to say Dr. Selms. They're both in orchids, you see, so there's always been a friendly rivalry to see who can publish the most papers, do the most research, find a new plant." Her smile is prim. "A healthy competition pushes people to do their best. The university encourages it."

Healthy, is it? Sheila thinks. Depends on how intense it gets. "Other competitors?"

"Well, Dr. Burns and Dr. Fairlee often go after the same grant money." Charlaine hesitates. She adds, "Of course, the competition for grants is pretty stiff these days. There's never enough money available. And equipment and research space is always an issue for everybody, especially for the junior faculty."

Miller looks up from the notes he is taking. "Speaking of research space, we understand that Dr. Fairlee wasn't authorized to build that greenhouse. Can you tell us about that?"

Charlaine's laugh has a tinny edge. "Oh, yes. Fairlee's Folly, people called it — in a good-humored way, of course. And yes, I understand that it was rather a spur-of-the-moment thing. He had some money left in a grant at the end of the semester and he got the idea and —" She gives a small, helpless shrug. "Professors are sometimes a law unto themselves, you know. They don't always follow the rules. A committee looked into it and recommended that the greenhouse be designated as a teaching and research facility and allowed to stay where it is."

"But we understand that there was hate

mail about it," Miller persisted. "And some vandalism. And that faculty members were upset enough to sign a letter to the dean demanding that Fairlee be fired. Who organized that?"

Charlaine shifts in her chair. "There were a few nasty emails and letters, I believe," she says reluctantly.

"We'd like to have any that you might have saved," Sheila says. She has glanced through the faxes that Denise sent. They are nasty, yes, but also anonymous.

"I'll look," Charlaine says. "I can't promise."

"Please do," Sheila says. "We would like to have a copy of the faculty letter, too. Who did you say wrote it?"

Charlaine pulled her brows together. "I'm sorry, but I really don't see where you're going with this. I mean, poor Dr. Fairlee must just have felt he couldn't —"

"Who wrote it?" Sheila repeats her question.

"Well, if you must know." Charlaine's mouth tightened. "It was Dr. Haley. He felt that allowing one professor to have individual research space put all the other professors at a disadvantage. And yes, he did urge that Dr. Fairlee be . . . terminated." Her mouth trembles as she seems to catch the implications of that word, and she hurries on. "I'll see if I can find a copy, but the letter was written some time ago. I can't imagine it had any bearing on Dr. Fairlee's suicide. Can you? I mean, can you, *really*?"

Sheila tilts her head. "I suppose the greenhouse will be reassigned. Do you have any idea who might get it?"

"Why, I don't know." Charlaine seems surprised by the question. "Perhaps . . . Dr. Selms, I imagine. That is, he works on orchids too, so it might be appropriate. Or Dr. Haley, or Dr. Burns. They are our most senior faculty. Why do you ask?"

Sheila changes the subject. "When we talked yesterday, you also mentioned that there is some *personal* competition in the department. What did you mean by that?"

"Oh, dear. Did I say that? I didn't mean to imply . . ." Clearly nervous, Charlaine picks up a pencil and twirls it between her fingers.

Sheila waits, saying nothing. She learned long ago that silence is often the best enticement to speak, especially for women. They're socialized to fill in the gaps when a conversation lags.

"You probably know that Dr. Fairlee is divorced," Charlaine says, at last. "There was some unpleasantness at the time, because Mrs. Fairlee — she goes by the name Walker now, Margaret Walker, Maggie — was unhappy about the division of their orchid collection, as well as financial matters. The house, for one thing." Her eyes glint.

"The divorce was unpleasant, then," Sheila said, taking notes.

Charlaine's face hardens. "Ms. Walker was *quite* unfair to Dr. Fairlee, which made the divorce very difficult for him. She came here and raised a serious fuss at a faculty meeting, in front of everybody." She taps the pencil on the desk. "Anyway, they *are* divorced, so it was quite understandable that Dr. Fairlee would . . ." Her voice trails away.

Miller doesn't have Sheila's patience. "Would begin dating someone in the department?" he asks. "Who would that be? Another professor?"

The secretary's face has paled, and the blusher on her cheeks — two rosy circles — stands out in contrast. Sheila isn't sure whether the cause is embarrassment, jealousy, or something else altogether. Finally Charlaine says, "Not . . . not another professor. That is, not exactly. I mean —" She bites her lip and her glance slides away. "I suppose I had better tell you before somebody else does, although I can't think why you're interested. This is all ancient history."

"Tell us what?" Miller asks.

"Dr. Fairlee and I did go out." She twists the pencil. "Together."

"Over what period?" Miller is making notes.

"Not long. Maybe . . . five months. Six at the most." Her lips are trembling and she presses them together. "Seven, perhaps. Then it seemed best to end it, and he began seeing someone else."

Seven months. Long enough for a relationship to feel permanent. Sheila can understand the woman's discomfiture. Who had ended it? Charlaine? Or Fairlee? And why?

"He began seeing someone else — in the department?" she prompts gently.

"No." Charlaine draws in her breath. "But the girl's father is in the department, which has made for the occasional awkwardness."

"Her name?" Miller asks, still writing.

There's another silence. Finally, Charlaine says, "Dr. Fairlee has been seeing Jennifer Haley. Dr. Haley's daughter. She's a graduate student in linguistics."

"That's the same Dr. Haley who tried to get Fairlee fired?" Miller's smile is cynical. "That could make for more than an 'occasional awkwardness,' if you ask me."

"I believe there may have been a few . . . interactions," Charlaine concedes. "Dr. Haley's daughter is some years younger than Dr. Fairlee."

Some years younger? Sheila thinks. If she's a grad student, there must be a couple of decades between them, at least. "And they were going together at the time of Dr. Fairlee's death?"

"I believe so, yes," Charlaine says stiffly. Her face is pale.

Miller opens another subject. "Security cameras." He leans forward. "Are there any in the building? Outside the building?"

Charlaine's fingers are shaking and she picks up the pencil again, gripping it tightly. "None in the building. Dr. Fairlee had one installed in his greenhouse after the orchid was stolen. Logan Gardner might know if it was in use. Outside the building — you'll have to ask security. There may be one in the parking lot." She looks from Sheila to Miller, then back to Sheila. "I simply don't understand why you are asking all these questions. Dr. Fairlee's suicide is a terrible tragedy, and I hope you can find out why he did it. But —"

"One more thing and we'll let you get back to work," Sheila says. "Can you tell us where you were and what you were doing on Sunday night?"

Charlaine tries to pull herself together. "*Me?* But why — ?"

Sheila smiles reassuringly. "It's just routine. You know that every cop has to ask that question."

"I suppose you do, but really —" Charlaine stiffens her shoulders. "I was at home on Sunday night. I live with my widowed mother. We turn off the television and go to bed at ten-twenty-five, right after the local weather. But I don't understand —"

"Thank you," Sheila says with a smile. Pointedly, she writes this information in her notebook and drops it in her bag. "You've been very helpful." She can hear voices in the hallway. Classes must be changing, she thinks, and she rises.

Miller rises also. "We may have more questions later. In the meantime, it would be best if you could keep this interview to yourself."

Sheila gives the other woman a direct look. "You can do that, can't you?"

Charlaine drops the pencil. "Yes. Oh, yes, of course," she replies. "Not a word. Absolutely." She glances at her wristwatch, obviously relieved to be rid of them. "Dr. Selms is probably in his faculty office, if you want

171

to talk to him now. It's on the second floor, just to the right of the stairs."

Sheila excuses herself for a stop in the restroom, then she and Miller step outside to confer. The sky is still gray and clouded, and a humid breeze is blowing from the Gulf. Looking around her, Sheila sees the young women moving swiftly and gracefully, as lithe and lovely as wild animals. There was a time, not that many months ago, when she ran a couple of miles every morning before breakfast and she longs to be able to do that again. For a moment, she resents the clumsy bump that bulges under her wrinkled maternity uniform like a watermelon on steroids. But she feels the baby stir and pushes the resentment away. She'll have her old figure back soon. And she'll have Noah, too.

"We need to reorganize," she says. "Rudolph's remarks about Fairlee's ex-wife concern me, especially the part about her raising a fuss at a faculty meeting. I think I'd better talk to Maggie Walker right away."

"You think the ex might have killed him?" Miller asks.

Sheila shrugs. "Walker certainly sounds like an interesting character — although that may be Charlaine's own special spin.

She had a personal stake in the situation. You picked up on that?"

"Yeah. She and Fairlee were dating — which probably translates to sleeping together — until she was supplanted by a grad student. That couldn't have been easy for her. She may be carrying a load of hard feelings toward Fairlee."

"Exactly." Sheila makes another note. "I'll get Connie to dig up an address for Charlaine and her mother. We'll want to check on her alibi. And while I'm talking to the ex-wife, you can interview Selms and Logan Gardner, the research assistant. Then Dr. Haley, Jennifer's father, and what's-his-name, Burns. The one who's been competing for grant money with Fairlee. Let's get alibis for everybody and take a look at those that Maxwell has been working on. Oh, and see what you can find out about that new security camera in the greenhouse. If it's operating, our killer may be on camera."

"We should be so lucky." Miller is frowning. "Charlaine gave the impression that most — if not all — of Fairlee's colleagues had it in for him, one way or another. I wonder if somebody coveted that greenhouse enough to kill for it."

Sheila nods. "And I'm curious about Logan Gardner. Get him to tell you about that vanilla project that he and Fairlee were working on."

"Vanilla?" Miller is puzzled. "You mean, like in tobacco? My father used some kind of vanilla oil to flavor his tobacco. He always said his homemade stuff was better than anything he could buy."

"Yeah? Well, Gardner was telling me that vanilla is an orchid."

"An orchid? Huh. How about that."

"A surprise to me, too. Anyway, the two of them — Fairlee and Gardner — were working on some sort of hybrid that's supposed to be disease resistant and have a high concentration of whatever makes vanilla vanilla. They were apparently planning to file for a plant patent, jointly. Gardner didn't want to talk about it, but he seemed pretty concerned about what was going to happen to his share of the project now that Fairlee is out of the picture. He said it might be a little 'tricky' to keep what belongs to him. See if you can get the details."

"I'll do it." Miller eyes her. "You didn't tell Rudolph that we're investigating a homicide. What about Selms? And these others? Do I tell them?"

"Use your judgment. When you start asking about alibis, they may want to know why. If it's useful, tell them, but warn them to keep it to themselves. And if we have to re-interview anyone, let's do it at the station, where we'll have them on camera."

Miller glances down at what he has written. "Looks like the interview assignments are gendered. I do the guys, you do the ladies. You want it that way?"

"You bet," Sheila says. "My ears are gendered, too. They may hear things yours won't, and vice versa. Sexist, probably, but that's the way it is." Wryly, she puts a hand on her belly. "And the women may be more comfortable with me in my current state. Maybe I look motherly. I certainly don't appear threatening."

"Yeah, you got that right," Miller says. He closes his notebook. "But I gotta say, you handled that secretary just fine. You got a lot out of her and she doesn't even know it."

The remark may be condescending, but Sheila hears the grudging respect in his tone and is pleased.

CHAPTER SEVEN

SPICE-SCENTED
VANILLA POTPOURRI

4 whole vanilla beans (okay to use lower grade)
3 cinnamon sticks
2 whole nutmegs
1/2 cup allspice berries
1/2 cup star anise
1/4 cup whole cloves
1/2 cup dried rose or other flower mix

For the Fixative:
2 tablespoons powdered orris root*
Vanilla fragrance oil

Snip the vanilla beans into half-inch lengths with scissors. Break up the nutmeg and cinnamon sticks and put them in a sturdy plastic bag. Hammer the bag cautiously (I use the flat side of a meat hammer) until the hard bits are crushed (but not powdered). Add allspice, anise, and cloves and shake.

For the fixative, pour 6–8 drops of vanilla fragrance oil onto the powdered orris root or other material. Place in bottom of a quart Mason jar. Add the contents of the plastic bag, then the dried flowers. Top with snipped vanilla beans. Cap the jar and allow fragrance to develop for about three weeks. Pour into a decorative bowl and place where you will enjoy the scent. Stir often to release the fragrance.

* A fixative helps to retain the scent. Fixatives besides orris root traditionally include calamus, clary sage leaves, oak moss, tonka beans, and vetiver root. Ground corn cobs (also called ground cellulose) and natural or dyed wood chips may be used.

Pecan Springs was settled in the middle of the nineteenth century by German immigrants who stepped off their sailing ships at the yellow-fever-ridden port of Galveston. They joined a wagon train and made their way west, struggling some two hundred miles through the wilds of the brand-new state and against the strenuous objections of the Comanche and the Apache, who still thought the land was theirs. They built their first homes of cypress logs from the trees that grew along the Pecan River. The hardy folk who survived those first challenging years built more enduring homes from hand-chiseled blocks of native limestone, removed with primitive tools and grueling physical labor from local stone quarries and transported to the building sites in mule-drawn carts.

My herb shop, Thyme and Seasons, is located in one of those early native square-cut limestone houses, an attractive two-story structure on the north side of Crockett Street, a couple of blocks east of the town square. I bought the building when I left the Houston law firm where I'd worked for most of my twenties, cashed in my retirement account, and moved to Pecan Springs. I was hoping that the move would settle me into a kinder, gentler life, quiet and drama-free. Boring, even. This pastoral vision has turned out to be unrealistic. Life just doesn't operate like that — or maybe it's me. Things happen. That's all I can say.

But the mornings always feel kind and gentle, somehow. In fact, the best part of my day is the early morning, when I unlock the front door and step into my shop. The

Crystal Cave (Ruby Wilcox's shop, through the door to the left) takes up half of the front of the building. Thyme and Seasons — a small space crowded with fragrant herbs and sweet-smelling herbal products — occupies the other half. The walls are stone, the floor is the original wide pine boards, much worn, and the ceiling is embossed tin. The beams are hand-hewn cypress.

If you were to come inside with me, you'd see antique hutches and wooden shelves stocked with herbal vinegars, oils, jellies, and teas. The pine cupboard in the corner displays personal care products: herbal soaps, shampoos, massage oils, tooth powders, cleansers, balms, and bath herbs. In the middle of the room, a wooden rack holds gleaming glass jars of dried culinary and medicinal herbs, as well as bottles of extracts and tinctures. Of course there are books — including a counter display of *China Bayles' Book of Days,* of which I am quite proud — and stationery and cards and gift baskets. Wreaths and swags hang on every wall, there are bowls of fragrant potpourri on the shelves (including some luscious vanilla potpourri that is Ruby's absolute favorite), and the corners are full of baskets of dried yarrow, sweet Annie, larkspur, statice, and tansy. On a pretty morning like this one, the golden sunlight slants across the wood floor, the room is flooded with light, and the mingled scents are delicious.

Outside the front door is a rack of potted herbs for sale, always something new for your garden, depending on the season. It's September and time to plant perennials, so that's what's on the rack right now. Rosemary, lavender, thyme, mint, sage, chives — and from the look of them, the sooner I water them, the better.

If we turn left and follow the stepping-stone path around the building, we can wander through the theme gardens — the Zodiac Garden, the Fragrance Garden, the Kitchen Garden, the Apothecary Garden, the Children's Garden — now filled with late-summer blossoms and herbs ready for harvest. Wander far enough, and we will find our way to Thyme Cottage, where Ruby and I held our "Not Just Plain Vanilla" workshop the day before, and which frequently serves as a bed-and-breakfast.

But instead of going to the cottage, we will turn to our left and step through the patio doors into Thyme for Tea, which is located just behind the shops. The tea room is lovely: stone walls, green wainscoting, tin ceiling, and narrow, deep-set windows. Behind that is the kitchen, where Cass Wilde practices her culinary magic for our tea room guests, as well as for the Thymely Gourmet and our Party Thyme catering.

The kitchen is where I was headed this morning. I was on my way to feed Khat, our imperial Siamese shop kitty, and then brew myself a cup of Earl Grey tea, toast a bagel, and slather it with my favorite orange marmalade. The first task was dispatched quickly. Purring loud enough to be heard at the Alamo, Khat settled himself to his morning bowl of chopped chicken livers, his charcoal tail twitching ecstatically. I can hear him humming his own version of "The Siamese Cat Song": *I am a former resident of Siam/There is no finer Siamese than I am.* When he came to the shop, Ruby — a great admirer of Koko, the clever cat-sleuth in the Cat Who mysteries — gave him the name of Khat K'o Kung. Khat takes his duties as Top Shop Cat very seriously and is a great feline favorite of all our customers.

With Khat attended to and my breakfast finished, I busied myself with early morning shop duties — dusting, sweeping, and getting ready to greet the day's first customers. I kept an ear out for the Victorian shopkeeper's bell over the front door, not because I was expecting people just yet, but because it rings occasionally, with a silvery, half-amused tinkle, even when the door is closed. It is a brief reminder that our shop ghost is still hanging around. She is a previous resident — Annie Duncan, honored by the Historical Society's plaque beside the front door — who gets our attention by humming her favorite folksong ("Annie Laurie") or by ringing the bell over the door. When she has something really important to say, she communicates by rearranging the magnetic letters on the bulletin board behind the counter. Happily, Annie has a sense of humor, so while her manifestations may be a little unsettling, they are rarely frightening.

In fact, over time, I have discovered a certain sympathy for our ghost. I remind myself that it must be pretty frustrating to go through eternity with something terribly urgent that you are just dying to tell somebody, and no way to get the message across except by ringing a bell or rearranging colored plastic letters on a board. But now that Ruby and I have discovered her identity, it seems that Annie has said all she wants to say — for the moment, anyway. She rings the bell every now and then, sometimes teasingly or even emphatically, when Ruby and I are alone and she wants to join the conversation. Or simply to remind us that there are things in our universe that are beyond our human ken. But mostly she seems content to hang out in the shadows and watch what's going on in her house. She's a companionable spirit, so this doesn't bother me. And of course Ruby, who is psychic, is entirely in synch.

No bells this morning — yet. I stowed the dust mop in the closet, unlocked the front door, and flipped the CLOSED sign to OPEN. I was putting the change into the cash register when Ruby arrived, bouncing through the connecting door from the Crystal Cave to say "Isn't it a simply *gorgeous* day?" and show off her eye-popping outfit: clingy tangerine-print leggings topped with a lime-green batwing-sleeve gauze tunic and several strands of neon orange and electric blue beads. With her curly, copper-red hair, she was a sight for sore eyes. All six feet plus of her.

Ruby had cooked dinner for Amy and Kate the night before and was bubbling over with happy news. Grace's tonsils were much better. Kate had felt the baby move. Amy got promoted to head vet technician at the Hill Country Animal Clinic. If I could have gotten a word in edgewise, I might have mentioned Carl Fairlee's suicide. Ruby knows Maggie, of course, although I'm not sure she had ever met Maggie's ex-husband, now deceased. But she was so fizzy-full of good tidings that I decided not to darken her day.

After a few minutes, Ruby finished her report and went back to her shop to light a stick of incense and put on some music, and before long, both the fragrance and the melody were wafting into my shop. Today's scent turned out to be a sunny citrus, which (according to Ruby) encourages customers to feel energetic and generous. The CD she was playing — something light and rhythmic called "Rainbow Fields in the Sun" — would no doubt reinforce the mood. Looked like we were in for a happy day.

Until Beverly Selms arrived, just before noon, with some startling news.

She showed up at an especially inopportune moment.

I was ringing up items for Mrs. Birkett, the senior Crockett Street resident, who had just purchased a half-dozen vanilla beans, four ounces of cinnamon sticks, and a mixed assortment of whole spices. At the same time, I was answering the phone, taking reservations for lunch at Thyme for Tea, and keeping an eye on Ruby's shop while Ruby (harried, but still as cheerful as a ray of sunshine) was managing the seating in the tea room. Jasmine, our current server, was tending to the dozen already-seated customers. Cass was in the kitchen, putting the finishing touches on today's menu items: a choice of seafood or vegan quiche; a cup of tomato-basil soup; fresh greens tossed with a vanilla vinaigrette and topped with feta, cucumber, red onion, tomato, pecans, and fresh mint from the garden; and carrot cake with a vanilla cream-cheese frosting. To die for. Really.

"China, I wonder if you would have time to come and see me," Mrs. Birkett said, in her high-pitched, scratchy voice. "I have a new renter in the little house next door, and something about her is worrying me. I'd like to talk to you about it."

The old lady doesn't always hear very well, and I know that her arthritis sometimes bothers her. But she still manages the big house and the smaller rental cottage she inherited from her grandmother, and her mind is as agile as ever. She's not the kind of person who worries without a good reason.

"I'd love to," I said, "but this is a pretty frantic time right now. Could we —"

185

"Wonderful." Her old blue eyes rested on me with an odd intensity. "How about breakfast tomorrow? We'll have ourselves a quiet, leisurely hour before we start our busy days."

When I hesitated, she nodded at the vanilla beans she had just purchased. "I'm planning to make my famous strawberry vanilla breakfast omelet. Will that tempt you?"

The bell over the door — the *closed* door — rang peremptorily. Our ghost and Mrs. Birkett go back a long way, to the time when Mrs. Birkett was a little girl and Annie was in her last years.

With a chuckle, I pointed up to the bell. "You and Annie are ganging up on me." It was only partially a joke. I have learned to take Annie quite seriously. "Would eight o'clock be too early?"

"Eight will do very well, thank you." She gathered up her bag as the phone rang again. "See you tomorrow morning, dear."

"Tomorrow morning," I promised. I waved goodbye as I picked up the phone, gave the caller a quick recap of our luncheon menu, and jotted down two more names on the reservation form.

That's when I looked up again and saw Beverly Selms standing at the counter in front of me, crisp and well-groomed and every inch the real estate broker in a navy jacket and slacks and a cream-colored shell with a silky red scarf. She was not smiling.

"Oh, hi, Beverly," I said brightly. "I'll be right with you. I just have to take these reservations to Ruby."

I scooted off, handed Ruby the names, and got back behind the counter just in time to pick up the phone again and log another reservation, this one a single. The name — Karen Taylor — sounded familiar but I didn't have time to ponder. I jiggled my eyebrows apologetically at Beverly, took the name to Ruby, and was back again, breathlessly.

"Sorry for the interruptions," I said. "Can I help you find something?"

Which was not the right question. Beverly didn't look like she wanted to shop. She looked like she wanted to fire somebody, and the sooner the better.

"I've caught you at a bad time, I know," she said, trying to downgrade her scowl to a frown. She wasn't very successful. "But there's something I really think you ought to hear."

"Oh?" I said uneasily. Judging from the doomsday look on her face, I wondered whether I should duck and cover. The

187

phone rang again, but this time, feeling a little cranky, I took the initiative.

"Please hold," I said, and punched the button. "So sorry," I said to Beverly. "Tell me what's wrong."

"What's wrong," she said in a grim voice, "is that my husband is being *questioned.*"

I didn't recoil or gasp in surprise, but that was primarily because I was confused. "Questioned?" I asked blankly. "By whom? About what?"

Her look said that she had expected me to be more astute. "Why, by the police, of course. About Carl Fairlee. A detective named Miller came to Dan's office this morning and asked a lot of questions. Dan says he was very *rude.*"

"Uh-oh," I said, under my breath. In my professional experience, the police are occasionally rude. But they are not usually rude to important, well-connected people like Dan Selms unless they have reason to suspect —

"Uh-oh is right, damn it!" Beverly's eyes flashed. "The detective asked all kinds of irrelevant questions about Dan's relationship with Carl, their plant-collecting business, their rivalry, and that ugliness over Carl's greenhouse." Her eyebrows registered contempt for such nosiness. "Why, he even wanted to know where Dan was the night Carl died."

"The detective was checking your husband's *alibi*?" Now I was surprised. If that's what he was doing, it obviously meant that the cops now believed that Fairlee —

"Yes. Which is absolutely, unequivocally outrageous." Beverly rolled her eyes. "I can vouch for him, of course. All they have to do is ask me."

I am too well-mannered to point out that a wife's corroboration of a husband's whereabouts don't count for terribly much in the grand scheme of things. And anyway, Beverly was too irate to hear that. So instead, I started to say what had not yet been put into words.

"If the detective is checking alibis, that must mean the police have reason to think that Dr. Fairlee did not —"

I didn't get to finish.

"Exactly. He did not kill himself. After asking Dan all those snoopy questions and treating him as if *he* had pulled the trigger, the detective finally announced that Carl Fairlee was murdered. *Murdered!* Apparently somebody shot him and tried to make it look like suicide."

"No kidding," I breathed.

"No kidding." Beverly pulled her dark

eyebrows together. "So they have fastened on poor Dan as a person of . . ." She waved her hand impatiently. "A person of consideration, or something like that. I don't remember the term exactly."

"A person of interest," I said. I stared at Beverly for a moment. From Maggie, I knew there had been bad blood between Dan Selms and Carl Fairlee, going back a couple of years. And McQuaid's story about Dan's part in the fiasco of the greenhouse was fresh in my mind. When it came right down to it, I wasn't surprised that the police were considering Beverly's husband as a person of interest. If I were advising him, I'd tell him to start looking for a lawyer. A *criminal* lawyer.

But all that glimmered out of my mind when I thought of Maggie.

"Murdered!" I let out my breath. "Oh, poor Maggie. This will be so dreadful for her."

Beverly's lips were compressed into a taut line. "I don't know why you'd say *that,* China. She and Carl are divorced. And if you're thinking of the children, murder might be easier for them than suicide. At least they would know that their father didn't desert them."

"That's ridiculous," I said flatly. Whatever

had happened, whoever had killed him, their father was dead. That loss would haunt them forever, even after the killer had been caught, brought to trial, and sentenced.

But Beverly had thought of something else. "What will really make it hard for them," she said, straightening her shoulders, "is if it turns out that *she* is the one who killed him."

"She?" I blinked. "She who?"

Her reply dripped pity for my thick-headedness. "Why, Maggie, of course. Who else?"

"Maggie?" Naughty me — I hadn't even guessed. "But why in the world would you think —"

"Why?" she repeated. "Really, I am surprised at you. Weren't you a criminal lawyer? Isn't the spouse — in this case, the *ex*-spouse — always the first to be suspected? And Maggie certainly isn't known for her gentle personality. She and Carl battled like a couple of demented prizefighters over the divorce settlement, and especially over those orchids. Why, she went to the campus and raised hell with him at a faculty meeting, calling him every name in the book, right in front of everybody. She was hysterical. Dan said that if she'd had a gun with her, she

would probably have shot poor Carl on the spot."

"It wasn't about orchids," I said. I remembered when Maggie had confronted him on campus. It had happened when she was distraught about having to sell the house out from under the children. She felt they ought to be able to continue there until both kids were out of high school. And while it wasn't very smart, she confronted him at the faculty meeting because he wouldn't return her phone calls or her emails.

But Beverly was going on. "In fact, Logan Gardner — Carl's research assistant — told Dan that it was Maggie who broke into the greenhouse a couple of weeks ago and stole that rare orchid of Carl's. Logan saw her skulking around the building that night. Dan has told the police, so they'll probably be onto her right away."

I narrowed my eyes. "Rare orchid?"

"Oh, maybe you didn't hear about that. It's called a 'demon orchid,' because the central part of the blossom looks like the face of a devil and the pink-striped petals look like claws. It was collected from the jungles of Colombia. It's endangered, and quite, quite rare. Logan says it was Maggie who stole it."

"If it's endangered, how did Carl get it?" I

asked, thinking of CITES and the prohibition against orchid export and import. Had somebody smuggled it into the country and sold it to Carl? Or had Carl himself done the smuggling?

Beverly chuckled wryly. "Dan asked Carl that question, too, but he didn't get an answer. Still, it's worth saying that Carl refused to allow the campus police to look into the theft — probably because he didn't want anybody asking how he came by that orchid." She pulled her brows together. "I'm sure that Dan related all of this to the detective. I hope the cops search Maggie's greenhouses. I'll bet they'll find it."

I took a breath. "Maggie can be a little unpleasant sometimes." An understatement, and I knew it. I hurried on. "But she would never break into somebody's greenhouse and steal a rare orchid. She's just not that kind of person."

But the minute the words were out of my mouth, my lawyerly self was reconsidering. Maggie was the kind of person who might steal an orchid if she thought the orchid had been smuggled and she intended to set the matter right. She was also perfectly capable of blowing her cool, losing her temper, and hurling hysterical threats. Yes, she might steal an orchid. But that didn't mean she would murder somebody, not even her ex-husband.

I was about to say this to Beverly when her cell phone chimed. She took it out of her jacket pocket. "My timer," she explained, turning it off. "A reminder that I have an appointment to show a house." She looked pointedly at the hold button blinking on my phone. "And I'm sure you have things to do, too. I apologize for taking up so much of your time. But I thought you ought to know that Carl didn't kill himself."

"Thank you." I managed a smile. Beverly was wrong about Maggie, but I was glad she had let me know what was going on. We said goodbye, and I pounced on the hold button. "Hello," I said breathlessly. "Are you still there?"

"I'm still here," a low, rich voice said. "Hi, China. It's me — Kate Rodriguez."

"Oh, Kate!" I said, stricken. "Sorry to keep you on hold. I got sidetracked by something here at the shop." Something like a friend being accused of theft — and murder. Should I call Maggie and offer a shoulder to cry on? She probably needed more than that.

Kate cleared her throat. "I apologize for calling at a busy time, but I was wondering if we could get together — soon."

"Sure," I said. "I'd love to. I've been meaning to congratulate you on your baby."

"Yeah." Kate sighed. "Well, that's what I want to talk to you about, China. Amy and I had dinner with Ruby last night, and she told us what you said about having an agreement with Ron. The baby's father."

"Oh, *that.*" I was paying attention now.

"Right. That." She hesitated. "The thing is . . . well, we *don't* have an agreement. And Ron is getting a little pushy about the baby. I'm at the point where —" She was trying to sound casual, but I could hear the concern under her words. "I think I need some advice. Could we, like, just talk?"

"Of course," I said sympathetically. "When?"

"As soon as possible. And please, don't mention this to Ruby — or Amy. I don't want to . . . well, worry them." Her voice darkened. "At least, not until I know whether there's something to worry about."

"Well, then, how about coming out to my house after supper tonight? It'll be quiet there, and we can talk as long as we like. Seven, seven-fifteen, maybe?" For supper, I was planning to experiment with a balsamic vanilla sauce that would dress up a simple baked chicken dish. The meal ought to be quick and easy to assemble. I'd be out of the kitchen by the time Kate showed up.

"Terrific." Kate huffed out a relieved sigh. "I can't thank you enough, China."

"Thank me when we've finished talking," I cautioned, and she laughed, nervously. "See you this evening."

I hung up the phone and went back to work — or rather, I tried to. But my mind wasn't on it. I was chewing on several possibilities and wondering what, if anything, I could or should do about them.

Specifically, I was considering whether I should call Maggie and offer not just my sympathy but my help, although at the moment I couldn't think what sort of help I should offer. Although I certainly didn't want to get into the middle of a murder investigation, I couldn't help feeling that I should be doing something to support her. But *what*? Should I go out to the garden center and talk to her?

I was thinking about all this when the door opened and a woman came in. "Hi," she said, pausing in front of the counter. She had assertive hazel eyes, a firm jaw, and a square face bare of makeup and neatly framed by short, straight brown hair. She wore jeans, a bright green cotton roll-sleeve blouse, and tennis shoes. "I called in a lunch

196

reservation a little while ago. I'm Karen Taylor."

"Oh, right." So that was why her name had sounded familiar. "You attended our vanilla workshop yesterday. You're the nurse, aren't you?"

She nodded. "That's right. I work at the Adams County Hospital, in the ER. After I left here yesterday, I went on the computer and looked at some of the medicinal research you mentioned." She gave me a rueful grin. "I also found a ton of hype, of course. People are touting vanilla as God's great gift to humankind. A cure for gout and arthritis, better than Prozac for depression, even a treatment for sickle-cell anemia." She tilted her head. "But I also read that our stomach enzymes destroy the main chemical, vanillin, which means that it only works in test tubes. If it's to have any effect at all, it will have to be modified before it can be useful to humans."

I was impressed. People don't always ask the right questions about the medicinal information they find online, some of which is way over the top and unreliable. Karen Taylor was clearly an exception.

"I'm glad you're interested enough to sort out what's credible and what can't be trusted," I said. "But until there's more research . . ."

"Oh, yes, we always need more research, don't we?" We both chuckled. "Actually," she added, "it was my daughter who was interested in vanilla. Her curiosity prompted mine." She gave me an odd little smile, half-forlorn. "I *have* come for lunch, but I was also hoping to get a better look at your vanilla plant. I'm thinking of buying one of my own. As a reminder."

I wasn't sure what she meant by that last remark, but I returned the smile. "I'm sorry, Ms. Taylor," I said. "I took it out to Sonora after the workshop."

"Oh, please. Call me Karen." She cocked her head. "Sonora is the garden center you were talking about, isn't it? Owned by Maggie Walker?"

"Yes, that's the place." I smiled. "My vanilla plant thinks it's heaven."

"I'm not sure how long I'll be in Pecan Springs. I'm at the hospital on a temporary assignment. But the place where I'm staying — just a few blocks down the street, actually — has a greenhouse window in the kitchen. I'd love to have a small vanilla plant."

"Then you'll want to see what Maggie has," I replied. "In fact, I was just thinking of going out to Sonora. Would you like to go with me?"

"That would be wonderful!" she said eagerly. "What time?"

I considered. I was sure that Ruby would be willing to watch the shop if I left for an hour or so. "How about right after lunch?" I suggested. "But I'd better call first and make sure that Maggie's there today. There's been a death in her family, and she might not have come in this morning."

"A death?" Karen's brow furrowed. "Oh, that's too bad. Somebody close?"

If I had thought about it, I might have found the question a little odd. But I was caught up in the conversation, so I simply answered. "Yes. Her ex-husband. Dr. Fairlee taught botany courses at the university. I audited his graduate seminar on vanilla. Those photographs I showed at the workshop yesterday were taken on our field trip to Veracruz a few years ago."

"I was going to ask you if I could take another look at those photos. I've traveled in that region recently, and I'm interested." She gave me a curious look. "But you're saying that your professor has died?"

I nodded, feeling no need to go further. But she persisted.

"How did he die?" She tilted her head. "Sorry. Occupational habit, I guess. Nurses always want to know the details."

I hesitated. But there was no need for reluctance, surely. The police were already interviewing persons of interest, so the story would likely be all over the news tonight. In fact, I'd bet that my friend Jessica Nelson, the *Enterprise*'s top crime reporter (more accurately, its *only* crime reporter), was already pursuing the story. So there was no good reason not to answer Karen's question.

"I'm afraid he was murdered," I said regretfully. "Shot to death, in fact. In his greenhouse at the university."

She blinked, taken aback. "Mur . . . murdered!" Her hand went to her mouth and her eyes grew large. "But that's —" She drew in a breath. "I mean, really? *Murdered*?"

I was a little startled by her reaction, since she didn't know the man. "Shocking, I know," I said, wanting to soothe her. "Pecan Springs is a great place to live, but it has its fair share of crime. And bad people can do bad things anywhere."

She opened her mouth to ask another question, but Ruby interrupted her. "Ms. Taylor?" she called from the door of the tea room. "Your table is ready."

While Karen was being seated, I telephoned Sonora. Ruben answered the phone and when I gave him my name and asked for Maggie, he said that she had come in that morning but had left after a couple of hours and wasn't expected back.

He dropped his voice. "Actually, Ms. Bayles, she was planning to stay for the rest of the day. But she changed her mind after the police chief came to see her this morning. She went straight home after that. She said she had to talk to her kids."

"The police chief? Sheila Dawson?"

I wasn't exactly surprised to hear this. Since the cops had decided that Dr. Fairlee's death was a homicide dressed up like a suicide, interviewing the victim's ex-wife would be at the top of their to-do list.

"That's her," Ruben said. "Chief Dawson, preggie as all get-out. The boss was closeted with her for nearly an hour." He sucked in a breath, and I guessed what was coming next. "I just happened to be working not far from her open office window, and I heard something pretty shocking. It turns out that Dr. Fairlee didn't kill himself. He was . . . *murdered*." The pause before *murdered* was almost long enough to insert *wait for it.*

I didn't want to spoil his performance by letting on that I already knew this. "Oh, my stars," I breathed, with appropriate dismay.

"You've got to be *kidding,* Ruben!"

"No! It's true, I swear it! Just like CSI! The chief said that whoever killed him wanted to make it look like suicide, which they didn't know until they saw the autopsy report this morning. And on top of that, Chief Dawson seems to think that the boss might have been involved somehow or another. She's told her to go to the station and get fingerprinted, and not to leave Pecan Springs. Like she's a *suspect.*" Another breath. "Actually, I'm thinking Ms. Maggie needs a lawyer. Do you suppose you could —"

"No, I couldn't, Ruben," I said sternly. "And I hope you won't go around telling everybody about this. That would not be helpful to your boss. Let's just leave it between the two of us. Okay?"

He backpedaled hastily. "Oh, absolutely," he said. "Sorry. I know you're a special friend, or I wouldn't have —"

"And I'm grateful," I cut in. "I'll give her a call." I added, "Oh, and if a woman named Karen Taylor shows up this afternoon, she'll be looking for my vanilla plant. Please point her in the right direction. And you might be able to sell her a baby vanilla."

"I'll be glad to do that." Ruben sounded chastised. "If you talk to the boss, tell her

202

we've got everything under control. I don't want her worrying about the garden center, on top of everything else."

A moment later, I had Maggie on the phone. "What are you doing for lunch today?" I asked. I knew she would be distressed, so I made my voice as cheerful and upbeat as I could.

"You've heard the news about Carl?" Without waiting for an answer, she said, "Sheila Dawson came to see me at the garden center this morning, China. Carl didn't kill himself. He was *murdered.*" There was a moment's silence. "I don't want any lunch. And I don't want to see anybody."

"Uh-uh," I said. "You need to eat, Mags. I'm coming over and bringing lunch from the tea room. It's quiche today — do you prefer seafood or vegan?" I added, "Are the kids there? I'd be glad to bring some for them."

There was another silence. Then, finally, "Lyle's gone out, but you can bring vegan for Chelsea, if you want. She didn't want to go to school today, and I couldn't bring myself to force her." A pause. "And vegan for me, too, I guess." Her voice was unchar- acteristically meek. "Thank you."

"Don't mention it," I said. "Go lie on the sofa. I'll be there in a jiffy."

On my computer, I brought up Sonora's website and printed the map and directions. I went to the tea room door and told Ruby that something important had come up and I needed to take a break. "I'll be back in an hour," I promised. "Two at the outside. I'm not going far."

"Sure." She gave me a concerned look. "Is everything okay?"

"It's Maggie Walker," I said. "She's just heard that her husband was murdered."

"Murdered!" Ruby breathed. Her eyes widened. "Oh, my God, China. That's terrible!"

I nodded. "Apparently, it was made to look like a suicide, but the police now say otherwise. I'm sure the news has come as a shock. She needs to have somebody with her. I thought I'd take her some lunch."

"Don't worry about us," Ruby said. "Laurel can cover for you if I'm busy." In her characteristically Ruby way, she added, "You just do what you have to do. We'll manage here."

"Thank you," I said gratefully.

In the tea room, I stopped at Karen Taylor's table. "I'm afraid my after-lunch plans have changed." I handed her the page I'd just printed from Sonora's website. "Here's a map and directions to the garden center, so you can go on your own. When you get there, ask for Ruben. He'll show you where to find what you're looking for."

"I'm sorry we can't go together," Karen said. She started to say something else, stopped, and gave me a small smile. "Another time, perhaps."

"Another time," I agreed, and headed for the kitchen to fix three takeout lunches.

CHAPTER EIGHT

Breakfast was a century ago, maybe two, and Sheila is hungry enough to eat a wolf. So she picks up a green chili bagel with cheese and sausage and snarfs it down as she heads to Sonora for her interview with Maggie Walker. It is ten-thirty by the time she parks her squad car in the garden center lot and arrives at Walker's office. She breaks the news — that Fairlee's death is now officially a homicide — with a calculated abruptness meant to catch Walker off guard. It does. For a moment, the woman seems stunned.

"My God," she whispers in a dazed voice, shaking her head. "Suicide was bad enough — but *this*? I mean, Carl wasn't always a nice man, but who on earth would have *killed* him?" She closes her eyes and takes a deep breath. "How am I going to tell the kids?"

Walker's concern about the children

seems natural enough to Sheila and genuine, as far as she can tell. The boy — a college freshman — is old enough to deal with the news, but Sheila shudders when she imagines telling a thirteen-year-old girl. When a parent is murdered, the children are victims, too.

To complicate matters, it turns out that the daughter is Walker's (hardly watertight) alibi for the night of the murder. Their home is no more than a ten-minute drive from the Plant Sciences building where Fairlee was killed. It would be easy enough for Walker to get in the car, drive to the campus, shoot the ex-husband, and drive home — all while the child was asleep. There and done and back in less than thirty minutes and no one the wiser. Sheila reminds herself that a wife murdering a hated ex-husband is hardly news.

On the other important question, the break-in at the greenhouse, Walker blinks, claims she knows nothing about it, and asks for details. She doesn't seem surprised, however, when Sheila tells her that the only thing that was taken was a rare orchid from Colombia.

"Carl had connections in the orchid trade," the woman says, "and they weren't all on the level, if you know what I mean."

She runs a hand through her spiky, green-tipped hair — an odd look, Sheila thinks, for a businesswoman. But maybe horticulturalists like to look funky. Or the green is meant to convey a message. Or something.

"No, I don't know what you mean." She takes out her notebook, hoping for something that might turn into a lead.

"Orchid smuggling," Walker says. She shakes her head energetically. "It's a big business these days. But I'm a reputable seller. I make it a rule not to buy wild orchids from anybody." The window in the small office is open. Voices can be heard outside, and the sound of music. Gershwin? Somebody laughs.

"Orchid smuggling?" Sheila asks, writing it down. "What's that?"

"There's a huge demand for rare orchids," Walker says. "And a global black market for new orchids found in the wild. Everybody in the horticulture business knows which airports to fly from with hand-carried plants — Taiwan, for instance, which doesn't belong to CITES. Smugglers hide them in suitcases and unmarked packages, or they put them in secret compartments in shipping containers. Or sometimes, they're right in plain sight. Customs inspectors can't tell one plant from another, so a smuggler can put almost anything down on a permit and get by with it. If it isn't flowering, it's impossible to tell that it's a rare species. And once plants have been smuggled in, they can be laundered through orchid shows or crooked nurseries. There are plenty of greedy and dishonest buyers out there." Her voice takes on an edge. "It's the collector's compulsion, you know. All they want is an orchid that nobody else has. They don't care how they get it."

This is all new information to Sheila and she's scribbling fast. "Dr. Fairlee was involved in this black market?"

"I didn't say that." Walker frowns. "I just know that he wasn't always careful about how he got plants or who he got them from." She pauses and her mouth tightens. "His girlfriend might know. You should ask her."

"His girlfriend?" Sheila prompts. She has the name she got from Charlaine Rudolph, but there is always the possibility of turning up somebody else.

"Jennifer Haley seems to be his current love interest." Walker adds, with revealing bitterness, "She's a grad student — he liked them young, you know." Her voice becomes sharper. "The younger the better."

"You make it sound as if there have been

other women in his life. Were there?"

"As in women-who-might-have-a-motive-to-kill-him?" Walker rolls her eyes in a comic mockery that suggests dozens. "Well, you might start with Charlaine Rudolph."

"The departmental secretary?" Sheila asks, as if this is news to her. "You're saying that *she* was involved with Dr. Fairlee?"

"For a few months," Walker replies. "Charlaine never got over it when he dropped her for young Jennie. But there were students, as well — even while we were married."

"Students? While you were married?" Sheila wonders if Walker realizes that she is revealing a possible motive for herself.

"Yes, students." Walker's voice is caustic. "Which of course gave Dan Selms heartburn. He had a couple of man-to-man talks with Carl about his unrestrained libidinous tendencies. Dan was afraid that the department might get a bad name. Or the university might get hit with a lawsuit for sexual misconduct."

"I see," Sheila murmurs, adding *maybe #MeToo?* to the note she has just made. She wonders if Selms will volunteer this information to Miller or if they will have to dig for it. It opens up a whole new avenue of investigation. "Do you know who these students are? Might one of *them* have killed him?"

"My gut reaction, no. But you might talk to Beth Craig, who was a friend of one of the girls. Dan Selms probably has other names." Walker considers for a moment. "And if I were making a list of potential suspects, I wouldn't put Charlaine at the top. She's kind of a cold fish. She might have felt betrayed when Carl dropped her for Jennie, but I doubt that she could have whipped up enough passion to kill him."

Sheila frowns. She understands what Walker is saying. But she has the feeling that Charlaine is a repressed woman who conceals depths of passion that aren't apparent to casual acquaintances. What's more, she had to see Fairlee every day. For a scorned lover who is years older than the young woman who replaced her, this must have been agonizingly, perhaps unbearably painful. Sheila draws a circle around Charlaine's name.

Walker is smiling crookedly. "I don't see sweet little Jennifer doing it, either. She's too wimpy. I was surprised to hear that she'd got up the nerve to move out of her parents' house."

But you're neither a cold fish nor a wimp, Sheila thinks, watching Walker's face as she speaks. Her police work has taught her that people keep secrets, sometimes related to the crime they are being questioned about and sometimes completely unrelated. But secrets all the same. Old angers, corrosive passions, festering wounds — any of these, all of these, can bleed into someone's response to even the simplest questions. Sheila can't guess what it is or whether it's significant, but there is something in Walker's replies that catches her attention. Secrets related to the long-dead marriage? To the divorce or to Fairlee's lovers? To his murder? What is Walker keeping to herself?

But there are no immediate answers to these questions, and anyway, Noah is telling her that it's time to pee. She pushes herself to her feet and tells Walker to come to the station that afternoon to be fingerprinted.

"And I must ask you not to leave Pecan Springs," she adds. "We may want to interview you again." In fact, she knows that they *will* interview her again, to try to pry her open and find out what she's concealing.

Walker's eyes widen. "You're saying that I'm a *suspect*?"

"Everybody is a suspect," Sheila says, "until we find your ex-husband's killer. I'm sure you want that as much as we do."

"Oh, yes," Walker says hurriedly. "Yes, of

212

course I do. I just . . ." She swallows. "Fingerprints. Yes."

Sheila hesitates at the door. "Restroom?"

Walker gets up. "It's a little hard to find. Let me show you." She glances down at Sheila's belly. "When I was as far along as you, I could never hold out for more than an hour at a stretch." They both laugh.

Ten minutes later, greatly relieved, Sheila is easing her bulk behind the steering wheel of her car and thinking that she is hungry. That bagel didn't come close to filling her up, and even though it's just eleven-thirty, she's ready for lunch.

She reaches for her cell and calls Dylan Miller. "Where are you on your interview list?"

"I finished with Selms and Haley and had a quick conversation with Gardner," Miller replies. "Told all three to report for finger-printing this afternoon, and be prepared to talk to us again." He pauses. "What about you?"

"Walker done, Jennifer Haley yet to do, and I want another go at Rudolph. But I could eat a horse, saddle and all, so I'm thinking of someplace where we can get lunch while we compare notes and see where we are." She is also thinking of a large cabrito fajita smothered in red sauce, with extra onions. Her stomach rumbles in anticipation. "What would you say to a back-corner table at Bean's?"

"Meet you there in ten," Miller replies and clicks off.

As Sheila drops her phone into her bag she is considering whether to run her bubble light and siren so she can get to Bean's a little faster.

Used to be, there were only a couple of places to eat in Pecan Springs, which was fine if you were in the mood for a bowl of red or a plate of fried catfish, not so great if you wanted something a little more varied.

But times have changed, Pecan Springers are getting more eclectic, and international cuisine is almost as easy to find as a bacon cheeseburger. Within a fifteen-minute drive, you can sit down to masala dosa, som tam, chicken rice with garlic and pounded ginger, pho, or a plate of bratwurst and spaetzle. Heading north on I-35? There's a smorgasbord of upscale eateries in Austin, where at least one swanky new restaurant is launched every week. Southbound, you'll find the same thing in San Antonio, especially along the Riverwalk.

But if what you want is a real down-home Texas place that puts fine Tex-Mex food on the table and plenty of it, you can't beat Bean's Bar and Grill. It is named for Judge Roy Bean, who called himself "The law west of the Pecos." Bean had a reputation as a hanging judge, although he sentenced only two men to hang and one of them got away before they knotted the rope.

You'll find Bean's just a couple of blocks off the square, next door to Purley's Tire Company and across the street from the Old Fire House Dance Hall. Definitely, defiantly downscale, the place features an old-fashioned saloon bar along the right side of the dining room, a couple of pool tables in the back room, and TV sets tuned to ESPN and Fox. The ceiling is stained with the tobacco smoke of generations, and the tables and chairs are green, red, yellow, blue — whatever color was on sale at Banger's Hardware the week somebody got around to painting them. A carved wooden Indian stands in the corner with a sign around his neck that instructs his politically correct friends to refer to him as a Native American, and wagon wheels hang from the ceiling, wound with rusty barbed wire laced with strings of lights in the shape of red and green jalapeño peppers. Signed photographs of Texas news-makers line the walls: Willie Nelson, LBJ, Buddy Holly, Ann Richards,

Dubya, Janis Joplin, Stevie Ray Vaughn, the Apollo 13, Selena, Beto, Bevo (the UT longhorn mascot) and Reveille (the A&M collie mascot, who has a Twitter account), and so on and so forth. There is a never-ending parade of Texans seeking fame and glory.

The place is already crowded and noisy when Sheila comes in. The usual noon-hour games are in progress in the pool room at the back, and the sharp *crack!* of a cue ball punctuates the buzz of diners' voices, the clatter of dishes in the kitchen, and the nasal sound of Willie and Waylon on the jukebox. The Missouri Pacific tracks are less than fifty yards away on the other side of the parking lot, and every now and then, the rumble of a passing freight train drowns out everything else. The noise makes Bean's a good place to meet for a working lunch. Nobody can overhear you. You can barely hear yourself.

Miller, already seated at a table in the back corner, puts up his hand to catch her attention. Sheila glances at the hallway that leads to the ladies' room, coyly designated *Heifers* on a sign beside the door. (The men's says *Bulls,* of course.) Whenever she comes into a restaurant these days, she automatically notes the location of the restroom and estimates the distance and how long it will take her to get there.

But she doesn't need it at the moment, so she threads her way through the tables to join Miller, stopping to say hello to people she knows — the mayor, a couple of city council members, the manager of the Sophie Briggs Museum, the director of the library. She sees quite a few acquaintances, actually, which can be a bit of a nuisance when you go to Bean's at the lunch hour. (It's not a place to meet a secret friend.)

As she sits down, burly, red-haired Bob Godwin — owner, manager, and general factotum — saunters up with a red plastic basket of warm tortilla chips, a crockery mug of hot-as-hell salsa, and a frosty pitcher of iced tea to put out the flames. Bob is a stocky, broad-shouldered man with a gingery goatee and reddish hair as short and bristly as a scrub brush. A proud veteran, he is wearing a black T-shirt that displays an American flag and the blood-red proclamation, *Freedom ain't free. Some of us paid an arm and a leg for it.* He is accompanied by Budweiser, his golden retriever, who is wearing a blue bandana and a pair of canvas saddlebags. Bud totes wrapped snacks and beer bottles from the bar to the tables, and money and credit card chits from the tables back to the bar. Since customers have an unhelpful habit of tipping the dog with food from their plates, Bob has hung a sign around Bud's neck: *If you feed me, Bob will bite you.*

"How y'all doin' today?" Bob takes an order pad out of the navy blue apron tied around his waist. When they say they are fine but hungry, he grins, showing two gold teeth. "Cabrito kabobs is good." He gestures toward the chalkboard menu behind the bar, under a colorful sign: *7-Course Texas Dinner: A 6-Pack & a Possum.* "Or there's the reg'lar. Ribs, meatloaf, chicken-fried, catfish, and chili. What'll it be?"

"The kabobs will do it for me," Sheila says with a little regret, since she would rather have a burrito, which is heftier. But Bob's cabrito kabobs — marinated in lime juice, soy sauce, and garlic and grilled with cherry tomatoes and chunks of onion, pineapple, and green peppers — are justly famous, with rice and guacamole on the side, so she's content.

"Chicken-fried for me," Miller says, spooning sugar into a quart-sized glass of iced tea. As every Texan knows, chicken-fried is not fried chicken. It is a cube steak pounded into submission with the pointy side of a meat hammer, dredged in egg and seasoned flour, crispy-fried, and served under a thick blanket of black-pepper gravy. Bob's chicken-fried is fork-tender and comes with mashed potatoes, sweet corn, and coleslaw.

"Got it," Bob says cheerfully. He grins at Sheila, and his approving glance drops down to her belly. "So when's the big day, Chief Lady?"

"First weekend in November," Sheila says.

"First weekend in — !" Bob's jaw sags and his eyes get big. "No way! That's opening day!"

Sheila widens her eyes. "No kidding?" she says, as if she is flabbergasted by this news.

She isn't, of course. Blackie, Bob, and most of their friends are deer hunters, and the opening of whitetail season is sacrosanct, like Christmas or the Texas-Oklahoma football game. Sheila has often advanced the opinion that the first Saturday in November would be a perfect day for an alien invasion. Half of the male population of Pecan Springs would be found hanging out in their deer blinds or tramping through the cedar brakes hoping to get a buck with a halfway decent rack. The aliens would be unopposed.

Bob doesn't disappoint. "First weekend!" He pretends great alarm. "Well, all I can

219

say is that you better launch that bambino early or hang onto him for an extra two–three days. I'll have a talk with that man of yours. Can't let him miss out on openin' day just because his woman is havin' a baby."

"I'm sure we can work something out," Sheila says.

Bob says, "Damn straight," and leans toward Miller. "Listen, I heard about that guy gettin' hisself murdered up there on the campus over the weekend, Dylan. You arrested anybody yet?"

"Where'd you hear that, Bob?" Sheila asks sharply. They haven't released the cause of death yet.

"One of the docs at the hospital was in a little while ago." Bob drops his voice. "Said Doc Berry did the autopsy. Wasn't suicide, like was first thought. Shot, he was, right in the head. You got any leads yet?"

"We're working on it," Miller says in an even tone. "What are you hearing?" This is not a frivolous question, since a lot of the news that travels around Pecan Springs walks in through Bob's front door. Bob himself has a soft spot in his hard heart for the Blue Brotherhood, to which he has finally, if grudgingly, admitted Sheila. He can be relied on to tell what he hears, although what he hears isn't usually very reliable.

"Ain't heard nothin' yet, but I've got my ear to the ground," Bob promises. "I'll holler if something turns up, bro." He winks at Sheila and adds, "You hang in there, pretty lady. Just a few more weeks and you can go on full-time diaper patrol." He pockets his order form and leaves, Bud at his heels.

Sheila has known Bob for years and has developed a tolerance for his humor. She is more amused than offended by his mildly sexist comments. Miller doesn't find it funny, however.

"How in the bloody hell do you put up with crap like that?" he wonders. "It would drive me up the damn wall."

"Comes with the territory," Sheila replies. "Try being a female cop for a week or two and you'll see." She empties a couple of envelopes of pink stuff into her iced tea and gets down to business. "What did you dig up this morning? Anything useful?"

Miller, who is a methodical interviewer, pulls out a small notebook and begins with Dan Selms, whom he saw first. Selms proclaimed himself "shocked and appalled" to learn that Fairlee had been murdered, but Miller believes the news wasn't a surprise.

"Looked to me like he knew this already — maybe guessed it." Maybe more than that, Miller adds. "Selms' wife is his alibi, but they have separate bedrooms, so he's still on the suspect list." A possible motive: anger at Fairlee for the trick he pulled with the greenhouse. But there is more.

"Selms told me that Fairlee ripped off his — that is, Selms' — research on plant DNA," Miller goes on. "He made it sound like penny-ante stuff, hardly worth mentioning, but he was downplaying it. When I talked to Haley, he said that —"

Sheila interrupts. "Did Selms happen to mention anything about Fairlee's sexual involvement with students?"

"Nope." Miller raises both eyebrows. "Where'd you hear *that*?"

"Fairlee's ex-wife, Margaret Walker. She claims that Fairlee's 'unrestrained libidinous tendencies' gave Selms some serious heartburn. Not from a moral angle, apparently. She says he was scared that the department might get a bad name or that the university might get sued. According to Walker, Selms had a couple of talks with Fairlee, cautioning him to cool it." With a small smile, she adds, "I don't remember hearing of somebody being killed to save his employer from a lawsuit. But it's not hard to imagine a

#MeToo revenge motive for murder." She's thinking of the Salvagings in *The Handmaid's Tale.*

"Damn." Miller is staring at her. "So there could be *students* with a possible grudge against Fairlee?"

Sheila shivers. "Your guess is as good as mine. The ex-wife suggested that Selms might know who they are. It's worth asking him. Or Haley. Or both." She snags a tortilla chip and backtracks. "So what were you saying about Haley and Selms' research?"

Miller scribbles *students* and *#MeToo* into his notebook, adds a question mark, and underlines them. "What Haley says is that Fairlee ripped off Selms' orchid-DNA research, and it was *not* penny-ante. It was a great big deal — or it would have been if Selms had formally reported the plagiarism to the department's tenure committee, which Haley chairs. Haley says they would certainly have investigated. If they had found Fairlee guilty, the committee would have recommended revoking his tenure." He grinned crookedly. "Haley called it 'defrocking.' Apparently, putting your name on somebody else's research is a giant-sized no-no."

"So why didn't Selms report it? Seems like a convenient way to get rid of a bad-

223

boy faculty member who is causing everybody great grief."

"I asked Haley that same question. He fumbled around and finally advanced the opinion that Selms kept quiet because Fairlee had some kind of leverage over him. Blackmail, in other words."

"Blackmail!" Sheila reaches for another chip. "Interesting collegial relationships in that department. Was Haley specific about the leverage?"

"He hinted that he knew but was reluctant to say. I didn't push him, thinking we would include that question when we haul both of them — Selms and Haley — down to the station for a second interview. If Fairlee was blackmailing Selms and Selms felt he had to put a stop to it, murder dressed up to look like suicide might seem like a viable solution."

Sheila takes out her notebook and makes a note of her own. "Maybe Charlaine Rudolph can tell us something about the blackmail, if that's what it was. All the department paperwork crosses her desk, and I'm sure she catalogs every scrap of faculty gossip. Plus, she was sleeping with Fairlee for a while, according to the ex-wife. If Fairlee was blackmailing her boss, she's likely to know it."

At that moment, Bud trots up to the table with two cold bottles of beer in his saddlebags. He noses her knee politely. "Sorry, not ours," Sheila says to the dog. Two tables over, a fat guy with tattoo sleeves calls, "Hey, Bud, over here with those beers," and Bud corrects his mistake.

Miller's dark eyebrows have gone up again. "Fairlee was sleeping with Rudolph *and* students?" He makes another note. "Plus his current girlfriend. He was one busy guy."

"That's Walker's story," Sheila says. "She's bitter. Understandably, I guess. She wound up losing the house in the divorce."

"Bitter enough to shoot her ex?"

"Possibly," Sheila replies. "Her alibi is weak — a thirteen-year-old daughter, asleep in another room. Plus, she's hiding something. I don't know what, but it's *something.*" Another tortilla chip, warm and crispy. "So what did you make of Haley?"

"Typical professor, pompous, stuffed shirt, full of himself. He was 'horribly distressed' to hear that his colleague didn't commit suicide, which he seemed to feel was a natural end to a totally misspent professional life. Specifically, Fairlee's sins included plagiarizing research, hogging more than his share of departmental travel funds, and building that greenhouse, which gave him the research space that enabled him to get even more grants. On reflection, Haley allowed that Fairlee was such a first-class jerk that it wasn't much of a surprise that somebody knocked him off. A world-class favor to students, the department, and the university."

"Ha," Sheila says. "With all that baggage, Haley'd better have a world-class alibi."

"No alibi at all. His wife was in San Antonio for the weekend, with one of their daughters. He was home, in his study, reading."

"Too bad," Sheila murmurs. "We've got more than enough suspects. It would be good to whittle down the list." She pauses. "Did you get anything out of him about his daughter and *her* relationship to Fairlee?"

"Yep. He was candid on that point, too. Both he and his wife hated the idea of Fairlee and their Jennifer getting it on together — for the girl's sake, Haley says, but there was clearly more to it than that. He didn't even try to hide his relief that his potential son-in-law is dead." Miller picks up his iced tea and takes a sip. "But here's something else. According to Haley, the daughter had been seeing Logan Gardner before she got involved with Fairlee."

"Oh, yeah?" Sheila raises both eyebrows. "So Fairlee stole her from his research assistant? Which presumably didn't make Gardner happy."

"Right. Haley says Gardner took it hard, very hard. However, the Haleys weren't in favor of that relationship, either. Haley says Gardner cuts too many corners, and his DNA research is sloppy. Hard to tell how much of that is Haley's ego talking, though. He doesn't think highly of anybody's research but his own."

"A hotbed of intrigue," Sheila says. "I feel sorry for Jennifer already." She sips her iced tea. "What about the orchid theft? Anything there?"

"Hey, that's the fun part." Miller licks his thumb and turns a page. "Selms suspects that Fairlee staged the theft to cover the loss of a plant that died from his carelessness. Haley thinks Logan Gardner took it and that the orchid — the 'demon orchid' is what he called it — is worth a ton of money."

Sheila thinks about Walker's tale of orchid smuggling and wonders whether the stolen orchid is part of a larger black-market scheme. "Does Haley have any evidence for his suspicion?" she asks.

"Nope. Just his opinion. The guy has lots

of them." He turns another page. "And get this. Haley also says that Gardner was expecting Fairlee to file a plant patent in *both* their names. Fairlee apparently filed it in *his* name only, thus cheating Gardner out of both professional recognition and potential income. Gardner was pissed when he found out, according to Haley. He made threats."

"So that's what Gardner meant when he said it might be a little tricky to keep what belongs to him," Sheila says. "We need to know when Gardner found out about Fairlee's patent filing."

"Yeah. That's crucial. And here's more about that demon orchid. Selms says Gardner told *him* that Fairlee's ex-wife took it. Said he saw her skulking around the building the night of the break-in. She apparently has a key."

"Huh," Sheila says. "Walker claims to know nothing about that theft."

Miller shrugs. "Apparently Selms didn't buy the story, either. In fact, when I asked Selms who he thinks killed Fairlee, Gardner is at the top of his list."

"You talked to Gardner? He has an alibi?"

"I had only a few minutes with him. Says he was home alone, working on his dissertation, so no alibi. What's more, it turns out that he's licensed to carry. *He* didn't tell me that," Miller adds. "I checked the DPS files."

"Ah," Sheila says, her interest piqued. Being licensed to carry means (among other things) that Gardner was required to submit his fingerprints to the Department of Public Safety. His prints should be in the system. "But AFIS didn't pick up a match for that partial from the suppressor," she reminds Miller. "Which should mean that Gardner is not our guy."

"The print is pretty smudged," Miller says doubtfully. "Maybe it just wasn't good enough for AFIS. We'll get a fresh set and check." He adds, "Neither Selms nor Haley are licensed to carry. They're not in the DPS system."

Which doesn't mean that they don't own guns — legally. Texas does not require gun owners to be licensed, just those who want to carry their guns around with them, concealed or otherwise. She asks, "How about Walker and the Haley girl? Are they in the DPS files?"

"I didn't ask," he says, and reddens slightly.

"Sexist," Sheila says, and grins.

"Here you go, pretty lady," Bob says, sliding a plate of kabobs in front of Sheila, and

229

an equally large plate of chicken-fried steak in front of Miller. "Sorry it took so long. The kitchen is pretty busy."

There is silence for a few moments as they dig into their food. The cabrito is tender and flavorful, the vegetables are grilled perfectly, and Sheila no longer regrets the burrito. While she is eating, she updates Miller on her interview with Walker.

She concludes with, "The most significant thing, I'd say, is her claim that Fairlee was getting it on with Charlaine Rudolph *and* with students. We need to check this out with both Rudolph and Selms. Gardner may know about the students, too." She pushes her plate back and reaches for her napkin. "And if this case isn't complicated enough, there's apparently a lucrative international black market in orchids. Walker is saying that Fairlee might have been receiving and selling smuggled plants. If so, Gardner is likely to have known about it. I'm wondering whether that 'demon orchid' might have been contraband."

Miller is staring at her. "Black market? Smuggled *orchids*?"

Sheila chuckles. "Yeah. Who knew? Let's put this on our list of things to talk to Gardner about. Selms and Haley as well. If this smuggling business is a real thing, people will at least have heard rumors."

Miller makes a note. "Your take on Walker?" he asks, going back to his chicken-fried.

"She's carrying a load of long-term anger and hostility toward Fairlee. She owns a large business, so she has strong planning skills. Plus, she strikes me as having a short fuse. And her alibi — a daughter, asleep in the house — is weak. I told her to go to the station this afternoon for fingerprinting. And warned her against leaving town. The usual."

"So far, then," Miller says, "we want formal statements from Gardner, Selms, and Haley — the old man, not the girl — and Walker. Is that right?"

"And Rudolph." Sheila sips her iced tea as Miller adds Rudolph's name to his list. "Heard from Parsons on the search of Fairlee's apartment? Or from Donnelly on Fairlee's computer and phone? If there's anything to Walker's suggestion that her ex might have been involved in some sort of smuggling scheme, there's likely to be something in the phone. Or the computer."

Miller shakes his head. "Nothing from Parsons yet, and Donnelly had just gotten into the phone when I talked to her a little while ago. But Maxwell checked in. She's finished interviewing the twelve faculty members with offices in the Plant Sciences building. None of them were on the premises over the weekend. She's got to confirm a few alibis, but she says they all seem reasonable."

"Good. Glad that's taken care of. Next on my interview list is Jennifer Haley. Meanwhile, you can get started on those formal statements — and the fingerprints. Maybe we'll get lucky and find a match for that smudged partial on the suppressor." She pushes her chair back.

Miller laughs. "Don't bet on it." He's reaching for the check that Bob has left under the salsa cup, but Sheila stops him.

"Mine," she says, picking it up and pushing her chair back. "I'll take care of it at the bar."

"If you insist," he says with a shrug.

"I insist." She doesn't want to argue. She is headed for the restroom. She is halfway there when she hears a woman calling to her.

"Chief Dawson! Hang on a moment, Chief. I have a question for you."

It's Jessica, Girl Reporter. Sheila picks up her pace. Jessica will have to wait. She needs to get to the *Heifers*.

Urgently.

CHAPTER NINE

Outside of Mexico, vanilla grows in tropical climates such as Madagascar, Tahiti, Java, and Bali. For vanilla plants to thrive and produce a commercially viable crop, farmers have to invest knowledge and a great deal of skilled labor. But vanilla is especially vulnerable to weather and other conditions that can cause huge price fluctuations and seriously affect farmers' livelihoods. And there is the competition from synthetic vanilla, which is much less costly to produce and is widely substituted for real vanilla in an increasing variety of products.

Countering these forces, Fair Trade is an international program that promotes better working conditions and more bargaining power for farmers. Fair Trade practices enable vanilla farmers to build stronger businesses and form long-term ethical relationships with buyers. Fair

Trade farmers are better able to control their lives and contribute to their communities. While Fair Trade vanilla may cost us a little more, the increase in price is more than made up for by the higher standard of living it provides to those who grow it.

China Bayles
"Vanilla: The Ice Cream Orchid"
Pecan Springs Enterprise

Maggie and her daughter Chelsea live not far from the campus in one of a quartet of almost identical condos at the end of a quiet, wooded cul-de-sac off Lampasas Road. The cool, calm September morning had given way to a hot and windy midday, and the temperature was pushing ninety. We needed rain, but while Houston and Galveston had been soaked by tropical downpours all summer, the Hill Country had to make do with scattered showers. In fact, the summer had been so dry that the weather service had issued another red flag alert, warning that conditions were ripe for wildfires. Urban dwellers don't think about this often enough, but the trees that surround our neighborhoods and blanket our rolling hills are a conflagration just waiting for an igniting spark — a careless smoker, a powerline arc, a bolt of lightning. It wouldn't take much to set things off.

I parked in the driveway and got out, carrying the lunch takeout boxes in a plastic sack. Maggie's condo is attractive but small, nothing like the larger, more comfortable home in which she raised Lyle and Chelsea and which had been swallowed by the divorce. When Maggie moved in, she landscaped it with xeriscape plants from the garden center — yuccas, salvia, lavender, santolina, and a large agave in an attractive pea gravel mulch, along with a graceful desert willow.

And beside the drive was a glorious pride-of-Barbados in full bloom, flaunting its frilly orange-and-yellow blossoms. Every time I see this plant — a traditional abortifacient — I remember something I read years ago, written by Maria Merian, a seventeenth-century botanical illustrator who lived and worked in Barbados: "The Indians, who are not treated well by their Dutch masters, use the seeds of this plant to abort their children, so that their children will not become slaves like they are. They told me this themselves." At the time, of course, an abortion denied valuable human property to the slave's owners, so the plant was a powerful defense of women's bodies and a potent tool of revenge — which meant that its use had to be a carefully guarded secret.

When Maggie answered the door, she was wearing blue scrub bottoms and a loose purple knit top. Her spiky green-tipped hair was standing straight up, as if she had been running her fingers through it. Her eyes were red and puffy, and she was barefoot.

She said, "Thank you for coming, China," and burst into noisy tears. I put down my bag and pulled her into my arms, rubbing her back and making soothing noises.

"It was bad enough to hear that Carl had committed suicide," she sobbed against my shoulder. "But murder is so much worse. I managed not to cry in front of Chief Dawson, but now I can't stop. Who could have done such a terrible thing? And *why*? Carl caused trouble for a lot of people. But he didn't deserve to be shot!"

I wanted to say that nobody, ever, deserved to be shot. But I only murmured, "I know, I know, dear." And rubbed a little harder.

A few minutes later, we were in the kitchen. Housekeeping has never been Maggie's strong suit. Dishes from the night before were stacked in the sink, and the table in front of the large kitchen window still bore the remains of breakfast: bowls of half-finished oatmeal, empty juice glasses, a puddle of spilled milk, a plate of cold toast.

But the fluorescent-lit plant stand beside the table was bright with several pots of blooming orchids, set in a gravel-filled tray. One of the orchids was growing on a sphagnum-covered branch in its own private terrarium, a domed glass container about eighteen inches high, fitted onto a dark plastic base. Inside the terrarium was a small thermometer that registered both the temperature, 74 degrees, and the humidity, 85 percent. I bent over for a closer look at the plants, noticing that the exotic scent of their flowers masked the unmistakable perfume of the kitty box in the corner. The kitty, Maggie said, was with Chelsea, who was having a nap. Hearing that her father had been murdered had thrown her into another tailspin. Lyle had come home from A&M to help Maggie deal with the details. But he had gone out on an errand, so it was just Maggie and me for lunch.

I put the boxes on the kitchen counter, opened the soup containers, and set one of them in the microwave while Maggie piled the breakfast dishes in the sink and cleaned off the table. She had dried her tears, although there was still an occasional hiccup. She brightened when she saw the carrot cake.

"Oh, that's lovely!" she said, trying to

237

sound normal. "I have some vanilla ice cream we can use for topping. You know, since your workshop on vanilla that I came to last year, I always look for ice cream that has real vanilla in it. I try to buy Ben and Jerry's, because they work with Fair Trade vanilla farmers."

I was glad that our segment on Fair Trade vanilla had made an impression, but that wasn't why I had come. I said, "Do you want to talk about your visit with Sheila Dawson this morning?"

Maggie sighed heavily. "Honestly, China, I just couldn't believe what she was telling me — that Carl was murdered, I mean. I kept thinking there had to be some mistake. But the chief obviously knew what she was talking about. And she was *very* professional." She set out a pair of plates, bowls, and glasses on the table. "Even though she is also very pregnant. I have to say that it felt a little weird to be talking to a pregnant cop."

I took the first soup container out of the microwave and put the second in. "Did she have any information about how he died? *New* information, I mean. From the autopsy report, maybe?"

"Well, she said that the stippling — whatever that is — showed that the gun wasn't close to his head." Maggie arranged table-ware and put folded paper towels, in lieu of napkins, beside our plates. "And that his hands were clean, although I don't know what that's supposed to mean, either."

I guessed that Maggie didn't watch *CSI*. "If his hands don't show traces of powder residue, it means that he couldn't have fired the gun. And if there's no stippling on the skin — sometimes called tattooing — the gun was probably more than an arm's length away." I slid the slices of quiche onto our plates and added the salad. "Are you sure you're okay talking about this?"

"More or less." Maggie took a pitcher of iced tea out of the fridge and filled our glasses. "It . . . it doesn't seem real. I mean, it's like we're talking about some dead guy in a movie, not about my husband." She pulled up a chair and sat down. "My ex-husband." There was a moment's silence, and when she spoke, her voice broke. "My kids' father. Somebody I used to love. After all that's happened, it's sometimes hard to remember I loved him. But I did. Once."

"I know," I said quietly. I took the second soup container out of the microwave, filled the second bowl, and put both bowls on the table, along with our quiche and carrot cake, waiting for their topping of vanilla ice cream. I joined her at the table, and we picked up our spoons and began on our soup.

"Did the chief tell you what time he was killed?" I asked.

"Sunday night between eight o'clock and midnight." She looked at me. Her brown eyebrows were a hard, straight line across her forehead. "She wanted to know where *I* was during that time."

"Well, did you tell her?"

"Why wouldn't I?" she countered. "It's no big secret. I was right here in this house, with Chelsea, where I always am at that hour of the night. It's not like I have a glittering social life, you know. I don't go out partying or dancing." She sighed. "I don't even have a boyfriend, damn it."

"Do you and Chelsea sleep in the same bed?" I asked. "In the same room?"

"Of course not." She bent over her soup. "Chelsea's bedroom is downstairs, and mine is up. I'm a pretty light sleeper, but Chelsea sleeps like a stone. With her door closed." A pause, and then a very quiet, "Oh," as she understood the implications of what she had just said. She looked up at me with a twist of her mouth. "Well, there's nothing I can do about that. The chief will either believe me or she won't."

I let the silence lengthen while I began on my quiche, considering how I should ask the question that was bothering me. Finally, I decided that it was better to come straight out with it. "I heard that somebody broke into Dr. Fairlee's greenhouse last week and stole a rare orchid. Did the chief ask you about that, too?"

"You heard about that?" Maggie fiddled with her spoon, not looking up. "Yes, she asked."

No surprise there. "And you told her . . . what?"

She pushed her soup bowl away and reached for her quiche. "What was I *supposed* to tell her?"

"The truth, I hope." I met her eyes, challenging her. "Did you?"

"Of course I did," she snapped. "Why would I steal one of Carl's orchids? Don't I already have enough of the damned things?"

I got up from my chair, took the terrarium from the plant stand, and set it on the table between us. The spindly plant under the glass dome boasted a single, weird-looking bloom. The three pink-striped, claw-tipped sepals were clustered around a wine-purple center that looked remarkably like the face of a devil with two pink eyes and pointed purple ears. It was the plant Beverly Selms had described to me. The demon orchid.

Maggie bit her lip.

Bluntly, I asked, "Is this the orchid you took from your ex-husband's greenhouse?"

No answer.

"Because if it is," I went on, "you have to tell the police. I'm saying this as a friend, Mags, but a lawyer would say the very same thing. If the cops discover that you've stolen the orchid and lied about it, they will assume that you're lying about your alibi for Sunday night." I paused. "Are you?"

She leaned forward, her eyes intent on mine. "No, I'm *not,* China. I was right here with Chelsea, all night. Caitie is the same age — you wouldn't leave her in the house alone at night, and I wouldn't either. And I didn't kill Carl. There were many times when I hated him and wished him dead, but there were still times when I . . . I loved him. And he was my kids' father." Her voice was sharp and fierce. "I didn't kill him! And I don't know who did, damn it! If I knew, I'd tell you. I'd tell the cops. I'd scream it from the rooftops."

I believed her. But I wasn't letting her off the hook. "Did you take the orchid?"

Her eyes went to the plant on the table and her shoulders slumped. "Yes. *Telipogon diabolicus.* I took the damn thing. Chelsea was staying with Carl that night, so I could come and go as I pleased. He never worked in his greenhouse on weekends when he had his daughter with him."

"Did you tell the chief that you took it?"

"No." She let out a long, trembling breath. "What made you think it was me?"

I took a bite of my quiche. "Because you were identified. Somebody saw you in the Plant Sciences building the night the orchid was stolen."

"Somebody saw me?" She dropped her fork with a clatter. "Who?" Her voice quavered and she took a deep breath. "Who says they saw me? Was it the girl?"

"The girl?"

"That sweet young thing Carl has been sleeping with. Jennifer. Dr. Haley's daughter." She sighed. "She thought he was in love with her, but he was only screwing her to piss her father off, and everybody in the department knew it. Everybody except Jennifer."

I didn't want to let on that Jennifer was news to me, so I nodded and kept on eating. Maggie took my nod as encouragement to continue. She had clearly been storing up enough bitterness to fuel a big bonfire, and she was ready to torch it.

"Jennifer wasn't the first one, either, you

know." She drew a ragged breath. "Those field trips to Veracruz to study vanilla?" Her voice hardened. "Wine, some great Mexican food, exotic settings — worked every time. He would pick the one he wanted, seduce her, and when they got back to campus, he and the girl would hook up for a month or two. After that, he was on to somebody new. *That* was the man I was married to, China. I should have divorced him a decade ago."

"Yikes," I muttered. I finished my quiche and pushed the plate away. "All that was going on when I went on that field trip to Veracruz? I didn't have a clue."

"That's because you went for the *vanilla,*" Maggie said in a meaningful tone. "You weren't interested in sleeping with the professor."

"True," I agreed uncomfortably. "Definitely true." Still, why hadn't I noticed? I'm usually a pretty observant person. But perhaps none of the women interested him. Or maybe he was watching his step because he knew I was a friend of Maggie's, or because of the accident that had killed Shelley Harmon and drawn so much negative attention to his field trips.

Maggie frowned. "We've gotten off the subject. Was it Jennifer Haley who saw me in the building the night the orchid was

244

stolen? She hangs out there a lot. And how in the world did *you* find out about it? Do the police know?"

"Yes, the police know," I said. I wasn't going to tell her that Logan Gardner had told Dan Selms and that Selms had told the cops — that would just produce another harsh outburst. "I can't tell you who saw you, Maggie. The bottom line is that you were seen, and the chief knows it. If she decides that there's a connection between the theft and the murder, she will get a warrant to search your house and your greenhouses for the orchid."

I touched the demon orchid's bloom. "For *this* orchid. You need to come clean with them before that happens."

She narrowed her eyes. "Come clean?"

"Yes. If you cooperate with the police and tell them what you did and why, they may be less likely to attempt to connect the theft and the murder." I paused. "Maybe it'll help if you tell *me* why you took it." That's a tactic her lawyer would use, if she had one. If she could put it into words now, she would find it easier to tell the police later.

"It's . . . complicated." She looked down at her hands.

"I'm sure." I prompted her. "You prob-

245

ably had several reasons, some better than others."

She touched the orchid. "I know it sounds petty, but I took the *Telipogon* because I knew it mattered to Carl. Somebody gave it to him, and he was thrilled with it. I wanted to hurt him. To get even for taking my *Dendrobium*. For forcing the sale of the house. For being such a creepy *jerk* about those students. For everything."

"That's not petty," I said.

She paused, took a breath, and came up with more. "I also took it to remind him that if I wanted to, I could get him into a helluva lot of trouble with CITES." She narrowed her eyes and her voice was hard. "And remind both of us that I wasn't on the short end of the stick *all* the time."

I was surprised. "Sounds like you wanted him to know you took it."

"Of course I wanted him to know." Her eyes flickered defiantly. "I told him, didn't I?"

"You *told* him?" That was news. "Did he try to get it back? Did he threaten to have you arrested?"

Her lips curved upward in a small smile, and she shook her head.

"Why not?"

"Because I told him that if he did, I would

turn him in to the CITES police. They might give me a hard time, but they would go after him. He's the one who arranged for that plant to be smuggled into the country — and not just that one, either. If they raided his greenhouse, they would find other illegal orchids, some that he and Dan brought back years ago, others that he'd gotten lately."

"You *told* him this?"

"I texted him." Her voice was edged with an ironic humor. "I reminded him that if he got into trouble with CITES, he would lose his job. On top of that greenhouse debacle and the dead girl in Mexico, that would give the university everything they needed to revoke his tenure."

I didn't get past her first sentence. She had *texted* him? I leaned forward and met her eyes. In my sternest lawyerly voice, I said, "Maggie, your ex-husband was murdered. It is routine for the cops to take the victim's phone. Depending on its security, it may take them a little while to unlock it. But they will. And when Chief Dawson reads your text, she will have evidence that you lied to her about the theft. Since you lied about that, she will conclude that you lied about not leaving the house on Sunday night. As Carl's ex-wife, you may already be a person of interest in their investigation. But if you're not now, you damned sure *will* be when they see that text."

For a long moment, Maggie stared at me. "So that's why they want my fingerprints. I'm a person of interest."

"At least. When they see that text, they'll probably upgrade you to suspect." I kept my eyes on hers. "It depends on what else they've got."

Her face crumpled. "Suspect!" she wailed. "What . . . what can I do, China? If the police think I've had anything to do with Carl's death — anything at *all* — the kids will be devastated." She buried her face in her hands. "Lyle is trying to be brave, but Chelsea is already overwhelmed." She gave a muffled sob. "I don't know what to do. Please. Please *help* me!"

Help her? A huge part of me — my usually reliable common sense, my resolution to stay out of police investigations, my longtime and much-repeated reluctance to use my legal experience — said no. *Nope, nada, negative.*

But even a friggin' idiot could see that Maggie needed help.

Help from a lawyer. A good lawyer. Well, maybe not necessarily a good lawyer. Even a half-bad lawyer could probably get her out of this mess.

Assuming, that is, that she hadn't killed him. Although to tell the truth, now that I thought about it, I wasn't so sure. As I've said, in her worst moments, Maggie can be a puffer fish, highly toxic to anybody who doesn't handle her carefully. I have seen her lose her temper and fling a pot or tear into Ruben and her other employees for not doing their jobs. Was it possible that she had gone to see Carl at his greenhouse, that they'd quarreled, and that a gun had gone off — accidentally, or even on purpose?

Yes, that was possible — not likely, I thought, or even probable. But *possible.*

On the other hand, I have always agreed with something I heard in a law school lecture: "One person on your side, no matter what you've done. That's what makes the justice system work. That's what keeps us a free people, under the law."

One person on your side, no matter what you've done. I could be on Maggie's side for one afternoon, couldn't I? It is true that I left the practice of law some years ago, but I've kept up my bar membership. And this should be a fairly simple matter, standard defense attorney strategy. Maggie cooperates with the cops by surrendering the orchid and explaining why and when she took it. If the situation morphed into something else, or if it looked like she might actually be charged with a crime, I could step aside and hand the case over to Charlie Lipman. He had represented Maggie during the divorce. I knew he'd be glad to represent her in this, if it went further.

I took a deep breath, opened my mouth, and heard myself say, "I suppose I could call Chief Dawson and arrange for you to talk with her this afternoon. All you have to do is —"

"If I go," Maggie broke in, "will you go with me?"

I looked at her. "Have you told me *all* the truth? You're not hiding anything that might raise its ugly head and bite you?"

"Yes. All of it. There's nothing else to tell." She dropped her eyes. "Except that I — but that doesn't have anything to do with Carl's death. I only —"

"Whoa." I frowned. "*What* doesn't have anything to do with Carl's death?"

"I . . . Are you sure you need to know this?"

I folded my arms. "If I go with you — you got that? *If?* — I need to know everything. Everything. Understand, Maggie? Do not leave anything out."

She gave me a long look. "Well, if you

must," she said at last, heaving a melodramatic sigh. "I went to see Jennifer."

Jennifer Haley. The other woman. The *young* other woman. "When?"

"A couple of weeks ago." Maggie pulled her brows together, reflecting. "No, it was last week." She thought a minute. "Last Wednesday. Or Thursday."

"Why?"

"I wanted to . . . well, I thought she ought to know that there had been others. That she wasn't the first, by a long shot. That she probably wouldn't be the last and —" An uncomfortable shift in her chair. "Of course, she wasn't happy with what I told her. In fact, she seemed a little —" A vague gesture of the hand. "A little angry, I guess you'd say. I was sort of surprised. I thought she might be hurt. I didn't think she'd be *angry.*"

"Angry. Angry at you?"

"No, not at *me,* silly. Why would she be angry at me?" A little eye-rolling here. "I was telling her something she probably already knew, deep down. She just didn't want to admit it because then she would have to acknowledge that her parents were right. She was angry at Carl, for being such a jerk. And also at herself, for believing him. And for hurting Logan."

251

My eyebrows went up. "Logan Gardner? You're talking about Carl's research assistant?"

Logan and I had become friends on the Veracruz trip, and we had made it a point to connect several times afterward. I had even invited him to speak at one of my vanilla workshops. But while he was good to look at and he certainly knew a lot about vanilla, his talk was a little dry and academic for my workshoppers. He mostly spoke about the disease- and drought-resistant hybrid he'd been working on with Carl Fairlee. The two of them were planning to patent it together, but since Logan had done the break-through hybridizing, they had agreed that the new hybrid would be named for him: *Vanilla planifolia gardneri.* He was proud of that, especially because they expected to license it to vanilla farmers through the Fair Trade program. It sounded like it might even be a lucrative idea, if they could make the business end of it work.

But what would happen to that jointly owned patent now that Carl Fairlee was dead? Would the survivor — Logan — earn *all* of the money, or would some of it — half of it — go to Fairlee's estate? To Maggie and/or her children?

The thought that Maggie might profit

from her ex-husband's murder made my lawyerly self rather uneasy, although the rest of me did not for a minute believe that Maggie would kill him in order to inherit his half of a vanilla patent — or even his half of their joint orchid collection.

What the police might choose to believe, however, was an entirely different matter. I've seen them chase after some wild and woolly theoretical motives. Killing for a patent? It was something they would probably consider.

"Yes, Logan Gardner," Maggie said, answering my question. "Jennifer was his longtime girlfriend, you see. They had been together since their undergraduate days and were planning to get married when Logan finished his PhD and got a job that paid enough to live on."

I frowned. This was complicated. "When you went to see her, you didn't threaten her? Or try to intimidate her, or —"

"No!" Maggie exclaimed, offended. "Of course I didn't *threaten* her! What kind of a person do you think I am? I felt sorry for her. I wanted her to have a realistic view of things, that's all."

I wasn't convinced. But I returned to the more pressing subject. "Are you willing to give Carl's orchid to the police this afternoon?"

"But the cops won't know how to take care of it!" she exclaimed. "They'll *kill* it, China! And it's very, very special. The researchers who found this species said that there were only about thirty in a small patch of jungle in southern Colombia — a patch that has already been wiped out by road construction. I can't just —"

"The correct answer," I said emphatically, "is yes. I'll suggest that the cops return the orchid to the greenhouse immediately. Somebody — probably Logan — will be taking care of Carl's plants."

There was a long silence, and then, at last, a sigh.

"Yes," Maggie said, her eyes still on the orchid. "If you think giving them the orchid will keep me out of trouble with the police, I'll do it. I'll do *anything* to keep Chelsea from being hurt any worse than she is already. And Lyle, too. Both of them."

"Then I'll call the chief and arrange a meeting for this afternoon. But before I do that, there's one more thing. You may be asked if you have any idea who might have killed Carl. In my experience, if you can offer the detectives a legitimate lead to follow, they are likely to be more . . . accommodating. And a lead can direct their attention from you to somebody else. I don't want you to volunteer any information — that will look like you're too eager. But if they ask, what can you tell them? Who might have had a reason to want your ex-husband dead?"

"I don't know." She took a deep breath. "And anyway, I hate to accuse —"

"You're not accusing anybody, Maggie. You were married to the victim. You knew him better than anybody else. Based on that experience, you're suggesting possibilities. That's all. Possibilities."

With luck, of course, one of those possibilities might turn out to be the real deal and not a red herring. But that wasn't my business right now. My business was to get Maggie off the hook. And keep her off.

"Well," she said slowly, "there's Dr. Haley. Matthew Haley. He tried to get Carl fired after that stupid business with the greenhouse. And he was angry — really angry, I mean — that Carl was sleeping with his daughter. He and his wife tried everything they could to put a stop to that."

"Okay, Haley. Who else?"

She frowned. "Dan Selms, I guess. They were very good friends once, but Dan has been mad at Carl ever since he built the

255

greenhouse. It made Dan look . . . well, sort of dumb. Like he didn't know what was going on in his own department."

"That was a while ago, though, wasn't it? Isn't that bad feeling water under the bridge by now?"

"Yes, but there have been other things, too, some of them recent. Dan claimed that Carl stole some research from him and published it under his name. I know they had heated words over that not very long ago." She pursed her lips. "And of course, there's Logan."

"Ah," I said. "Because Carl stole his girl-friend."

"But there's more to it than that. Carl and Logan were developing a new hybrid vanilla plant. It's supposed to produce more pods and be resistant to *Fusarium oxysporum* — *Fusarium* wilt. If it is, it could be worth a lot of money."

"Oh, right," I said. "Logan spoke about his plant at one of my workshops. He was proud of the research that went into hybrid-izing it. He and Carl were applying for a jointly owned patent. And the plant would be named for him."

She shook her head. "That was what they planned, but that isn't what happened. Carl applied for the patent in his name only.

Plus, he named the plant for himself. *Vanilla planifolia fairleei.*"

"In his name only?" I was startled. "But Logan was expecting that the orchid would be named after *him.*"

"Yes. What's more, Carl didn't even bother to tell Logan what he was doing. Jennifer said that Logan was furious when he found out. You can't blame him for feeling cheated. It must have been a huge disappointment."

I stared at her. Had Maggie just put her finger on the motive for Carl Fairlee's murder? Well, whether she had or not, it was certainly something the police would want to hear. It was time to call Sheila and set up an interview appointment.

I was reaching for my cell phone when I heard a small voice.

"Mom?"

A girl about Caitie's age was standing in the kitchen doorway. It was Chelsea. She was wearing a pink shirt, pink shorts, and pink flip-flops and hugging a worn teddy bear close to her. Her brown hair was tousled, her eyes and nose red from weeping. She was thirteen, but she looked like a vulnerable nine or ten.

"Hi, baby," Maggie said with a quick smile. "Are you feeling better? Ms. Bayles has brought you some lunch. Tomato soup and really yummy quiche. Want some?"

"I guess so." Chelsea took the vacant chair as her mother got up to get her lunch.

"Hi, Chelsea," I said with a smile.

"Hi." Chelsea rested her chin on her teddy bear's head. "Thank you for bringing some lunch," she said, minding her manners. "And please tell Caitie I'm sorry I couldn't talk when she called last night. I . . . I wasn't feeling too good."

"I'll tell her," I said. "She was worried about you. She'll be glad to know you're okay."

"I'm not okay," Chelsea said, hugging her bear. "Not really. My dad's dead." Her brown eyes filled with tears. "Somebody *killed* him."

"I understand," I said. "And Caitie does, too." Both Caitie and I lost our fathers to violence, and neither of us has really gotten over it.

"But you *will* be okay," her mother said with a forced cheeriness. "We'll get through this, all of us together, won't we?"

There was a silence. Finally, Chelsea said, in a choked voice, "Excuse me. I have to go to the bathroom." Still carrying her bear, she left the room.

"Chelsea is a daddy's girl," Maggie said with a half-irritated sigh. "She blames me for the divorce. It's been pretty hard these last couple of years. And now *this*."

I nodded. "I was about to contact Chief Dawson and make an appointment for you to talk to her this afternoon. But what about Chelsea? Are you okay with leaving her by herself?"

"She won't be by herself." Maggie glanced up at the clock. "Lyle just had a few errands. He'll be home in less than an hour."

"Thanks," I said, and sent a quick text to Sheila's private cell number:

MS. WALKER WOULD LIKE TO COME TO THE STATION AND MAKE A STATEMENT THIS AFTERNOON. I WILL BE WITH HER. WHAT TIME IS GOOD FOR YOU?

The reply came almost immediately.

CAN U HAVE HER IN MY OFFICE @ 3:30, COUNSELOR?

I reported Sheila's text to Maggie — all but that last word. The chief and I have been friends for a long time, and she knows I've resisted a great many efforts to push me back into lawyer mode. She had to be wondering what had prompted my change of heart.

"I guess there's no point in putting it off." Maggie put Chelsea's plate on the table, along with a glass of milk. "Might as well get it over with early this afternoon."

I replied to Sheila:

THANK YOU, CHIEF.

I looked at the clock. It was nearly one. "Chief Dawson wants to see us at three-thirty. That'll give me time to catch up on a couple of things at the shop and go home and change. How about if I pick you up at three-twenty? It's only a ten-minute drive to the station."

"I guess," Maggie said, without enthusiasm. "See you then."

CHAPTER TEN

Sheila's encounter with reporter Jessica Nelson is more productive than either of them might have expected. Jessica doesn't want to ask just one question. She has several in mind, and she has followed Sheila into the Heifers', which is empty except for the two of them.

"What's this I'm hearing about orchid smuggling?" Jessica asks through the door that Sheila bolted behind her when she retreated into the toilet stall.

Sheila lobs the question back to her. "What *are* you hearing about orchid smuggling, Jessica?" Under the stall door, she can see that Jessica is wearing to-die-for red spike heels.

"That Dr. Fairlee was into it big time," Jessica says. "Quite a few of the orchids in his greenhouse come from the black market. Some are from Thailand and Java, others from Guatemala and Colombia. He sold them at orchid shows for a very tidy markup."

Surprised, Sheila blurts, "Where did you hear all this?" She gives the red heels one last covetous glance and flushes. She loves heels. But with all the weight she is carrying out front, they're out of the question. She would end up flat on her face. "Who told you?"

"You know I don't rat out my sources," Jessica reminds her in a slightly aggrieved tone.

"Huh." Sheila pushes the door open and the reporter steps back. A lively young woman with boy-cut blond hair and a sprinkle of freckles across her nose, she is wearing a red blazer over a black V-neck top, white pants, and those luscious red heels. But behind that girl-next-door face, easy smile, and bouncy walk is a savvy reporter with a quick brain and plenty of street smarts.

Sheila goes to the lavatory and turns on the water. "This is a murder investigation, Jess. You don't want to obstruct justice, do you?" Looking into the mirror, she meets Jessica's eyes. Her voice is mild but firm when she says, "Seriously. Where are you getting this information?"

"From an anonymous informant." Jessica

262

folds her arms. "Actually, I got the tip on this part of the story — the black market in orchids — *before* Fairlee was shot. I was already researching it when I learned that the guy was dead. Which adds a twist to my story, of course."

So that was why Jessica had pounced so quickly on the news of Fairlee's death. Deliberately, Sheila squirts soap on her hands, rinses them, and shuts off the water. "Your tipster. Somebody here in Springs?"

Most likely, Sheila thinks. Somebody local, who follows Jessica's work in the *Enterprise*. She remembers Jess' reference to Fairlee's "girlfriend" in their earlier telephone conversation. Could Jennifer Haley be her anonymous tipster? But Jessica is an enthusiastically creative reporter who knows how to use a search engine and is constantly talking and texting on her cell phone. Her information could be coming from just about anywhere.

Jessica doesn't answer the question. Instead, she says, "I would like to include a couple of paragraphs about this angle in my story on the murder — in the online version that goes on the paper's website this afternoon. Would I be too far off the mark if I say that the cops are exploring a possible connection to orchid smuggling?"

Sheila yanks a paper towel out of the dispenser and dries her hands. "If you wrote that, you would be right. You would also be right if you said that the police would like to talk to anyone who has purchased an orchid from Dr. Fairlee in the last couple of years. People can call the department's information number and ask for Dylan Miller. We would also like to hear from anybody who *sold* plants to Dr. Fairlee." There. That could bring in a key witness or two, if they were lucky.

"Hot damn." With a wide smile, Jessica jerks a thumbs-up. "Thanks, Chief. I'll get that out there as quick as I can. And I'll be digging some more."

"Terrific." Sheila wads up the towel and throws it in the trash bin. "And when you're ready to give me your tipster's name, I'll be all ears."

But Sheila doesn't have to wait for a clue. As she and Miller are leaving the restaurant, she sees Jessica at a table for two in a distant corner. She is bending over to say something private to a good-looking man with sun-bleached blond hair and a dark summer tan. Fairlee's research assistant, Logan Gardner — undoubtedly her source.

In the parking lot with Miller, Sheila reports her conversation with Jessica. "We definitely want to find out what Gardner knows about orchid smuggling," she says. "I'm on my way to talk to Jennifer Haley right now. Let's get Gardner in for an interview this afternoon — with both of us. We need to lean on him for names."

Miller nods. "What time?"

Sheila frowns. Connie has texted to tell her that she has an afternoon appointment with a woman named Fernandez, another possible replacement. "An hour? Hour and a half?"

"Works for me," he says, and takes out his cell phone. "I'll set it up right now."

Sheila puts a hand on his arm. "Don't call him while he's with Jessica Nelson, Dylan. Hold off until they're finished with their lunch and are going their separate ways. Shouldn't be long now."

With a nod, he pockets his phone. "See you later, Chief." He grins. "Feels like we might actually be getting somewhere, huh?"

"Depends on your definition of 'somewhere,' " Sheila says with a chuckle, and he laughs.

As Sheila gets into the squad car, she thinks that whatever happens with the case, at least it has had the effect of warming her relations with Dylan Miller.

■ ■ ■ ■

China Bayles' text appears on Sheila's phone as she is getting out of her car in the parking lot at Jennifer Haley's apartment.

MS. WALKER WOULD LIKE TO COME TO THE STATION AND MAKE A STATEMENT THIS AFTER- NOON. I WILL BE WITH HER. WHAT TIME IS GOOD FOR YOU?

Sheila is surprised. China had a successful decade-long career as a criminal defense at- torney in Houston. But she left it behind when she moved to Pecan Springs and she's resisted several invitations to step back into the legal game. So why has she agreed to bring Walker to the station? And why does Walker want to make a statement? Sheila's skin prickles. Is there a confession coming? But she doesn't hesitate. She texts:

CAN U HAVE HER IN MY OFFICE @ 3:30, COUNSELOR?

That should give her time to talk to both Haley and Gardner. She smiles to herself, knowing that China will understand the wry question behind "Counselor."

China replies:

THANK YOU, CHIEF.

Sheila nods, satisfied.

According to the secretary in the Linguistics office, Jennifer Haley has no classes on Tuesdays, and Sheila hopes to catch her at home. The young woman lives in a typical student apartment building, an older two-story complex on Brazos Street, within walking distance of the campus. The building is flamingo-pink stucco with a tile roof and pseudo-Spanish wrought iron gates, flanked by spiky yuccas. As Sheila takes the stairs to the second floor, she notices that the air is rich with a blend of Mexican and Asian cuisines, spiced with the fugitive scent of marijuana.

When Jennifer answers the door, she is clearly startled at the sight of a pregnant police chief holding up her badge wallet. "I'd like a few minutes of your time, Jennifer," Sheila says.

The girl is in her mid-twenties but looks like a teenager. She has straight brown hair, a freckled, plain-featured face, and doe-like brown eyes behind dark plastic-rimmed glasses. She's wearing green pedal pushers and a yellow sleeveless top that makes her olive skin look sallow. The living room behind her is furnished with a dark purple sofa and chair, a battered coffee table, a television, a brick-and-board bookcase double-stacked with textbooks, and a desk and chair. On the desk is a laptop computer surrounded by stacks of books, some of them open.

Watching Jennifer closely, Sheila adds, "I need to talk with you about the murder of Carl Fairlee."

The girl turns pale. "Mu-murder?" she stammers. "Murder?" Her voice rises. "My father told me last night that Carl was dead. But he said that he'd . . . he'd killed himself. He —"

She breaks off. Her hand goes to her mouth. Her face is so white that every freckle stands out and she sways.

"Sit down," Sheila commands, taking her arm and pushing her to the sofa. She goes into the tiny but tidy kitchen, finds a glass in a cupboard, fills it with water, and makes Jennifer drink. After a moment the girl is able to talk.

"Murdered," she whispers. Her eyes are shut. "Are you sure?"

"Yes," Sheila says. "The killer wanted us to think it was suicide, but there's no doubt. Someone shot him."

"I can't believe it! Who would —" Shaking her head, she opens her eyes. "But maybe you already know. Have you caught him — or her?" She bites her lip. "Whoever did it, I mean."

"Not yet," Sheila says, noting the correction. "But we will. I'm hoping you can help." She takes out her notebook and sits down on the sofa. "What can you tell me about your relationship with Dr. Fairlee, Jennifer? Obviously, the more we know, the better."

After a hesitant start, the words spill out, as if the young woman is relieved to talk. Most of what Jennifer tells her, Sheila already knows, at least in outline. She and Fairlee had been a couple for several months and had been talking vaguely about getting married. No, they hadn't set a date. No, they weren't even engaged. Carl insisted they wait until her parents came around to the idea, but it had been slow going. And then there were the second thoughts.

"It got so unpleasant at home that I finally decided to move out and get my own place," she says, with a vague gesture around the room. "Carl and Dad just couldn't get along. Dad doesn't . . . didn't trust him, I guess is the best way to put it. And Carl has never cared about whether people like him."

"Didn't trust him?" Sheila asks. "Why not?"

Jennifer speaks reluctantly. "Well, there was that trouble about the greenhouse, of course. And the accident that happened on that field trip in Veracruz — which wasn't Carl's fault at *all*. I mean, how could anybody hold him responsible for a girl getting shot?"

A girl getting shot? When? Where? This is something Sheila hasn't heard about. She wants to ask, but she doesn't want to interrupt the flow of Jennifer's story. She makes a quick note in her notebook.

Jennifer takes off her glasses and wipes her eyes with the back of her hand. "But Dad says that Carl doesn't . . . didn't play fair, that he used people. That he took advantage."

"Took advantage? Of whom, specifically?"

"Of friends. Of guys on the faculty." She puts her glasses back on, speaking reluctantly. "Of students. Girls."

"Girls?"

"I didn't pay much attention," Jennifer says hastily. "I thought Dad was just being . . . Dad. He's always controlled my mother and he likes to think that he can control me. But then —" She stops.

"But then *what,* Jennifer?" Sheila asks

gently. "Come on. I need to know. It could be important."

Jennifer's voice is subdued. "Well, Carl's ex-wife came to see me a few days ago. It was sort of a last straw, actually. I don't think I was very polite. But on top of what I already knew . . . well, she gave me a lot more things to think about. Where Carl was concerned, I mean. I could see that I might have been . . ." She shifts uncomfortably. "A little naïve."

"What did Ms. Walker say that made you think that?"

Jennifer studies her laced fingers. "That while she and Carl were married, he'd had several affairs with students. That I wasn't the first and I wouldn't be the last." She takes a breath. "That I made a terrible mistake when I . . ." She drags the back of her hand across her mouth.

"When you broke up with Logan Gardner?"

Jennifer's eyes are big behind her glasses. "You know about that?"

"Yes, we know," Sheila says compassionately. She's made mistakes like that herself, several of them. Every day, she counts herself lucky that she and Blackie are together. If they hadn't been patient with one another, hadn't reached for each other in the dark places, it could easily have gone a different way. "I understand that you and Logan were pretty serious."

Jennifer nods slowly, unhappily. "We were talking about getting married when he finished his research. We'd even planned how many kids we were going to have. But that had to wait until he finished his dissertation and the plant patent came through. He and Carl were working on this vanilla orchid that they were going to patent together, which is kind of a big deal. Commercially, I mean. But then Carl, he —" She turns her hands over helplessly. "Carl started hitting on me, and I just . . . I guess I was blown away. I had stars in my eyes or something. I didn't . . . I couldn't say no." She slides a glance at Sheila. "Logan tried to tell me that I was making a mistake, but I didn't listen. After a while, he got disgusted and went away. I couldn't blame him."

"When did this happen?" Sheila asks, wondering whether Jennifer understands that she is giving Gardner a motive for murder — yet another motive, added to that patent business.

"Last spring." Tears flood her eyes. "I know I hurt Logan — *a lot.* And then, after I found out about Carl and the other woman, I . . . I told him I was sorry." Her voice drops. "I know it sounds like a cliché. But it's too late. The harm has been done."

Sheila is writing in her notebook. "Carl and the other woman?" she prompts, keeping her voice level, not looking up. "What woman?"

Jennifer takes a breath, lets it out. "The one he was . . . seeing."

Pretending detachment, Sheila continues to scribble. "This is a fairly recent development, I take it."

"The last two weeks. When Carl's ex-wife came to tell me all that stuff about his extracurricular love life, I'm sure she thought she was telling me something I didn't know." Jennifer's mouth is tight. "But she wasn't. By that time, I'd already found out that he was interested in somebody else."

"And who would that be?" Sheila tries to keep the interest out of her voice.

"I don't know." Jennifer pushes her glasses up on her nose. "That is, I don't know her name. I don't think she's from the university, and she's older." A wan smile. "Older than me, I mean. And not a student."

"So you've seen her, then. What does she look like? How old?"

"Well, she's sort of ordinary, I'd say.

Brown hair, short. No makeup. About as tall as me. I don't know how old — maybe mid-forties? Attractive, I guess, in a mature kind of way." The word *mature* is said with the unconscious disdain of the young. "The day she came to the greenhouse, she was wearing jeans and a blue Adams County Hospital T-shirt. You know, one of those shirts they give away at the half-marathon fund-raiser."

Sheila is making quick notes. "And when did you see her?"

"Twice. Once in Carl's greenhouse, in the morning. Another time in the afternoon in the parking lot, in her car." Jennifer shifts uncomfortably, remembering that she has neglected her hospitality responsibilities. "Maybe you'd like something to drink? I could get you some iced tea."

"I'm fine, thank you," Sheila says. "In the greenhouse, in the morning — what was she doing there? Did you get her name?"

"Her name? No." Jennifer smiles slightly. "I was watering the plants when she came in — that's what Carl always liked me to do, if I was around in the morning. He didn't bother to introduce us. She had brought him a plant, some sort of rare orchid he was interested in."

"A rare orchid?" Now we're getting somewhere, Sheila thinks. Maybe.

"A demon orchid, he called it. I looked at it later, and I could see how it got its name. It was in bloom, and the blossom looked sort of like the face of a devil." Jennifer pauses. "He collected weird orchids, you know. He was into cloning and hybridizing — he loved coming up with new plants. He'd load up his van with the best ones and take them to orchid shows and meetings and stuff. That's where he sold them. I went with him a lot of times."

Ah, Sheila thinks, remembering the plant tags and traces of soil she and Miller had found in Fairlee's vehicle. And remembering what Maggie Walker had said about smuggled plants being laundered through orchid shows or crooked nurseries. "Maybe you remember the names and locations of two or three of the shows?" she prompts.

"Oh, sure," Jennifer says easily. "We went to the Heart of Texas Orchid Society in Austin, the North Texas show, up in Richardson, and the Oklahoma show, in Oklahoma City." Her face clouds. "It was a lot of work, getting everything ready. Logan had to help, too, so that was awkward. But the shows were fun, and I learned a lot about the orchid business."

"I understand that there's a big demand

for rare orchids," Sheila says. Offhandedly, she adds, "So much so that plants are sometimes smuggled into the country. Do you know anything about that?"

"A little, maybe," Jennifer says. "Logan wrote a paper once about orchid smuggling, and I typed it for him. I was surprised, actually. I mean, everybody knows that drugs are smuggled into the country. But *plants*? That seems really weird." She became more animated. "Logan found one case where a guy smuggled over thirteen hundred lady's slipper orchids into California — they're supposed to be medicinal, he says. Like a sedative, or something? Anyway, the orchid cops set up a sting, and the smuggler sold them thirteen thousand dollars' worth of plants. They arrested him and he got a fine and a year in jail." She pauses. "Is that what you're talking about?"

"Something like that," Sheila says. "The orchid that the woman gave to Dr. Fairlee. Was that a plant that might have been smuggled into this country?"

"I don't think so." Jennifer frowns. "I mean, I didn't think about that at the time, but I suppose it was possible. All I know for sure is that Carl was super pleased with it — at least for a while." With a note of irony in her voice, she adds, "It's the one that was stolen, you know. When that happened, it made him really mad."

"Did he tell you who he thought stole it?"

"No." Jennifer shakes her head. "But Logan did," she adds unexpectedly. "He told me it was Carl's ex-wife. He saw her in the building the night the orchid disappeared." She hesitates. "I don't think he told Carl, though. Logan was pretty mad at Carl by that time. He figured that if she wanted the plant bad enough to steal it, she should have it."

Mad at Carl. Sheila makes a note, then goes back to the subject. "The woman who gave Dr. Fairlee the orchid. You said you saw her twice. When was the other time?"

"With Carl." Jennifer looks back down at her hands. "She picked him up in the parking lot behind the Plant Sciences building. He got in her car and . . . and kissed her."

"Kissed her how? Quick and friendly, like a peck on the cheek? Passionately?"

"It definitely wasn't a peck on the cheek." Jennifer's voice is so low that Sheila has to strain to hear. "Then they drove off together."

"When was that? Do you remember what kind of car she was driving?"

"One afternoon last week. Tuesday, I guess. Or maybe Wednesday." Jennifer makes a little face. "I'm not very good when it comes to cars, but I recognized that one. It was one of those funny-looking Beetles."

"A Volkswagen? What color was it? What year?"

"Yes, a VW. It was green. Dark green, maybe sort of metallic. I don't know what year it was. Not exactly new, but not one of the old ones."

"Did you notice the license plates? Texas? Out of state?"

"Sorry, no."

"Did you ask Dr. Fairlee about her?"

"Are you kidding?" Jennifer says incredulously "I couldn't do *that.*" She pulls her brows together. "This woman . . . Do you think *she* might have killed Carl?"

"We'll certainly look into it," Sheila says, making a note to check with security about that camera in the parking lot. She looks down at what she has written. "A moment ago, you said that Logan was mad at Carl. How do you know? Did he tell you?"

"Yes. We're not together — as a couple, I mean. But we still talk." She bit her lip. "I guess I maybe still sorta care about him."

Sheila nods sympathetically. Jennifer doesn't seem to have a great deal of insight into herself or understand why she made the choices she'd made or how they might

278

shape her future. But she is still very young. Knowing yourself comes with maturity — and sometimes not even then. She asks, "Was Logan angry with Dr. Fairlee about your relationship with him, or was it something else?"

"Well, he definitely wasn't happy about Carl and me," Jennifer says slowly. "He thought I was making a mistake, and he doesn't mind telling me so, whenever he feels like it." She pauses, reflecting. "But there *was* something else, recently. The patent I mentioned? Carl and Logan had been working on a hybrid vanilla plant for several years. The idea was that they were going to patent it in both their names and license it, together. Logan had collected and cloned several plants when he was an undergraduate, and Carl had contributed some of the ideas and of course the lab space. But Logan had done most of the work and was writing his dissertation on it." She frowns. "Anyway, Carl went ahead and filed for the patent — in his name only. Logan just found out a few days ago."

"And he was angry?"

"Wouldn't you be?" Jennifer counters. "I told Carl it was a terrible thing to do, but he laughed at me."

"Which made you feel . . . how?"

Her voice becomes thin and she looks away. "I was angry, too. At Carl. For treating Logan like . . . like he didn't matter."

How angry? Sheila wonders, although she doesn't think this young woman is capable of pointing a gun at someone and pulling the trigger — and lying about it later. "Wimpy," Maggie Walker had called her, and that's probably right. Still . . .

"Dr. Fairlee was killed on Sunday night," she says, "sometime between eight and midnight. Where were you at that time?"

"Me?" Jennifer is startled. "I was with a girlfriend here in the apartment complex. We had an exam in Psycholinguistics on Monday morning. We studied together."

"All evening?"

"From maybe seven until twelve-thirty or so," Jennifer said. "I don't mean we studied all that time. Actually, we drank a bottle of wine and we watched a TV show — *Poldark,* on PBS." She smiles dreamily. "Aidan Turner is *so* hot."

"Your friend's name, please? Her phone number?"

Jennifer gives her friend's information and watches uneasily as Sheila writes it down. "That's when Carl was . . . was killed?" she asks timidly. "I'm not a suspect, am I?"

"That's when he was killed, yes. And no,

you're not a suspect, at this time." Sheila closes her notebook. "But we may want to talk to you again. And we would like your fingerprints, for purposes of exclusion. Can you come down to the station later this afternoon?"

"Yes, I guess so," Jennifer says. She gives Sheila an apprehensive glance. "What I said about Logan being mad at Carl — I hope it doesn't get him in trouble. Logan's a good person. I know he wouldn't harm anyone."

"We're only interested in the facts," Sheila says in a reassuring tone — the usual evasive cop speak. But it seems to satisfy Jennifer, who nods and looks relieved.

Sheila's phone dings and she glances at the new text: Connie, letting her know that Fernandez, one of the job applicants, has arrived and is waiting. She texts quickly:

ON MY WAY.

But she has been wanting to go to the bathroom for the last fifteen minutes, and she doesn't think she can put it off until she gets back to the station.

She clears her throat. "I wonder — would you mind if I used your restroom?"

"It's not very neat," Jennifer says. "But sure. Whatever. Down that hall, first door

281

on the right."

It isn't neat. There are wet towels in the bathtub, panties and a bra on the floor, and makeup scattered over the counter. But Sheila pays no attention, does what she has to do (with great relief), and thanks Jennifer, who gives her belly a curious look and asks the inevitable question.

"Early November," Sheila replies. Noah does a quick backflip and she puts her hand on him. "Six more weeks." Only six weeks? It feels like an eternity.

Jennifer is wistful, "You are so lucky. A career and kids, too. If I hadn't —"

With a sigh, she breaks off. But Sheila knows what she is thinking.

Back at the station, Sheila goes to her office, sits down behind her desk, and glances at the clock. She's late, so she has only fifteen minutes to spend with Lucia Fernandez before Logan Gardner is supposed to show up. She'd better get started.

The woman on the other side of the desk is in her early thirties, a dark-haired Latina with flashing eyes and a determined chin. She is dressed in a businesslike red-blouse-navy-skirt combination and is wearing low heels.

"Ms. Page has already discussed the position with you?" Sheila asks. "It's a temporary situation. Could be weeks or a few months. Maybe even a little longer." She wishes she could pull out the lower drawer and hike her feet up on it, or at least kick her shoes off. But she doesn't think that would be a good idea. Wouldn't look professional.

"We talked about the job, yes, ma'am," Lucia Fernandez says. She is perched warily on the edge of her chair. "It sounds really interesting, and I'm honored that Ms. Page thought of me for the position. But I've decided it's not right for me. I'm sorry," she adds. She bites her lip. "I mean, I'm *really* sorry."

Sheila is taken aback. Fernandez works in Dispatch, so she knows the entire department by name — all the street cops, the detectives, everybody. Plus she has excellent evaluations from her supervisor as an independent thinker and creative problem solver. To Sheila, Fernandez looks like the person who could come closest to filling Connie's shoes, when they're empty. So what's wrong? Why is she saying no?

"I'm sorry, too," Sheila says frankly. "You come highly recommended, Ms. Fernandez. Do you mind telling me why you don't want to work in the chief's office?"

It can't be the money, Sheila thinks. She knows what Fernandez is earning in Dispatch, and Connie's job pays substantially more. Then *what*?

"Oh, it's not that I don't *want* to work here," Lucia replies earnestly. She meets Sheila's eyes without flinching. "I mean, I'd jump on it like a duck on a June bug. If I could."

"Well, then, what's keeping you?" Sheila asks, genuinely puzzled.

"It's my three kids." Lucia straightens her shoulders. "They're in elementary and middle school and I'm a single mom. Ms. Page says she works late three or four nights a week and sometimes comes in on Saturday. Evenings and weekends, I've got the kids' supper and homework and soccer and band practice and stuff, not to mention grocery shopping and the laundry and the dentist and the dog and the cat. So I can't do like Ms. Page does. If I took the job and had to say no to staying late . . . well, that wouldn't be so good, now, would it?"

She glances down at her hands, with their square-cut, unpolished, no-nonsense nails — working hands, Sheila thinks — then looks up again. "I would really like to work with you, Chief. You're my hero. You maybe don't know it but you are a hero to all us women in Dispatch. In Personnel, too. But I don't want to disappoint you. I need to stay where I can have reg'lar hours and time to do my other job, which is taking care of my kids. I gotta do that one *right.*"

Sheila's first reaction is to argue with the woman. She is opening her mouth to tell Fernandez that she has completely misunderstood the situation, when she stops herself, frowning.

"To tell the truth," she says, "I wasn't aware that Ms. Page worked late all that often. I should probably talk to her about that."

Oh, come on, now. She wasn't aware? That's ridiculous. She knows damned well that Connie — who has no children and lives alone — rarely leaves the office before she does. And *she* works until six-thirty or seven or even later nearly every night. It's a good thing that Blackie likes to cook and doesn't mind doing the grocery shopping, or they would be eating out four or five nights a week.

But who says her assistant has to keep the same hours she does? Or that *she* has to stay so late so often? And won't this arrangement have to change after the baby comes? Maybe it would be smarter to change it now.

Sheila clears her throat. "If the job was defined as eight-to-five, five days a week, no overtime, no exceptions, would that work for you?"

"It would work for me, sure." Lucia gives her a narrow look. "But I kinda doubt it would work for you. You think, Chief?"

"I don't know," Sheila says honestly. She laughs a little. "But I know I'm going to have to change my habits when the baby comes. Maybe I should start now."

Lucia echoes her laugh. "Well, good luck with that. And if you need any baby tips, you come to me. I know a lot about babies. Dumb as a rock with my first, but I learned fast. Had to, way things turned out."

"Thanks," Sheila says, liking her even more. "And about the job. I'd appreciate it if you could keep an open mind on the subject until we can get back to you. Maybe we can work something out about the hours."

"Be glad to do that." With dignity, Lucia gets up to leave. "Thank you, Chief. I appreciate your consideration."

When she has gone, Sheila punches a button on her desk phone and when Connie answers, she says, "Got five minutes to talk about Fernandez?"

A moment later, Connie sits down in front

of the desk. "I was impressed with her," she says. "What do you think?"

Sheila regards her. "How often do you work late?"

"Whenever necessary."

"How often is that?"

"Oh, maybe a couple of times a week." Connie lifts one shoulder slightly, lets it drop. "Or three." Her smile is crooked. "When you do. Usually."

"Do you *have* to? I mean, if I weren't staying late, would *you*?"

"Well, it does move the work along. I mean, what if you want something and I'm the only one who knows where it is? Which happens," Connie adds. "Especially when we're doing budgets. And reports to the city council." She pauses. "And planning."

"But you won't be here," Sheila points out. "And your replacement won't know where anything is."

"True," Connie says wryly. "But she can phone me and ask. It's not as if I'm dropping off the face of the earth." A wisp of a smile comes and goes.

Sheila sighs. "I wish you weren't going." Noah shifts. "Especially now."

"I know." Connie echoes her sigh. "I wouldn't if I didn't have to. But I do. And I *want* to, actually. My sister —" She stops.

"Well, Lillian has been managing Mom for three years now, while I've been able to do what I want. That's not been exactly fair, and it's time I helped out. You know?"

"I know." Sheila says, wondering if the guys who work for the PSPD ever have to make choices like this. They probably don't, because somebody at home has their backs. A wife, usually. Or a mom or a sister. Somebody. She hesitates. But to be fair, there's Blackie. He's a guy, and he has *her* back.

Connie gives her a searching look. "Fernandez has kids, doesn't she?"

"Three. And she's a single mom. She's thinking about their school stuff, and the laundry and shopping. Late hours and Saturdays don't work for her."

Is that what *her* life would be like if she had three, she wonders. But she's not going to have three, just two, because three is too many and one isn't enough — it's not fair to a child to be raised alone. And she's not going to be a single mother, either. Blackie will do his share, and they will have child care and help with the house —

"You might give Fernandez a couple of weeks to see if it works out," Connie suggests. With a lopsided grin, she adds, "And I don't suppose it would hurt you to quit at five every day, like normal folks." She pushes herself out of the chair. "But don't forget that you're seeing Billie Jean first thing in the morning. I think she has lots of potential. And she's single. No kids to complicate things."

Potential. Sheila sighs, remembering Billie Jean's blouses. And her bloody nails. How can somebody with two-inch acrylic talons manage a keyboard? There must be a trick to it. But being single would definitely be a plus. Billie Jean probably wouldn't complain about staying late — unless it began to cut into her social life.

She stands up, feeling bulky and awkward. "Anything on that green VW?" She had phoned it in on her way back to the office after her interview with Jennifer Haley.

"Not yet," Connie says apologetically. "There's been another computer outage at the DMV. They put me on hold forever, and when I finally got through, the woman said I'd have to call back."

Sheila shakes her head. "It would be nice if somebody at the Department of Transportation actually got things straightened out over there." She adjusts her wrinkled maternity top. "China Bayles should be here by the time I get back from the ladies'. Put her and Walker in the interview room. And tell

Miller I want him in on this. Maybe we'll learn something useful about the Fairlee murder."

CHAPTER ELEVEN

When it comes to the real thing, the scarcity of vanilla is creating another problem: the growing number of vanilla producers who silently substitute a shorter, quick-cure process for the traditional longer curing. Quick-cure vanilla often begins with unripened beans and does not result in the same fine quality that is produced when fully ripe beans are cured for several months. Producers who aren't concerned with quality get faster results, farmers get paid more quickly for less work, and buyers get a product that looks and even smells like vanilla.

But people who know say it's not the same thing. Not the same thing at all. Something to think about while you sip your $4.65 vanilla latte.

China Bayles
"Vanilla: The Ice Cream Spice"
Pecan Springs Enterprise

I intended to go home and change clothes before Maggie's interview with the police, but that didn't happen. There were customers with questions waiting for me. When I was finished with them, a couple of new volunteers showed up to work in the Zodiac Garden, one of the dozen or so theme gardens around the shop. I spent the next half hour showing them how to dig, divide, and replant the garlic (a Mars-ruled herb) and making sure that they knew the difference between mullein and comfrey (herbs of Saturn) and the lamb's ear that had wandered over from the neighboring Children's Garden and needed to be sent back.

By the time I'd gotten everything sorted out, it was too late to drive all the way home and back again. So I would be behaving like a lawyer in my slightly grubby Thyme and Seasons T-shirt and jeans. But Maggie and I were an evenly matched odd couple, for when I picked her up, I saw that she was wearing purple sneakers and had traded her scrubs for black jeans and a green roll-sleeve shirt the same shade as her green-tipped spiky hair. To top things off, she was carrying the terrarium in her arms. It was so tall she could barely see over it.

On the drive to the station, I outlined our game plan. "The interview will probably be video recorded. I'll make a brief statement, then ask you to tell how and why you stole the orchid and why you're surrendering it. The chief or maybe the other detective — there will likely be two — will ask you some questions. You may think they are dumb or deliberately offensive questions, but what you think doesn't matter. If you know the answer, say it. If you don't, say 'I don't know' and leave it at that. Don't explain, don't speculate, don't guess, don't volunteer." I slid her a stern glance. "Do *not* volunteer. You got that?"

Maggie rolled her eyes.

"I'll take that as an affirmative," I said. With emphasis, I added, "What's more, if I tell you *not* to answer a question, don't answer it. There's a reason, and I know what it is. They know, too, but that won't stop them from asking. Understand?"

"I'm sorry I agreed to do this," Maggie growled. "I didn't kill Carl. I don't know who did. I can't help the police. I —"

"You don't have a choice," I said bluntly. "You stole the friggin' orchid, Mags. If the cops think that plant is somehow connected to the murder, you'll be in a world of hurt. So face up to what you did, admit it, and let's get past this thing before it morphs into something else altogether." Like a murder charge, I thought. Or obstruction of justice. "Okay?"

"Okay, okay." She hunched her shoulders. "No need to get belligerent."

"I am not belligerent. I am authoritative. Lawyers are paid to be authoritative."

She gave me a suspicious look. "How much am I paying you?"

"I'm a cheap date." I pulled open the ashtray where I keep parking meter change. "The customary fee is a dollar, but you can dump your loose silver in here."

"Thank you." She fished in her purse, pulled out some change, and dropped it into the ashtray. While her bag was handy, she checked her phone. "Lyle isn't answering my texts," she said with a frown. We had left Chelsea watching a kids' movie on TV. Her brother hadn't come home yet. "I wonder if I should have asked a neighbor to come over and keep an eye on Chelsea."

"She's thirteen, Maggie." I turned left onto Guadalupe, heading west, and slowed for a guy pushing a baby stroller loaded with twins. "She's old enough to stay by herself for a couple of hours, isn't she?"

"You're right. But she's more fragile than she looks. Today is a very bad day for her, because of her father. And Lyle *promised.* How do you get kids to keep their promises?" She sighed. "Most of the time, I don't have a clue about anything, China. As a mom, I mean."

"It's hard, isn't it?" I said. "Sometimes we just have to make it up as we go along. Nobody is going to get it right every time. All we can do is the best we know how — and hope it will be enough."

It was a stupid answer, riddled with clichés. Later, I would wish I'd been able to come up with something better.

I parked my Toyota in the lot behind the police department. On one side of me was a black Dodge Ram hiked up on monster tires, with a shotgun in a rear-window gun rack. On the other was a gray Chevy Volt with a baby carrier and a stuffed giraffe in the back seat and a bumper sticker that declared *Arms Are For Hugging.* It takes all kinds to make a world, I guess.

Maggie and I went in through the back door. Connie Page, Sheila's longtime assistant, showed us to a gray-walled, gray-floored interview room that was as small and bleak as any I had seen back when I was a real lawyer. It was empty except for a scratched wooden table, four chairs, an inconspicuous camera high in one corner, and a one-way window set into one wall, so viewers in an adjoining room could watch. I couldn't help thinking about all the people, heavy with despair and hopelessness, who had sat in these chairs and poured out truths and half-truths and lies. I was glad that walls can't talk. We wouldn't want to hear their stories.

If Connie was surprised at the way we were dressed, she was polite enough not to mention it, just brought us some coffee, said "The chief will be with you in a moment" and disappeared. Maggie put the terrarium on the table, and we sat down. She began chewing on her thumbnail and casting wary glances at the camera and the window.

I took a notebook and pen out of my bag and put them on the table in front of me. "It's okay, Mags," I said, patting her arm. I knew why she was nervous. Any time you have to sit down with a cop, you immediately remember the times you've jaywalked or parked where you shouldn't or failed to return a library book and now have a humongous unpaid fine. It's stupid, of course, but it's a universal paranoia and completely understandable.

Maggie was muttering "I don't think I want to do this," when Sheila and Dylan Miller came in and took the chairs on the other side of the table. I noticed that Miller's jaw muscles tightened at the sight of Maggie's green-spiked hair and my Thyme and Seasons T-shirt. Maybe he thought we ought to have dressed up for the interview. Sheila looked tired, I thought. And awkwardly, uncomfortably pregnant under her rumpled maternity uniform. She's a beautiful woman, but pregnancy hasn't been easy for her. Her usually shiny blond hair was straw-like, and there were dark circles under her eyes. Our smiles were marginally cordial, one professional woman greeting another professional woman, both of us here on business (possibly adversarial business) and pretending we aren't friends.

After introductions, Sheila pointed a remote to the camera, clicking it on. "We record all our interviews, Ms. Walker. We'll make a transcript of the proceedings, and you and your attorney" — she nodded at me — "may have copies of it and the video. Now, why don't you tell us why you wanted to talk to us this afternoon."

I led off with a couple of boilerplate sentences and added a brief paragraph of Maggie's professional credentials. Then: "Ms. Walker wishes to fully and completely cooperate in the matter of the orchid she took from Dr. Carl Fairlee's greenhouse on the night of Sunday, September twelfth. She is surrendering the plant." I nodded at the terrarium. The single bloom had dropped off and the plant looked more like a dime-store markdown than a rare and valuable orchid.

I went on: "It is Ms. Walker's intention to make it very clear that her action had nothing whatever to do with Dr. Fairlee's subsequent death. She merely wants to clarify the circumstances and hopes that the orchid can be placed where it can get proper care. It is a very rare plant. She will make a brief statement now, and answer your questions." I sat back.

Maggie spent the next few minutes telling them what she had told me — why she had stolen the plant and when and how. "I had a key to the building," she said. "But I didn't have a key to the greenhouse, so I had to jimmy the door. I tried to be careful not to cause any serious damage."

When she got to the part where she texted her ex-husband to let him know that she had his orchid, Sheila said, "If you have your phone, I'd like to see those texts."

I asked for Maggie's cell, scrolled through the texts until I found what she had sent to her ex-husband, and read them aloud. "I assume you have Dr. Fairlee's phone, so you'll see the texts there," I added. "But in case you haven't been able to unlock it yet, I'm forwarding them to you now." I suited the action to the words.

Miller leaned forward. To Maggie, he said, "Stealing the orchid — that didn't have anything to do with its value? You're sure you didn't take it because you planned to sell it and make a lot of money?"

Maggie shook her head. "No. No way. I could lose my business, doing something like that." She made a rueful face. "I know it was stupid to take it, though. It could get me in a lot of trouble with the orchid cops. That's one reason I'm glad to let you have it."

"And what did you say its name is?" Miller asked.

"It's called the demon orchid," Maggie said. "*Telipogon diabolicus.* Somebody imagined that the bloom looked like a devil." She spelled the Latin binomial while Miller wrote it down. "Telipogons are notoriously hard to cultivate," she added. "The species is native to mountain cloud forests, and temperature, humidity, and light all have to be controlled. Just keeping it alive is an achievement. That's why it's in this terrarium."

"Tell us again why you took it," Sheila prompted. Cops always ask you to repeat your story several times. They're looking for contradictions, inconsistencies, holes, and outright lies. Which is why it's always easier to tell the truth in the first place. You don't have to remember which lies you've told. And if you're asked to repeat, you don't have to sort through several versions of your story.

Maggie made a little face. "It probably sounds childish, but I took the plant to show Carl that he couldn't push me around all the time. I knew how much he wanted that particular plant, and I wanted to hurt him. To get even for taking the orchids that belonged to me. For making me sell the house just so he could have the cash — which he didn't need. For making it hard for me to keep the kids in their school." Defiantly, she added, half under her breath. "For being such a damned jerk all the time I was married to him."

Under the table, I pinched her knee. She had said everything she needed to say on that score. It was time to stop.

Sheila's notebook was open on the table. She turned a page, read something, and looked up. "When we spoke earlier, you said that your ex-husband 'wanted that plant in the worst way.' How do you know he wanted it?"

"Because he told me, one afternoon when he came over to pick up Chelsea, our daughter. He was bragging about it. That he was going to get one." Her face darkened. "He just *had* to tell me. That's how he was."

"Do you know how he got it? Where he got it?"

"Why?" With a serious expression, Maggie cocked her head. "I mean, why does it matter where he got it?"

I was puzzled by this line of inquiry, too, but we weren't asking the questions. I leaned toward Maggie. "If you know, say so," I whispered.

Maggie sighed. "All I know is that Carl had been trying to find this particular plant ever since he'd heard about it, maybe a year or so. He said he had a buyer for it."

"A buyer?" Miller asked. "Who?"

"A collector who lives in Colorado. Carl said the guy was willing to pay a pretty penny for it, so he was surprised when somebody offered it to him for free."

"For *free*?" Sheila's eyebrows went up. "He didn't pay for it?"

"That surprised me, too," Maggie said. "I mean, of course Carl would happily *take* it, if it was offered." She gestured to the plant in the terrarium. "I know it doesn't look like much at the moment, just a few straggly shoots and some green leaves growing out of a bunch of moss on a branch. But when it was found in southern Colombia, there were only thirty of them, and their part of the forest has since been wiped out by road construction. There may be more somewhere in that jungle, but maybe not. Somebody went to quite a bit of trouble — and even more risk — to bring this one into the country. You'd expect to pay real money for it. Thousands of dollars, maybe."

"To *smuggle* it in, you mean," Sheila said. "Illegally. Maybe with other orchids."

"I don't know about the other orchids," Maggie said. "But yes. That *Telipogon* had to have been smuggled in. It didn't get here by itself."

"And who would that smuggler be?" Miller inquired.

"I don't know. Carl wouldn't have told me, even if I'd asked." Maggie's mouth twisted. "He liked secrets."

Sheila looked down at her notebook. "Do you know anybody who drives a late model VW Beetle — green?"

"A green Beetle?" Maggie's eyebrows went up. "I don't know of anybody who drives a Beetle, period. Around here, it's mostly SUVs and pickup trucks."

Sheila looked disappointed, but persisted.

"And you can't even guess who might have given Dr. Fairlee the orchid? A man or a woman? Somebody from the university, maybe?"

It was time to intervene. "No, she can't guess," I said firmly. "She has already said she doesn't know. It's time to move on." I was still mystified about this line of questioning. It sounded like the orchid might be crucial to their investigation in ways I hadn't understood, and I made a mental note to ask about it later.

Sheila nodded and changed the subject. "You know Logan Gardner, I believe, Ms. Walker." When Maggie nodded, she said, "Did you know that he and Dr. Fairlee had been working on a hybrid vanilla plant for several years?"

"Yes," Maggie said.

"And that he — Dr. Fairlee, that is — had filed a patent in his own name for that plant?"

"Carl told me he was filing, yes. And yes, that he was filing in his name. He even named the plant for himself." She smiled faintly. "He was calling it *Vanilla planifolia fairleei.* He said he thought it 'had a nice ring to it.'"

I was surprised. Hybridizers name plants for themselves all the time. It's like an

303

author's name on a book. It's a status thing — gets your name out there into the trade and sells plants. But I also knew that Logan had done most of the work on that orchid and expected it would be named for himself: *Vanilla planifolia gardneri.* That's what he had told the women in my vanilla workshop.

"Did you know that Gardner expected that the patent would be filed jointly?"

"Yes," Maggie said cautiously.

"Was Mr. Gardner disappointed when that didn't happen?"

Maggie glanced at me. I gave my head an imperceptible shake. "I don't know," she said. "It wasn't any of my business. Look, if you're trying to get me to say that Logan —" I put my hand on her knee and she stopped.

Miller took up the same line of questioning, from a different angle. "Were you aware that Logan Gardner and Jennifer Haley were planning to get married — *before* she began a relationship with your ex-husband?"

"Yes," Maggie said slowly. "I hated to see —" She bit off her sentence without waiting for my signal. *Good girl,* I thought.

"Any idea how Mr. Gardner might have felt about the professor stealing his girl-friend?" Miller pressed. "As well as his patent. Two pretty big rip-offs, seems to me.

Don't you agree?"

I could see where they were going with this. They were targeting Logan Gardner, who must now be their chief person of interest. They were already setting up a possible narrative for the prosecution, based on at least two strong motives. If Logan didn't have a solid alibi, he could be in serious trouble. Of course, their focus on him would take Maggie off the hook, which was a good thing. But I wasn't going to further their ambitions.

I held up my hand. "Hang on, Detective. My client has no way of knowing how Mr. Gardner felt about any of this. She would only be speculating. Not her job." I was a bit taken aback by how easily *my client* had slipped out and how natural it sounded. I should watch my tongue.

"Okay," Miller said, playing the game. "I'll put it a different way. Ms. Walker, did Gardner ever tell you how he felt about losing his girl or being cheated out of his patent?"

"No," Maggie said firmly. "He's never said anything to me on either subject. In fact, I haven't seen Logan in several weeks." And that, I hoped, was that — although if I were Logan Gardner, I would definitely start looking for a defense attorney. A good one.

305

"I believe that does it for us." Sheila closed her notebook and used the remote to shut off the video camera. "Thank you for surrendering the orchid," she said to Maggie. "We'll get the transcript typed and give you a call when it's ready for you to review and sign." She paused. In a sympathetic tone, she added, "Dr. Fairlee's body can be released at any time. I understand that the children are the next of kin."

"Yeah." Maggie nodded somberly. "The kids and I know Carl wanted to be cremated, so we'll go ahead with that. No funeral — there'll be a memorial service at some point, but we're not sure when."

Sheila nodded. "Before you go, Detective Miller can take your fingerprints." She frowned at the terrarium. "And we need to find a place to keep the orchid."

Which meant that they believed it was evidentiary — but evidence of what? Obviously, there was something here that I didn't understand. I doubted that Logan was a killer, but I've been wrong on that score before. Maybe he was involved with orchid smuggling, and Dr. Fairlee had threatened to blow the whistle. Or maybe it was Fairlee who was involved with black-market orchids and *Logan* who had threatened to blow the whistle. The subject offered several possible permutations; happily, none of them were my business. The plant was, however.

"That orchid is very nearly one of a kind," I said, "and Ms. Walker wants to make sure that it survives. She's an experienced orchidist. She'll be glad to keep it in one of her orchid greenhouses at Sonora Garden Center."

Miller shook his head. "Not a good idea. We'll keep it here."

I raised my eyebrows. "If you think the orchid might be needed at trial at some future date, it wouldn't serve any good purpose to let it die in an evidence locker. How about keeping it in the chief's office?" I glanced at Sheila. "I have a lighted plant stand I'd be glad to loan you."

"Does it come with your personal agreement to water the damned thing?" Sheila was scowling. "My thumb is totally black. If it's left to me, it will be dead in a week."

"I do house calls," Maggie volunteered.

"House calls?" Miller sounded skeptical.

"Sure," she said. "I'll water it, feed it, make sure the light and temperature are okay. Lots of people want to have plants but don't have the time or the knowledge to keep them healthy and growing." With a smile, she added, "For you guys, no charge. I'll do it as a public service."

"You won't get a better offer," I said. "Pro bono."

Sheila yielded. "Sounds like a plan," she said. "Ms. Bayles, could you bring the orchid to my office, please? You can wait there while Ms. Walker's prints are being taken."

Sheila doesn't personalize her office. In it, there was nothing but reference books, cop magazines, and stacks of computer printouts on the gray metal bookshelves; a large map of Pecan Springs and Adams County on one wall; and a computer and a glossy-green plastic philodendron on her desk. No plants to water, no doohickeys to dust, no framed photos and only the minimum number of certificates and diplomas on the wall. The terrarium containing the orchid stood out because there was something in it that wasn't man-made. Sporting a brand-new orange evidence tag and identification number, it sat on a bookshelf.

Sheila sat down and immediately bent over to unlace her duty oxfords. "Thanks for bringing Walker in, China." With a whooshing sigh, she kicked her shoes off, pulled out the bottom drawer of her desk, and propped her stockinged feet on it. "Her statement tied up at least one major loose end. The plant theft."

"You look tired, Smart Cookie," I said with concern. "You feeling okay?"

"I *am* tired." She made a face. "Noah isn't, though. He thinks this is all just one great big rodeo. After the bronc busting, there's the calf roping. He's ready to ride."

I laughed sympathetically. "All that, and murder, too," I said. "So where are you in the Fairlee case? Looking at it from the outside, it seems pretty complicated."

Sheila pursed her lips. "You're not asking as Walker's lawyer, are you? If you are, you know I can't answer."

"Nope. I'm asking as me. I suited up today as a pinch-hitter, just to be sure that the orchid theft got resolved before it morphed into something it wasn't."

"Suited up?" Sheila asked, with an ironic glance at my T-shirt and jeans.

"In a manner of speaking," I said. "If Maggie needs any more legal help, she'll call Charlie Lipman. He'll be glad to arm-wrestle you over the facts of the case."

"If you're just you and agree to keep your lip buttoned, I can tell you that we're still pretty much nowhere." Sheila made a rueful face. "What we have are a number of apparently unrelated puzzles and no way to connect them up."

309

"It sounds like you have more suspects than you need," I remarked. As a defense attorney, I loved it when there were several suspects — other than my client, of course — on whom I could pin the crime. Multiple suspects, especially those with strong motives, made it that much easier for me to persuade the jury that the prosecution had not made its case beyond a reasonable doubt.

"You got that right," Sheila said.

"Who's on your players' card? Not Walker, I assume. Speaking as a friend," I added hastily. "Not as her lawyer."

"Walker's still on the list," Sheila said. "She doesn't have an airtight alibi. But now that I know it was that stolen orchid she was hiding from me this morning, I'm probably okay with moving her to the bottom. As far as motive goes, we're looking at three suspects. Gardner is at the top. The professor took both his vanilla patent *and* his girlfriend. He has no alibi. He had a key to the building and access to the greenhouse. Plus, he has a license to carry, so he presumably knows how to handle a gun."

"MOM still gets people convicted," I said. In the hands of a skilled prosecutor, motive, means, and opportunity can persuade juries, even when there's no smoking gun. But I remembered what Beverly Selms had told me about the history of her husband's long relationship with Fairlee. "You're probably also looking at Dan Selms."

"Right. His wife is his alibi, which — as you know — can be challenged. As for motive, Selms had plenty of reason to hate Fairlee. That greenhouse, for one thing, which everybody says made Selms look like a total dolt. It must have been a sore that festered every time he went out and looked up at the roof. For another, we've been told that Fairlee apparently stole some of Selms' research and published it under his own name. And there seems to have been bad blood between them that goes back a couple of decades."

"You said there were three. Who's the third?"

"Jennifer Haley's father. He's got a mile-long list of grudges against Fairlee — he once even got a dozen faculty members to sign a letter demanding that the man be fired. Not to mention that he was royally pissed at Fairlee for sleeping with his daughter. And Haley was home alone. No alibi at all."

"I suppose you've surveyed the other faculty. Just to eliminate," I added. "The last thing you need is to come up with more suspects."

"You said it," Sheila replied emphatically. "But yes, Denise Maxwell, the campus security director, interviewed everybody who has offices in the Plant Sciences building. Their statements and alibis all have to be checked, of course, but she says nothing jumped out at her." She pulled her mouth down. "I was glad to have Denise's help. We're perennially shorthanded here. Besides Miller, Megan Donnelly is working on Fairlee's computer and his phone, and Gene Parsons is handling the searches — the victim's apartment, his office, and his vehicle. Which was used to transport plants, by the way. Jennifer Haley, the current girlfriend, said that Fairlee sold orchids at various orchid shows."

"Ah, the girlfriend. Maggie said she's a grad student." I raised my eyebrows. "Is she a suspect, too?"

"She says she was studying for an exam, with a friend. Haven't checked the alibi yet, but my guess is that she'll be cleared. I still need to talk again to the department secretary, Charlaine Rudolph, who is one of Fairlee's cast-off lovers. And I'd like to find the woman who gave him that orchid."

"You know it came from a woman?"

"Yeah, according to Jennifer. One possible

theory: Fairlee was involved with an orchid smuggling ring that brought plants into the country, then distributed them through orchid shows. His murder is related to that." She raised her shoulders and dropped them. "But that's all it is, a theory."

"No physical evidence? Nothing on the gun?"

"Stolen. There was a partial print on the suppressor."

"The suppressor? That's a little unusual, isn't it?"

"Right." Sheila's grin was bleak. "Suppressors are a big-city crime toy. We don't often see them here in Pecan Springs. Miller traced it to the original owner, who reported it stolen not long after he got it. We sent the partial print through AFIS and didn't get a match." She rubbed her face with both hands. "Not surprising — it was pretty smudged."

"Anything helpful turn up in the searches?"

"Not yet. The phone and the computer are both password-protected, and while Donnelly is plenty smart, all she has is on-the-job experience. As somebody said once, 'You fight the war with the army you've got.' Or something like that." She nodded toward the terrarium on the bookshelf. "And then

313

there's the orchid. Or maybe not."

"Ah, yes, the orchid," I said with a sigh. "I'm sorry Maggie couldn't give you more information about it. I'm confident that she's told us all she knows." I paused. "You said that Jennifer Haley saw the woman who gave Fairlee the orchid. Did you get a description?"

"Nothing terribly helpful. White, short brown hair, medium height, medium weight, middle age. Wearing jeans and a blue Adams County Hospital T-shirt, which could have been obtained anywhere locally, new or in a thrift shop, or even at the half-marathon, where they're handed out to runners. Jennifer saw her when she gave the orchid to Fairlee, at his greenhouse. On another occasion, the same woman picked Fairlee up in the lot behind the Plant Sciences building. He kissed her — not a casual kiss, according to Jennifer. So there seems to have been something going on between them. Besides the orchid, that is. The illegal orchid."

"She picked him up?" I asked. "What was she driving?"

With a smile, Sheila tented her fingers. "Now, that might be a little more helpful. It was a late model Volkswagen Beetle. Green, maybe metallic green."

"Of course. The Beetle you asked Maggie about."

That was indeed a little more helpful. Texans tend to drive big trucks and big cars. Forget about fuel efficiency — the bigger the better is our mantra. And green isn't our favorite color, either. Texans vastly prefer metallic bronze and brown. There couldn't be more than a couple of hundred green Beetles in the state. But maybe this one wasn't registered in Texas.

"Plates?" I asked.

"Jennifer didn't notice. Connie's running a registered vehicle check now. Trying to, anyway. The DMV computers are down."

I thought of something else and turned to look at the terrarium. It had a round base, some three or four inches high, into which the domed glass top fitted. "Do you know if the woman who supplied the orchid to Fairlee gave it to him in this terrarium?"

Sheila frowned. "I'd have to check, but I think I remember Maxwell saying that's how he reported the theft. Why are you asking?"

I pointed to the terrarium. "Both Maggie and I, and presumably also Fairlee, have handled that container. But we've touched only the outside. There may be a separate inside container that holds the soil — probably fir bark, which is the usual orchid-growing medium. Whoever assembled it might have left prints on the inside of the base. Or maybe even on the interior of the glass dome."

"That's a thought," Sheila said, brightening. "I'll have it checked right away." She dropped her feet to the floor, leaned forward, and pushed a button on her phone. "Connie, come in for a second." When her assistant came in, she pointed to the plant. "Please take that terrarium down to Miller and tell him to get somebody to disassemble it — carefully, without harming the plant — and see if they can pull any prints off the inside of the base and the dome."

As Connie took the terrarium, I said, "Hey, Con, how's Lillian?" Connie had worked for McQuaid when he served for a few months as the police chief, after Bubba Harris retired and before Sheila was hired. I had heard that her sister had cancer.

Connie pulled down her mouth. "Not so good. She's having surgery next week."

"Fingers crossed," I said. "Tell her we're thinking of her."

"I will." Connie glanced at Sheila. "Want some coffee, Chief? I'm going past the coffee machine."

"I wish," Sheila said wistfully. "But I've

already had mine for the day. No point in wiring the baby. You want coffee, China?"

"Thanks," I said. "I'm good."

After she had gone with the terrarium, Sheila shook her head glumly. "I just wish I could keep Connie forever."

I was startled. "She's going somewhere?"

"Afraid so. She's going to Dallas to take care of both her mom and her sister. You know that her mother has Alzheimer's?" When I nodded, Sheila added, "We're pretending that this is a short-term thing, but she has no idea when she might be back. This is something Connie feels she needs to do. All I can do is try to make it easy for her."

"Uh-oh," I said quietly.

"Yeah. I've been interviewing replacements." She pulled down her mouth. "As if anybody could come within a mile of replacing Con."

I could hear the pain in her voice. "Oh, Smart Cookie," I said sympathetically. "I am so sorry — now, of all times."

"This is making me understand just how much I depend on her." Sheila shook her head. "In fact, Connie is the only person in this whole friggin' department that I can trust a hundred percent. I can't begin to imagine doing this job without her."

"Ruby and I function that way a lot of the time," I said. "We back each other up, especially when things are difficult. Work wives, we call each other. After all, we're together for eight or nine waking hours a day. When we have a catering job, it can go to ten or twelve. More time than most married couples spend together."

"Work wives," Sheila said, as if she was surprised by the way the idea clicked with her. "Yes, that's exactly it. Connie and I just seem to —" She was interrupted by the short, sharp buzz of the phone on her desk. She answered it, listened a moment, then hung up. "Walker is fingerprinted and ready to leave. You can meet her in the lobby. And one of our suspects is waiting for Miller and me in the interview room."

I got up. "Go get 'em, Sherlock," I said. "Maybe your suspect will get the urge to confess and you'll make an arrest this afternoon. It *could* happen, you know."

"I suppose it could." Sheila got up, too. "But I have to go to the bathroom first."

CHAPTER TWELVE

BAKED CHICKEN WITH BALSAMIC-ORANGE-VANILLA SAUCE

1/2 cup chicken broth
1/2 cup balsamic vinegar
1/4 cup fresh orange juice
1/4 cup packed brown sugar
1/4 cup finely chopped green onions
1 teaspoon finely chopped fresh rosemary
1/4 teaspoon orange zest
1/2 teaspoon salt
3-inch piece vanilla bean, split lengthwise
Cooking spray
8 skinless, boneless chicken thighs
Salt and pepper to taste

Heat oven to 450° F. Combine first 8 ingredients in a small saucepan. Scrape seeds from vanilla bean; stir seeds into broth mixture.* Bring to a boil. Reduce heat and simmer, stirring occasionally, until reduced to 1/2 cup (15 minutes). While the sauce is reducing, coat the bottom of a roasting pan with cooking spray. Arrange chicken in a single layer. Salt and pepper to taste. Cover and bake at 450° for 10 minutes. Brush half of sauce over chicken; return to oven, uncovered, for 5 minutes. Brush remaining broth mixture over chicken; return to oven for 15 minutes, uncovered, or until a thermometer registers 180°. Serve over pasta or rice to 4 hungry diners.

*Bury the piece of vanilla bean in a canister of sugar. Wonderful in tea, coffee.

The delicious chicken dish we had for supper took no more than about ten minutes to assemble, fifteen minutes on the stove, and another thirty in the oven. The balsamic I used is an ordinary, off-the-shelf balsamic, tart and fruity but not as richly complex and tangy as one that is traditionally made and barrel-aged. The best balsamic is so pricey that I use it only *after* cooking, to add a final touch. I served the chicken with angel hair pasta (cooks fast), a green salad, and slices of Cass' carrot cake, brought home from the shop. McQuaid and Caitie chowed down with gusto, while Winchester waited beneath the table, alert for possible contributions.

When we were finished eating, Caitie went out to the chicken coop to discuss laying schedules with her girls. Several of her best hens hadn't finished molting, so production was down and she was worried about filling her egg customers' orders.

"I hope you'll be able to spare a dozen for me," I called after her. I was planning to make a vanilla custard for the next workshop session. If I'm going to the expense of real vanilla beans, I want real eggs, too.

"I'll tell them," she said over her shoulder. "But I can't promise."

At an age when most girls are jabbering nonstop into their cell phones, Caitie is unusually focused. Right now, her flourishing chicken and egg business takes all the attention she can spare from school and music. Her fifteen hens usually lay ten or a dozen eggs a day, with no time off on weekends or holidays. We pay her for those we use and she sells the rest to neighbors and friends, buying the feed out of her earnings and banking what's left. Toward college, she says, although the money her father left in trust for her education should take care of that, as well as grad school and more. Still, saving is a good habit for a kid. We encourage it.

These days, though, Caitie's chicken-and-egg story has a couple of new characters. Earlier, I mentioned Blackheart, the very valuable Ayam Cemani rooster that was chicken-napped along with Caitie's rooster at the Adams County Fair. What makes Ayam Cemani chickens so extraordinary is their astonishing color: their plumage is a shiny, glistening black, their legs and toe-nails are black, and so are their beaks, their tongues, their combs, and their wattles. Even their meat, bones, and inner organs are black — or so I was informed later. At the time, I was too busy liberating Black-heart to investigate down to the skin-and-bones level.

I also learned later that, back home in his chicken yard, Blackheart had an Ayam Ce-mani wife named Goodheart. Goodheart's fertile eggs, which are a very ordinary brown (really? not black?), sell on eBay for an astonishing $18 to $20 each. In gratitude for the safe return of her at-large rooster, Blackheart's owner gave Caitie a half-dozen of Goodheart's pricey eggs. *Fertile* eggs.

Caitie considered setting her six precious eggs under Dixie Chick. But she was afraid that Dixie might not be interested in invest-ing twenty-one days of her life in another hen's eggs — or that she might carelessly allow one or two of the eggs to get broken. So McQuaid helped her turn an old Styrofoam cooler into an incubator by inserting a twenty-five watt light bulb into one side and a plexiglass viewing window into the lid. She kept it in her bedroom (where else?), monitoring the temperature and humidity and turning the eggs before breakfast, after school, and when she went to bed at night. Her mother-hen diligence was rewarded when, after twenty-one days, all six eggs successfully hatched. The baby chicks were black as midnight, down to their tiny beaks and toes.

Now, Caitie has a new angle on the chicken business. She plans to keep a boy chick and two girl chicks and sell the other three when they are ten weeks old — for the going price of $150 each. Presumably her boy and girl chicks will grow into fatherhood and motherhood and produce their own fertile eggs. I have the feeling that whatever she does for a living when she's grown up, she will always have plenty of pocket change.

McQuaid, heading for his office, paused in the kitchen doorway. We hadn't talked about the investigation during dinner, but we had spoken by phone during the day, and he knew that Carl Fairlee's death had been ruled a homicide. "Any progress in the investigation?" he asked.

"I don't know if you'd call it progress," I said, putting the leftover pasta into the fridge. "I spent an hour at the PSPD with Maggie Walker this afternoon, making sure she didn't talk her way into a blind alley. Afterwards —"

"Whoa." McQuaid held up his hand. "You did what? I thought you were through with lawyering. Done with it forever. I hope this doesn't mean —"

"I wasn't lawyering. I was just helping a friend avoid a possible felony. When we were finished, Sheila updated me on their progress." I told him where the cops were in the case — and where they weren't.

"Sounds like the research assistant is their best bet," McQuaid said. "Gardner, is it?"

I nodded. "Sheila says he had both motive and opportunity, plus a familiarity with guns. But Carl Fairlee seems to have attracted enemies like flies. There is no shortage of viable suspects." I glanced up at the clock. "Did I mention that Kate Rodriguez is coming over tonight?"

"The lady who got pregnant with the turkey baster?" McQuaid raised one eyebrow. "No, you didn't. But I won't be in your way. I've got a few things to tidy up in the office, and then I'm heading over to the Banners'. Tom is having some guys over for poker."

Tom and Sylvia Banner are our neighbors. Tom is ex-Army, an Adams County reserve deputy, and a homesteader who has been a helpful resource for Caitie where the chickens are concerned. Sylvia, a talented spinner and weaver, tends a flock of Gulf Coast Native sheep on their thirty acres.

"I've got something for Sylvia," I said, taking a jar of Queen Anne's Lace jelly out of the cupboard. "I promised to give her this, and I keep forgetting. And tell Tom that all six of Caitie's black chicks hatched." Together, Tom and I had corralled the rooster rustler, who turned out to be a marijuana farmer, as well. It had been an action-filled encounter that ended with Tom being shot and me being questioned about my role in an officer-involved shooting.

McQuaid disappeared, Caitie came in and then went upstairs to do her homework. I was brewing a pot of after-dinner mint tea when I heard a car in the drive and a moment later, a knock at the kitchen door.

It was Kate, a tall, sturdily built woman in her early thirties. She has inherited a quiet beauty from generations of Latina foremothers: large brown eyes and heavy lashes, ivory-satin skin, high cheekbones, a full mouth, and straight dark hair. She was wearing denim leggings and a sleeveless red blouse.

"Hey, Kate," I said. "Come in." Winchester left his doggie bed and trotted over for an eager, inquisitive sniff of her sneakers and socks. Kate and Amy have a dachshund named Flossie, and her scent always intrigues Winchester. He couldn't wait for Kate to settle down so he could spend the next half hour with his nose on Kate's toes and his mind on flirty Flossie.

"I've brought a treat," Kate said, putting a box of assorted cookies on the table. "Amy and Grace baked this afternoon." She took one out and held it up. "Grace said she made this one especially for you." It was shaped sort of like an elephant and frosted with bright pink frosting. She took out another. "And if elephants aren't to your taste, here's a green dinosaur with purple paws. Amy dyed the frosting with Kool-Aid."

"Tell Grace her cookies are spectacular," I said with a chuckle. "Almost too pretty to eat."

A few minutes later, we were sitting on the front porch with our tea, a plate of cookies, and Winchester, who was mooning over

Kate's sneakers. The low western sun cast lengthening shadows across the grass, and twilight was beginning to fall across the late-summer landscape.

Over the years that McQuaid and I have lived here, we've added another twenty acres to the original three that came with our big old Victorian house. With all that space around us, it's easy to feel that we're alone here, on the edge of a wilderness that stretches all the way to the horizon. That isn't true, of course. The Hill Country is filling up fast, as gated communities swallow the woods and prairies. But this house has been here for a long time, and the land to which it belongs is still mostly wild. Our nearest neighbors, the Banners, are well out of sight, and Limekiln Road is a half mile away.

So Kate and I could relax in our wicker rockers and enjoy the view of a newly mown lawn and an old stone wall overgrown with wild greenbriar. (If you've ever tangled with this barbed vine, *Smilax bona-nox,* you will appreciate two of its folk names: cat's claw and blaspheme-vine.) On the other side of the wall is a woodland, a tangle of juniper, live oak, and mesquite trees. A doe and her twin fawns, still wearing their baby spots, were browsing in the shadows under the distant trees. On this side of the wall, a turkey hen was shepherding her brood of seven gangly half-grown poults toward the creek. The high-pitched thrum of cicadas filled the air, and from the woods, we could hear the plaintive, quavering call — *who-coos-for-you* — of the white-winged dove. Nearer, the last of the southbound migrating hummingbirds were visiting the honeysuckle on the trellis at the end of the porch, their wings making a soft whizzing sound.

"I was delighted when Ruby told me about the baby," I said, putting my teacup down and leaning back in my chair. "I had to laugh when she said that you and Amy had drawn straws to decide who got to be the mom. The birth mother, I mean," I added, since both of them are moms.

"There were good reasons on both sides," Kate said. "But I have wanted a baby for a very long time. This felt like the right time, given my age. Ron — my sister's husband — seemed like the right choice." She paused. "But as I said on the phone this morning, we don't have an agreement with him. Not a written one, anyway. I'm beginning to think that's not a good idea."

I leaned over and picked up Grace's elephant cookie. "You said on the phone that Ron is getting a little 'pushy' about the baby. What did you mean, exactly?"

She turned her empty cup in her fingers. "Well, it's kind of a long story. I suppose you remember about Grace's father?"

I nodded. Before Kate and Amy got together, Amy had had a brief and unhappy involvement with a young man who ended up as a victim of a double murder — a shocking event in Pecan Springs. He was Grace's father, but he died before the baby was born and was never involved in her life. Instead of a mom and a dad, Grace has two moms.

"Well, when Amy and I talked about having a second baby," Kate said, "we sort of assumed it would be like Grace's situation. The father wouldn't be an active member of our family." She made a little face. "We didn't actually talk it through, though. It was more like an unconscious assumption, I suppose you'd say."

"Makes sense," I said, nibbling on the elephant's trunk. "Trouble is, when assumptions are unconscious, we don't get to discuss them."

"Yeah. Well, that was our assumption going into this. Then some friends put us in touch with a fertility clinic in San Antonio. The clinic works with same-sex couples, and our friends had conceived a baby there, with an anonymous donor. So we drove down to San Antonio to talk to them and get started on the tests. And the paperwork."

"Ah, the paperwork," I said thoughtfully.

"Yeah." She sighed. "We were pretty naïve, I guess. We thought we could just . . . well, walk in, get it done, and walk out pregnant. But instead, there were all these tests, mostly because I'm older and this would be my first baby. And all kinds of forms to fill out, about my health and our marriage and what we were looking for in a donor. Physical characteristics, I mean, hair color, eyes, personality, education. It looked like the process was going to take forever, just to get through the first phase. And if I didn't get pregnant right away, there would be more tests and more paperwork and more trips to San Antonio — which is kind of a problem, when I'm trying to run a business."

"And that's where Ron came in," I said.

"Right. my sister Gail had a birthday party for their oldest son, and we got to talking about the situation. We all thought it was kind of a joke at first, when Ron said he'd be glad to volunteer. Everybody laughed, but then Gail said she thought it was a good idea, and just look at their boys, how healthy they were. Living examples of how our genes — her genes, which are also mine, more or less — mixed with Ron's genes to make strong kids."

"Which was pretty persuasive," I said.

Kate nodded ruefully. "Yeah, really. So Amy and I talked about it some more, and the next time we went to the clinic, we asked about it. They said, sure, we could do that, but Ron would have to drive to San Antonio and fill out a bunch of forms and go through all their tests. Like, tests for sperm viability and sexually transmitted diseases and things like that."

"Uh-oh," I said. "I see where this is going."

"Yes, exactly. Amy and I were already pretty sick of paperwork, and Ron said he couldn't see why his sperm had to be tested for viability when all anybody had to do was look at Clark and Charlie, their two little boys. We talked about it some more, and then Ron said, if we were going to do it, we should just *do* it. So we did." She ducked her head. "Not really, I mean. We didn't actually do it, but . . ."

"It's okay," I said, letting her off the hook. "Ruby explained. So did you get pregnant right away?"

"Not right away. It took several tries. In fact, Amy suggested that we ask you about herbs that might help. But then it worked, and everybody was happy." She smiled. "Amy and I are happy. And Ron is happy — really happy, I mean. This weekend, he was talking about how he hoped it would be a girl, since he and Gail already have two boys. Gail . . ." She sighed. "Gail is maybe a little jealous. She had trouble with Charlie and can't have any more. It's sort of like I'm having this baby for the two of us. She hasn't said that, of course, but that's the idea I'm getting."

The dynamics of this situation were fascinating. But troublesome. "So you and Amy were thinking that you wanted a donor who *wouldn't* be a father. And now you have a donor who wants a girl to go with his boys, and your sister is maybe wishing the baby were hers." At the look on her face, I stopped. "You see what I'm getting at, I guess."

Pressing her lips together, Kate nodded. "It's complicated, all of a sudden. And I can see that it could get even more complicated. I mean, I don't think it *would,* but who knows?" She stretched her legs, dislodging Winchester. "Anyway, after Ruby told us what you said, I thought it would be a good idea to ask you what some of the issues are. Legal issues, I mean."

I finished my elephant cookie and brushed

the crumbs off my lap. "Maybe I should tell you about an appellate court ruling that came down in Texas a few months ago. A single woman who wanted a baby made a deal with a good friend to donate his sperm. He said okay, as long as he didn't have any responsibility for the child. So they agreed — an oral agreement — that he would be just a donor, not a father." I paused. "The law makes a distinction, you see. Donors give sperm, and that's all they do. Fathers give sperm, but they are also parents and have parental responsibilities until the child comes of age."

Listening closely, Kate nodded. "Okay, I get it — so far."

"Good. But after the child was born, they changed their minds. The mom was still single and she thought it would be a good idea — in case something happened to her — if the dad was named on the birth certificate. The donor agreed. So they signed a document called an Acknowledgment of Paternity form, naming him as the father."

Kate squirmed uncomfortably. "This is a true story, huh?"

I held up three fingers. "Scout's honor. And then minds changed *again,* but this time, only hers. The mom had second thoughts and tried to retract the paternity acknowledgment, which upset the dad, because he'd decided he liked the idea of being a father. He got even more upset when the mom got married and her new spouse wanted to legally adopt the baby. The donor contested, and the case went to court. The new spouse claimed that the donor was *only* a donor and had no standing — no right — to fight the adoption."

"Ah," Kate said. "I'm beginning to understand why the distinction is important. So what happened?"

"The judge disagreed. She found the donor to be the legal father of the child, and since he opposed the adoption, she denied it." I grinned. "While she was at it, she granted him visitation rights and set his child support obligations, which maybe he hadn't counted on. Altogether, they were in court for a couple of years."

"A couple of years?" Kate was shaking her head. "Oh, gosh, China. We don't want *that* to happen."

"It won't," I said. "That situation isn't the same as yours, and the people involved made several mistakes that you won't make. But it illustrates some of the legal questions that can come up when you're not sure what you're doing."

Kate sighed. "Sounds like we should maybe have gone with the clinic and an anonymous donor."

"It might have been simpler, in the long run," I agreed. "But you're in a different place now, because you've already started the baby. The best thing would be for you and Amy to sit down with Ron and Gail and discuss the way you'd *like* it to work, ideally."

"Meaning, what Amy and I would like?"

"And what Ron and Gail would like. Does Ron want to be acknowledged as dad? How else does he want to be involved? Does he want to be responsible for the child's education? Health care? Is Gail okay with that? Do you like those ideas, or does any of that make you uncomfortable? Write everything down and discuss it. See where you agree and where you've got a conflict. If you want, I can look for some sample contracts that would give you an idea of the questions you'd want to tackle in this situation. And what you might need to do to protect your child."

Kate was nodding. "As I said, our idea of an uninvolved donor was mostly an unconscious assumption, and then we carried that over into our relationship with Ron. Thinking about it now, though, I can see the merits of acknowledging that he is our child's biological father. And that Ron's boys are half-siblings."

"Sure, if Amy agrees. And if yours is the kind of family that has a history of working things out together, rather than going to war." That got a smile out of her. I went on. "The best thing would be to get all the areas of agreement and conflict outlined. Then sit down with a lawyer who's up on the zigs and zags in current Texas law and can help you craft a contract that fits your situation."

"Would that be you?" she asked hopefully.

I smiled. "No, but I'll be glad to recommend somebody, when you're ready to get everything nailed down." I didn't have to think very hard to come up with exactly the right name. My old law school buddy, Justine Wyzinski, the Whiz, who practices family law in San Antonio. She would know how to unknot all the possible legal tangles, present and future.

"I'll talk to Amy tonight." Kate whooshed out her breath. "You have no idea how much better I feel, China. Thanks for helping me work through this."

"It's a start," I said. "Thank me when you and your family have agreed to something concrete." I leaned forward and peered at the plate of cookies. "What happened to the

336

dinosaur with the purple paws?"

"I don't know," Kate said. "I saw it there just a few minutes ago."

Lying beside the low table, Winston thumped his tail against the floor.

All three of us were up and out of the house by seven-fifteen the next morning. McQuaid drove off in his old blue pickup truck, on his way to the office that he and Blackie share in the strip center on Brazos Road, for an early morning meeting with a new client. I drove Caitie to the intersection of our lane and Limekiln Road and waited in the car until I saw her climb safely onto the big yellow school bus. Then I headed for Crockett Street, where Mrs. Birkett had promised to have breakfast waiting for me — a strawberry vanilla breakfast omelet, if I remembered correctly. I was already looking forward to it.

The late September morning was especially lovely, and the kaleidoscope of colors along the road into town was enchanting. Clumps of shining goldenrod, spires of purple prairie blazing star, and towers of Maximilian sunflowers bordered the highway. Colonies of flameleaf sumac glowed copper red in the new day's sun, their branches heavy with thick clusters of rusty red berries. Yellow cedar elm leaves fluttered like confetti-shredded sunlight onto the pavement ahead of me, and the cloudless sky above was that wonderful azure blue that heralds a low-humidity, haze-free day. My car radio — tuned to KZSM, San Marcos Community Radio — was playing old country-western favorites. I was happily humming along with George Strait's "Amarillo by Morning" and thinking about my conversation with Kate the night before, which had ended (it seemed to me) in a good place. I had the feeling that Kate and Amy would be able to work the kinks out of their baby-making, and that their child would be welcomed into a larger, inclusive, and loving family. It would be a *lucky* child, I thought, with so many grownups ready to love and protect her. Or him.

But my feel-good morning was abruptly fractured by the hard, flat voice of a radio announcer. "An Amber Alert has just been issued for Chelsea Fairlee, abducted last night from the bedroom of her home in Pecan Springs. Age, thirteen; sex, female; race, white; hair color, brown; eye color brown; height, four foot ten; weight, ninety-eight pounds. If you have any information about this missing child, please call 9-1-1 immediately."

I jerked bolt upright, clutching the steering wheel, catching my breath. My heart felt as if it were skipping every other beat and the feel-good morning was dust in my mouth. My first thought: Chelsea, sweet little Chelsea, taken from her bedroom? Who? How? And in God's name, *why? Why?*

My second thought: Caitie, cute as a pixie in her blue jeans and purple T-shirt and sandals, shrugging into her pink backpack and waving a jubilant goodbye as she climbed on the school bus. I wanted to turn around, race back to find the bus, and pull her off and into my arms, where I could hold her safe from all the ugliness of the world.

My third thought: Maggie. Oh, God, Maggie! Carl's suicide had morphed into his murder in the space of twenty-four hours. And now her daughter had been abducted. Was this an incredibly awful coincidence, or something else? Were the two events related? What was going *on*? Maggie must be out of her mind with worry. I reached for my phone.

I had to try the number several times to get through, and when I did, I knew that Maggie — who picked up the phone — was hoping that it was the kidnappers calling with a ransom demand. "Sorry," I said, "it's just me. China. I heard the Amber Alert on my car radio. How *are* you?"

To the cop on the other phone, Maggie said, "You can hang up, now, officer. This is a friend." Her voice was stretched thin, like a rubber band about to snap.

"Don't talk too long, Ms. Walker," a cop-voice said gruffly. "We need to keep this line open."

It took some doing to coax a coherent story out of her, but finally I had the gist. Lyle had left for College Station after supper the night before, anxious about an important Economics test this morning. Maggie and Chelsea had spent a quiet evening together, just the two of them. Chelsea was still deeply distraught about her father's death, so Maggie had done something she hadn't done for a long time — she'd read aloud to her daughter from *Anne of Green Gables,* one of the little girl's favorite books. When Chelsea dropped off to sleep, Maggie tucked her in, closed the door to her first-floor bedroom, and took a large glass of wine upstairs with her.

The day had been long and exhausting, the wine helped her fall asleep, and she slept deeply and without dreaming. When morning came, she got up, started breakfast, and went to wake Chelsea. That's when she discovered, to her horror, that the screen over the unlocked window had been cut and the window was open wide. Chelsea's teddy bear was lying forlornly on the floor beside the bed, and Chelsea was gone.

"Gone!" Maggie was crying. "She was kidnapped while I was asleep, China!"

"Do the police have any leads? Do they think it's connected to Carl's murder?"

"The cops are still here, looking around." Maggie gulped down a sob. "But leads — I don't know, China. I don't think they know anything yet. If they do, they haven't told me. And they haven't said anything about a connection."

"What about the chief?" I could hear voices in the background. "Is she there?"

"She was here, but she got an urgent call and had to leave. The detective who did the interview yesterday, Miller — he's still here." She gave a strangled, half-crazy laugh. "He tried to tell me that Chelsea might have done this herself."

"Done what herself?"

"Run away. He kept asking me whether we'd had a fight and what about her boyfriends. But she is still a little girl, China! The rest of the girls in her class may be boy-crazy, but if Chelsea has ever given a thought to boys, she hasn't mentioned it to me."

Just like a cop, I thought darkly, although I understood where Miller was coming from. For all he knew, Chelsea was a rebellious teen drama-queen who had run away with an older boyfriend in a bid for attention, while her mother was occupied with the legal and emotional aftermath of her father's death. But Maggie's daughter was a shy, quiet girl — a child still, really — who wouldn't do something like that. Who could have taken her? Where? Why? Why, why, *why*?

"Anyway, the detective has changed his mind," Maggie went on. She was making an effort to keep her voice under control. "He backed off the runaway idea when one of the cops found an empty injection vial beside the driveway. It was labeled scopolamine hydro-something. They think she was drugged."

"Scopolamine," I whispered. *Scopolamine.* One of the world's scariest drugs, also known as the "Demon's breath." It's an alkaloid derived from Datura and other plants in the *Brugmansia* genus of the nightshade family — more recognizable, maybe, under its common names, belladonna and angel's trumpet. I've seen these

342

psychoactive plants sold in nurseries without a warning label, yet they're so notorious that in their native jungles, mothers warn their children not to play beneath the beautiful trumpet-shaped yellow-ivory flowers, where they might breathe the pollen. All parts of these plants have a powerful narcotic effect that can knock you out and keep you out for hours. But this isn't a recreational drug you can readily buy on the street, at least in this country.

"Yeah," Maggie said. She took a breath and let it out. "Our driveway curves around the back of the condo to the garage, you know. They think the guy who took her gave her an injection that knocked her out. A predator who knew exactly what he was doing. Like, maybe he'd even been stalking her for a while." She swallowed a half-choked sob. "Oh, China, what am I going to *do*? They've got to find her. They've just *got* to!"

"You need somebody with you," I said. "I would come over right now, but one of my Crockett Street neighbors is expecting me for breakfast. It's sort of a duty call, though, and I can probably duck out in an hour or so. I'll phone Ruby and let her know what's happened. She and Laurel can pinch-hit for me at the shop and I'll spend the day —"

"No, you won't," Maggie broke in, trying to be tough. "I mean, I'd *love* it, but my sister is flying in from Chicago this morning. She decided to come when she heard about Carl. She'll be here in an hour or so. Edith is kind of . . . well, she's a little hard to deal with. Bossy. Take-charge. Dictatorial. She bugs the hell out of me. I wouldn't wish her on anybody, especially my best friend."

"Even bossier than you?" I asked, pretending incredulity. "I don't believe it."

She didn't laugh. "Oh, twice as bad. The minute Edith steps into this house, she'll declare that she's in charge of the investigation. It'll be all downhill after that. Go do your breakfast and go on to the shop, China."

I heard male voices and the scraping of footsteps in the background. Hastily, Maggie said, "I've got to go now. They want me to keep this line free in case the kidnapper calls, asking for a ransom." She stopped trying to be tough and her voice quavered. "Just pray that they find my little girl, China."

I thought of the last time I had seen Chelsea, standing in the kitchen doorway in her pink shirt and shorts and pink flip-flops, her teddy bear under her arm, her brown hair tousled and her eyes and nose red from weeping. I don't pray often, on the theory that we humans make our own messes and our deities have better things to do than to clean up after us. But this was an extraordinary situation.

"I'm praying, Maggie," I said.

And I was.

CHAPTER THIRTEEN

Connie stands up behind her desk as Sheila comes into the office shortly after eight a.m. "Oh, good, you're here. Billie Jean is —"

"I'm not here," Sheila says shortly. "I'm down the hall, in the interview room for the next hour or so. And I've made up my mind about filling your job. You're right. It won't hurt me to quit at five, like normal folks." She grins. "Let's go with Fernandez on a trial basis, say, for three weeks. If she doesn't work out, I'll consider Billie Jean."

"Yes, ma'am." Connie smiles. "I think you're making a good move." Her smile fades. Her mouth is set, her forehead creased with concern. "Any leads in the little girl's kidnapping?"

Connie has her own police scanner, so she heard the call from Dispatch at the same time Sheila did, in the middle of a six a.m. breakfast. Sheila left her egg and toast on the table, pulled on her uniform, called

346

Rambo, and dashed for her unmarked Crown Victoria. There aren't many Amber Alerts in Pecan Springs. Actually, there haven't been *any* since the beginning of the year, unless you count the eight-year-old who went off with his grandmother without telling his mother and had every police department between Austin and San Antonio on the lookout — until the grandmother's car was spotted at a favorite fishing hole on the Pecan River. The kidnapping of a child touches everyone who hears it. It's news. Big news, especially since this victim is the daughter of a professor who was murdered just a few days earlier.

Which simply cannot be a coincidence, Sheila thinks. It's all tied together somehow: the orchid smuggling, the murder, the kidnapping. She shakes her head regretfully. "No, no leads," she replies to Connie's question. "Not yet. But I'm about to talk to Jessica Nelson and Logan Gardner, so maybe that will change."

When the call came from Dispatch, Sheila had immediately phoned Miller and instructed him to send officers to check on Gardner, Selms, and Haley and determine their whereabouts from ten the previous night to the current time. Forty minutes later, the reports were in. Selms' and Haley's

347

wives vouched for their being at home in bed all night. Gardner's roommate, however, had a different story.

"Logan's got a girlfriend in Austin," he'd said. "He didn't come home last night, so I guess he's staying with her." But when he was asked for the woman's name and address, he'd only shrugged. "Never asked," he said. "None of my business." He had frowned. "So why are you looking for him? What's he done?"

"Put out a BOLO for him," Sheila said tersely, when the report came in. Twenty minutes later, though, she got a call from Jessica. The reporter had also heard the Amber Alert and had (of course) made an immediate connection to Carl Fairlee's murder. She and Hark Hibler, the *Enterprise* editor and publisher, had huddled quickly and come up with a decision.

"As journalists, Hark and I agree that it's our job to keep our sources confidential," Jessica had said. "But a child's kidnapping is an urgent and extraordinary situation. I have some information about Carl Fairlee's orchid operation that may help your investigation. I'm willing to talk to you. And my source has volunteered to come with me."

"Your source?" Sheila knew, of course. She had noticed Jessica having lunch with

348

Logan Gardner the day before. "That would be —"

"But this won't come free," Jessica said quickly. "Hark and I want access to the kidnapping story. Full access. As it happens."

"I'll do what I can," Sheila said. "That's the best I can do right now."

Jessica hadn't hesitated. "That'll work. Thanks, Chief."

Sheila had been reluctant to leave the Walker house, hoping that the kidnapper would call with a ransom demand, or a neighbor would arrive with information, or Chelsea — a cute, innocent-looking thirteen-year-old, to judge from her photo — would somehow free herself and find rescue. The thought of the little girl being drugged, then pulled out of her bed and dragged out the window made her shudder and want to clasp her hands around Noah, holding him safe under her heart and away from the real world and its frightening ugliness.

But there was nothing more to be done at the Walker house except wait for further developments. And Jessica Nelson was bringing Logan Gardner in. So Sheila had left Miller to continue the kidnap investigation — with the promise to call her cell the

349

minute something turned up — and had driven to the station, where Connie had been expecting her to interview Billie Jean.

"Can I get you anything, chief?" Connie asks. She is still wearing her look of evident concern, and Sheila wonders whether she combed her hair before she dashed out of the house. She knows she left without her makeup. She glances down to make sure that all her buttons are buttoned and is chagrined when she finds one gaping. How long has she been unbuttoned?

"Anything on the registration on that Volkswagen?" Sheila fumbles with the button.

"DMV says they're faxing a list that somebody compiled by hand, but I haven't seen it yet. Apparently, a few of their systems are back online, but not all of them." Connie gives a rueful shrug. "The official word is that they've experienced a minor 'security incident,' but one of my friends in Accounting over there says it's a system-wide hack. They won't admit it because they don't want the media telling the world they've been compromised."

Sheila rolls her eyes. "Probably the Russians. Well, if you can't get me that VW, make it three coffees." Answering Connie's unspoken question, she adds, "Jessica Nelson and Logan Gardner are waiting for me in the interview room. I came to get the orchid." She steps into her office and takes the terrarium from the shelf. She wants Gardner to positively identify it, to be sure that Walker hasn't pulled a fast one. If she has, China will have some explaining to do.

"Three coffees, coming up," Connie says. At the door, she pauses apprehensively. "Do you really think it's the Russians?"

"Probably not," Sheila says. "Probably North Korea."

Jessica is already seated in the interview room where she and Miller questioned Walker the day before. Sheila notices enviously that Jessie is wearing those luscious red heels, and that she looks terrific in a gray pencil skirt, a silky white tank, and a chunky red statement necklace. Her slender young figure and crisply professional appearance make Sheila feel ancient. And huge. As large as a rhino. No, an elephant. An awkward, ungainly, pregnant elephant. An elephant carrying twins.

"Hello, Jessica," she says, and puts the terrarium in the middle of the table. The orchid looks limp and spindly, as if it's about to expire. Without its bloom, there's nothing to distinguish it from any other orchid, so it would be easy for Walker to have slipped in a ringer.

With a smile, Jessica says hello. She is alone and Sheila frowns. "I thought your source was supposed to be here, too. Did he decide not to come?"

Instead of answering, Jessica looks up innocently. "Got any leads on the kidnapping?"

"Not yet," Sheila says. "The team is still at the Walker house."

"Full access," Jessica reminds her. "When you come up with something, I want to know."

"You'll get it when I can release it," Sheila says. She is about to say more when she hears the door open. Without turning, she says, "Thanks, Con. Just put the coffee on the table."

"It's just me," Charlaine Rudolph says apologetically.

"Charlaine?" Sheila whirls, surprised. What the hell is *she* doing here? The woman's primly coiffed auburn hair is unchanged (maybe it's a wig?), but today she is wearing a black skirt with a gray blouse and black beads and she has traded her tortoise-shell glasses for gold rims. She is carrying a brown leather briefcase.

"You were expecting someone else?" Jessica asks with a chuckle. "Like, maybe the hunky guy you saw me having lunch with?" She takes out a reporter's notebook and puts it on the table in front of her, with a pencil.

Damn, Sheila thinks, and hopes the BOLO will net Gardner. To Jessica, she says, "Actually, I was. It wouldn't be the first time I've been wrong."

Nervously, Charlaine takes a seat. She is putting her briefcase on the floor when Connie comes in with a tray — coffee, packets of sugar and pink stuff and a jar of powdered creamer.

When she has gone and everyone has coffee, Sheila picks up the remote that controls the camera. "How much of this interview is on the record, Jessica?"

"All of it, as far as Hark and I are concerned," Jessica says. "We're hoping that we know something that will help you find the girl." She pauses. "But I'd prefer that we not video this, if it's all the same to you."

"Charlaine?" Sheila asks.

Charlaine nods uneasily.

Sheila considers. Both of these women are here voluntarily. If something important emerges, she can always require them to return. She puts the remote on the table and takes out her own notebook.

"Let's get started then. Charlaine, maybe

you can help me out. Do you recognize this plant?" She gestures to the terrarium in the middle of the table.

Charlaine pushes her glasses up on her nose. "Well, I recognize the terrarium, so I suppose the plant is the demon orchid. The one that went missing from Dr. Fairlee's greenhouse." She leans forward, examines it critically, and shakes her head. "I'm glad it's been found, but I have to say that the poor thing looks simply terrible. You need to find somebody to take good care of it. Carl — Dr. Fairlee would just *hate* to see his precious orchid looking like a supermarket refugee."

"Thank you," Sheila says, and makes a note. She turns to Jessica. "For the record," she goes on, "you're here voluntarily because you want to discuss orchid smuggling — a story you're currently working on. I understand that Charlaine is here, and also voluntarily, because she is one of your sources. It's my understanding that this discussion may be relevant to the murder of Dr. Fairlee and perhaps to the kidnapping of his daughter, Chelsea. Correct?"

"It may be, although I don't have any direct evidence relating to either crime." Jessica gives Sheila a straight-on look. "Since the beginning of the year, I've been working on a story about plant theft and the international trade in stolen plants — not just orchids, but cactus, too. And I didn't start with Dr. Fairlee. I began my investigation at the other end, at the various points where many of the plants are coming into the US. During my investigation, I met a man in South Texas who accepts illegal plants as they are smuggled across the border at Brownsville, then redirects them — often via the postal service or FedEx — to collectors and growers around the country."

"You'll give me his name?" Sheila asks, making rapid notes.

Jessica doesn't hesitate. "I will. But I'm confident that he had nothing to do with Fairlee's murder or the child's kidnapping. He was diagnosed with terminal cancer three months ago. If you want to talk to him, you'd better hurry." She taps her pencil on her notebook. "He told me that one of his biggest customers lived right here in Pecan Springs. To say I was surprised would be an understatement. I was even more surprised when I discovered that his customer was a professor I once had for a botany class. And that this professor kept the smuggled plants right out in plain sight of God and everybody else, in his greenhouse on top of the Plant Sciences building."

"You're talking about Dr. Fairlee," Sheila says. She tastes her coffee, which is even more insipid than usual.

"Right. Carl Fairlee. I did some more digging, talked to more people, and identified him as the hub of an extended network of plant suppliers and buyers. He wasn't just doing legitimate academic research in that greenhouse, he was running an orchid-growing business. He obtained orchids from sources across the country and around the world, many of them legitimate. Enough, anyway, to give him a good cover." Jessica picks up her coffee, sips, makes a face, and puts it down. "However, he got quite a few of his orchids — the best ones, really — from the black market. In fact, at this moment, there are many rare, wild-gathered, illegal orchids and their offspring in his greenhouse. But one orchid looks pretty much like another unless they're in bloom, or unless you know its DNA, which most people don't. So it was pretty easy for him to conceal what he was doing."

Sheila remembers the hundreds of small glass jars with green plants growing in them. Cloned wildings? Rare orchids on their way to or from the black market?

"What did he do with the plants?" she asks. She has heard parts of this story from Jennifer Haley, but she's glad to have a corroborating informant.

"He sometimes sold the wild-gathered plants directly to people who were looking for specific species. But more often he used them for stock plants, propagating them in his greenhouse and selling them to collectors and hobbyists through regional orchid shows. He also worked with other registered orchid growers, supplying them with stock plants that they would then propagate and sell to their customers. In the trade, it's called orchid laundering."

"Fits," Sheila says wryly, jotting down the phrase.

"Plus, he had a website."

"A website?" This is news.

"I'll give you the URL. It's not under *his* name, of course. But it's his, and I can prove it." Jessica pauses. "I've been told that Fairlee made his academic reputation by studying the vanilla orchid. But the man lived and breathed orchids of all kinds, and he made them his business. The rarer and harder to find, the better."

"Margaret Walker — his ex-wife — is also in the orchid business," Sheila says. "Did you turn up any indication that her garden center is involved in this . . . this orchid laundering?"

"No," Jessica says. "So far as I know, Walker is legitimate." She pauses. "The people who are propagating these illegal orchids make a pretty reasonable argument, at least to my mind. They point out that tropical habitat is being destroyed. If they're left in the wild, these plants will soon be as extinct as the dodo bird. The best way to preserve a vanishing species is to put the plants in a greenhouse, propagate them, and distribute them. There's something to that, you know."

"There is," Sheila says. "But they need to change the law, not violate it." She frowns. Jessica's information is interesting, but it isn't specific enough. She needs people. Names, connections, a motive for murder — and for kidnapping. Something that will help her tie it all together.

"You say that Fairlee was a hub," she says. "Can you identify anyone in his network — supplier or buyer — who might have had a reason to kill him and kidnap his daughter?"

Jessica shakes her head regretfully. "I've been asking myself that same question, but I don't have any answers." She tears a page out of her notebook and slides it across the table. "I put this list together this morning

— a half-dozen names, addresses, phone numbers, all on the supply side. If there's a connection to the child's kidnapping or to Fairlee's murder, I hope you find it."

"Thank you." Sheila understands the deliberation that must have gone into the surrender of this list — the struggle, in Jessica's mind, between confidentiality and collaboration. Some people claimed that journalists who cooperated with cops would lose the trust of their audience. On the other hand, it has always seemed to Sheila that a reporter was more likely to lose her readers' trust if they found out that she'd refused to reveal important information about a murder.

But her heart sinks when she glances over the names Jessica has given her. There are no local people, nobody closer than Houston and Brownsville. The other addresses are in Los Angeles, Miami, San Francisco. She doesn't recognize any of the names.

"What about Logan Gardner?" she says. "He's not on your list, but he was in that greenhouse every day. He would be able to identify those plants. He must have known what was going on. Maybe he was even actively involved."

Sheila has already seen the video of yesterday afternoon's interview. Gardner conceded that he had a general idea about Fairlee's orchid operation, but he denies any involvement in it. He claimed to have been interested only in the hybrid vanilla orchid and apprehensive that he may have been cheated out of his share when Fairlee filed for the patent under his name only. Sheila could see Gardner as a possible murderer — he seems to have the strongest motive of anybody on their current list and is licensed to carry. But what possible motive could compel him to kidnap Fairlee's young daughter?

Jessica shrugs. "Logan told me he didn't want to know about Fairlee's orchid business. If he asked too many questions or looked too closely at the new plants coming in, he was afraid Fairlee might find a reason to kick him out of his doctoral program. He was banking on that vanilla hybrid to get him a teaching and research position at a university. It was supposed to be the open door to the rest of his professional life." She smiles crookedly. "But maybe you'll be able to get more out of him than I have. Especially if he's put in front of a grand jury."

Sheila looks at Charlaine expectantly. "I assume that you're here because you have something significant to contribute to this investigation, Charlaine." Somberly, she adds, "Let's not forget that a little girl is missing. Something you know may help us find her."

"Yes, I know," Charlaine says. "It's just awful, isn't it? Just horrible." She stirs uneasily in her chair, adjusts her glasses, and sighs. "Where do you want me to start?"

"How about at the beginning," Sheila suggests.

Charlaine nods. "Well, I guess it began when Carl — Dr. Fairlee — started coming into the departmental office more often. Mostly, it was just to chat about what was going on in the department." She smiles faintly. "He liked to stay current on the gossip. But then he started complimenting me on the way I kept the paperwork moving. There's a *lot* of it, and it has to be done right, or you have to do it again."

Sheila nods, remembering. She had thought she was escaping the bureaucracy when she moved to the police department. Wrong. She was only trading one bureaucracy for another.

"Well, Carl wasn't very good at that. Paperwork. I mean." Visibly nervous, Charlaine stops, clears her throat, and tries again. "He was a *very* smart man, you know, but he had never learned to type and he actually hated entering data into a computer.

361

He said it was because he made too many mistakes. He was afraid of misspelling those Latin plant names and he got his fingers mixed up when he tried to type numbers."

"Not a very good trait in a scientist, I should think," Sheila remarks drily. "Making mistakes, I mean."

"Actually, his wife had always done his typing." Charlaine clasps her hands in front of her on the table. "Anyway, he said he was worried because he didn't have a good inventory of his plants. I felt sorry for him, so I offered to help."

"Help how?" Sheila asks.

"I did a complete inventory, along with the source for each plant, the date he acquired it, and other notes. It was easier for me to do it on *my* computer, on a spread sheet. Every so often, I'd print it out for him. He would write his research notes on the printout, and I would type them in. That's how we kept it all up to date."

"I see," Sheila says. "You did this on your own time, I suppose."

"Oh, of course." Charlaine draws herself up. "I would never neglect my responsibilities to the other faculty members. Or to Dr. Selms."

"Of course," Sheila murmurs. "And by this time, you and Dr. Fairlee were . . . dating?" They were probably sleeping together, but that wasn't relevant here.

Charlaine colors, nods, and hurries on. "After I had been maintaining his plant list for a few months, Carl asked me if I would like to help him manage his sales at orchid shows. So I started going with him on weekend trips. It was actually a lot of fun — figuring out which plants to take, getting the tables set up, talking to customers, seeing how much they wanted what Carl had to sell. And they were willing to pay for it, too. But after a while, I began to realize that things were not quite . . . ." She pushes her glasses higher on her nose. "Not quite on the up and up, I suppose you might say."

"Can you be specific?" Sheila asks.

"Well, some of the plants went for astonishing prices — eight hundred dollars for a vial about the size of a test tube containing a stem with a single pair of leaves and roots like little white threads. It made me . . . well, anxious. I asked Carl about it, but he said that was just the way all businesses worked. If there's only one or two of something, the price will be quite high."

"Did Logan Gardner go along on any of these trips?"

Charlaine shakes her head. "It seemed to me that Carl deliberately kept him out. It was like he didn't want Logan in on that side of things." She pauses, then hurries on.

"Anyway, as time went on, I got more and more uncomfortable. Raising plants in a university facility, then selling them and keeping the money — well, it all seemed sort of underhanded, somehow. It wasn't fair to members of the department, especially to Dr. Selms, who has always tried to be a good friend to Carl, even when that wasn't easy."

"So Dr. Selms knew nothing about any of this?"

Charlaine shakes her head. "I don't think he wanted to know. Academic people are pretty *laissez faire.* They don't pry into what their colleagues are doing. And about that time . . ." She hesitates, sighs, and starts again. "Well, about that time, Carl told me he was seeing Jennifer Haley." She looks down at her clasped hands. "There had been others — students. But they were just passing fancies. I convinced myself they didn't matter, where Carl and I were concerned. He told me that Jennifer *did* matter, and that was the end of us. As a couple, I mean. He stopped asking me to go on trips with him, but he still wanted me to keep his plant inventory." She glances at Jessica. "Then Jessica came around asking questions and I learned about her investigation. She called it a 'research project.' "

"Well, it is," Jessica says with a small smile. "That's what reporting is, you know. One research project after another."

"So Jessica talked you into sharing Fairlee's plant records with her?" Sheila asks.

"Not right away," Jessica says. "She was pretty stubborn. She held out."

"I didn't want to be disloyal to Carl," Charlaine says. "But the fairness issue bothered me."

And so did his relationship with Jennifer Haley, Sheila thinks, but she doesn't say this out loud. She leans forward. "You have the plant inventories? And the records of the plant sales?"

"The files are on my computer. I've brought hard copies and a thumb drive." Charlaine reaches for the briefcase beside her chair and takes out several thick manila folders filled with printouts. "I think you'll find everything you need here," she says, putting them on the table. "The inventory lists the sources of his plants, as well as the names of people he sold to — dozens of them — and the amounts of the sales."

"Do you know whether he owed anybody money?" Sheila asks. "Did anybody owe *him* money?"

"He and his customers sometimes had some rather heated discussions about money," Charlaine says. "But I can't tell you much about that end of it. I was focused mostly on keeping track of the plants."

Sheila leans back in her chair and puffs out a breath. Her next question is blunt. "You seem to know more about Dr. Fairlee's activities — legal and illegal — than anybody else. Do you know who killed him? Or who might have had a reason to kidnap his daughter?"

"Oh, poor Chelsea." Charlaine's voice trembles and tears flood her eyes. "No," she says, barely above a whisper. "I don't know. I wish I did." She puts a hand on the stack of folders. "But maybe you'll find something in the records that will help. I hope you do."

Sheila turns to Jessica. "How about you, Jessie? Do you know?"

"I'm sorry, I don't," Jessica says. "While I've been calling this a smuggling ring, it's not exactly like the Mafia, you know. Most of these orchid people are ordinary folks who love these plants and want to have them and *share* them. They're worried that the orchids will become extinct if they don't find their way into the commercial trade. But they're prevented from trading the plants legally by environmental laws."

"Ordinary people?" Sheila says quietly. "They might not be the Sopranos, but they don't sound like the First Baptist choir, either. And *somebody* killed him. And took the child." Her cell phone rings. She reaches for it quickly, hoping it's Miller, with word that Chelsea has been found — alive.

It isn't Miller.

Sheila listens for a moment. Then, with a quick intake of breath, she stands, shoving her chair back so abruptly that it falls over.

"On my way," she says and clicks off. To the women at the table, she says, "This interview is over, at least for now." At the door, she pauses and turns.

"Come on, Jessica," she says. "You wanted access? You've got it."

CHAPTER FOURTEEN

MRS. BIRKETT'S STRAWBERRY VANILLA OMELET

1 cup hulled, halved strawberries
3 tablespoons liqueur (kirsch, brandy or
  Cointreau)
1/2 teaspoon vanilla extract
Seeds from 2-inch section of vanilla bean
4 eggs, separated
3 tablespoons sugar
4 tablespoons cream, whipped
2 tablespoons butter
Mint sprigs for garnish

In a bowl, toss the strawberries and the liqueur. Cut off 2-inch section of vanilla bean, split, and remove seeds with tip of knife. Add seeds and vanilla extract to strawberries and set aside to blend.

Beat together the egg yolks and sugar until creamy, then fold in the whipped cream. In a clean, dry bowl, beat the egg whites until stiff. Gently fold beaten whites into the egg yolk mixture.

Melt the butter in a nonstick omelet pan. Add the egg mixture, tilting pan to evenly cover the bottom. With heat-proof spatula, gently lift and push cooked edges toward the center so that uncooked mixture can flow underneath. Continue until no liquid egg remains and surface of egg is visibly thickened. Shake to loosen, using the spatula where necessary.

Stir strawberries. Spoon 2/3 onto half of the omelet, fold the other half over, and slide onto a warm serving plate. Cut the omelet in half, divide between two warmed plates, and top with remaining strawberries. Garnish with mint and serve immediately to 2 appreciative diners.

It was nearly eight when Mrs. Birkett opened the door to my knock and led me past the living room — comfortable with a doily-decorated recliner in front of the television and a pair of cats asleep on a corduroy-covered sofa — and straight down the hall to her kitchen, a light, friendly room at the back of her old two-story house. The room boasted cheerful ivy-patterned wall-paper, an old-fashioned Hoosier cupboard in the corner, and a wide over-the-sink window framed in ruffled green curtains, with a view of an immense elm tree and an attractive white-painted cottage next door. A large cage sat beside the window, and a stunning green parrot with an orange beak and splashes of red and blue under its wings preened itself on a perch.

Mrs. Birkett had inherited the house and the cottage from her grandmother, Jane Crow, who lived here for most of her life. Both are located at the foot of Crockett, where the street becomes a cul-de-sac, ending in the thick tangle of woods — junipers, live oaks, and wild pecans — that borders Little Cypress Creek. A couple of years ago, an out-of-town developer tried to buy up all the properties at this end of Crockett, aiming to tear down the houses and build a two-hundred-unit apartment complex. Mrs. Birkett not only refused to sell but rallied the other homeowners, most of them families with small children, against the idea. The developer finally gave up and went away, leaving Mrs. Birkett with a well-earned reputation as a neighborhood advocate. Thanks to her, the dense woods are still home to birds and squirrels and deer, and people can still walk the shaded trail along the creek.

Mrs. Birkett's grandmother was widely respected for her knowledge about the medicinal plants she grew in her backyard herb garden and gathered in the nearby woods along the creek and in the fields around the town. Back in the nineteenth and early twentieth centuries, doctors prescribed plant medicines almost exclusively, and Jane Crow kept the village pharmacy supplied and sold cultivated and wild-gathered herbs to those who sought her out. She had a stillroom just off the kitchen, where she distilled cordials, extracted essential oils, brewed herbal teas and beers, and concocted herbal medicines upon request — and she had a great many requests. Mrs. Birkett had lived with her grandmother as a child and treasures the memory of playing at her grandmother's feet while "Grandma Jane" worked with herbs.

A widow, Mrs. Crow supplemented her small income by renting the attractive two-bedroom frame cottage next door, which she owned. Despite its age, it has been well maintained. Mrs. Birkett rents it, furnished, to young women college students at an affordable monthly rate.

In fact, as I remembered, Shelley Harmon (the girl who died on Carl Fairlee's Mexican field trip) had lived in the cottage with one of her girlfriends while she was going to CTSU. The little house is a great deal more pleasant than a student apartment, and it isn't far from the campus. It's just a couple of blocks from our shops, too, where Shelley worked on weekends and during the summers of her junior and senior years. I had thought of her — such a lively, pretty girl — as I parked on the street and walked up the path to the porch. I wondered who was living in the cottage now and remembered Mrs. Birkett's reason for inviting me to breakfast. "I have a new renter in the little house next door," she had said, "and something about her is worrying me. I'd like to talk to you about it."

In the kitchen, Mrs. Birkett gestured to a chair at the round oak table in the middle of the room, a relic of a time when large families gathered for meals. "Come and sit down, dear," she said, and poured me a cup of coffee and a glass of orange juice. She wore a blue apron over her blue cotton housedress and her white hair was pulled up into a loose bun on the back of her head, giving her a distinctly grandmotherly look. "I've already halved the strawberries," she added, "and mixed them with a little Cointreau, so all I have to do is make our omelet."

"And I smell warm cinnamon buns," I said appreciatively. "And bacon. Yum!"

"Yum!" the parrot shouted. "Bacon. Oh, boy!"

"That's Mr. Spock," Mrs. Birkett said. "He belonged to a neighbor who couldn't keep him any longer, so he came to stay with me." She frowned at him. "He's a very clever bird with quite a vocabulary, but I'm afraid he's too noisy for me. I need to find him a new home."

"Live long and prosper," Spock replied cheerfully. "Bacon. Oh, boy!"

"His former owner was a Star Trek fan?" I guessed.

Mrs. Birkett nodded. "He only gets bacon when I cook a full breakfast. And I only do that when I have company. Thank you for giving me an excuse."

"You're welcome," Spock said, and cooed.

"My pleasure, definitely," I murmured. My mind was full of Chelsea's kidnapping and my heart was with Maggie, waiting in suspense for word about her little girl. But Mrs. Birkett didn't know Maggie or Chelsea and I wouldn't be doing her a favor if I darkened her day with the story. Instead, I sipped my coffee gratefully, focused my attention on my hostess, and asked her to tell me about the dish she was about to make.

"Strictly speaking," she explained, "this is a mousseline omelet. It's put together like a soufflé but cooked in a skillet on top of the stove instead of baked in a soufflé dish. It uses the French technique of beating the egg whites and yolks separately, then folding them together. A little cream makes it richer, so it's especially good with a jam filling or fruit."

"Logic is good," Spock announced. "Logic. Logic."

"Thank you, Spock," she said, in a half-irritated tone. As he replied, "You're welcome," she picked up a spoon and stirred the bowl of ruby-red strawberries. "But really, it's the vanilla that makes it special. I love to use the seeds when I have them, and of course, pure vanilla extract." She wrinkled her nose. "The synthetic stuff is okay in baked goods, most of the time. But this omelet requires the real thing, seems to me."

"So you're using the vanilla beans you bought at the shop yesterday."

"Of course," she said with a little laugh, pulling a pod out of a jar. She sliced a two-inch section from one end, split it, and scraped out the fragrant black seeds with the point of her paring knife. "I always like to do this just as I'm ready to use the seeds." She stirred them into the strawberries. "That way, you don't lose any of the magical fragrance."

I leaned forward and took a deep sniff. "It's easy to see why people are willing to work so hard for it," I said, thinking of what I had seen when I was in Mexico — and what I had read about vanilla robberies and even murders. But I kept that to myself, too. Sometimes we don't need to know *all* the details.

Mrs. Birkett dropped the pieces of split, scraped pod into a small glass jar filled with sugar, capped it, and shook it to mix. "I love vanilla sugar in my coffee and tea. Smoothies, too." She put the jar on a shelf, went to the fridge, and came back with a carton of eggs. "These are from Mrs. Sanger's little Leghorn flock," she said, opening the carton. "She lives on the next street over — close enough that I can hear her rooster crowing in the morning."

Spock cocked his head, fixed one bright eye on the eggs, and then lifted his head and crowed exactly like a rooster.

I couldn't help laughing, which encouraged Spock to crow again. "The eggs are very nice," I said, although these were white

375

eggs and not quite as large and pretty as Caitie's brown eggs. "But Spock is incredible."

"He is, isn't he?" Mrs. Birkett sighed. "You can almost carry on a conversation with that bird. I just wish he weren't so *loud.*"

"Logic is good," Spock said. "Make it so." Bobbing his head, he subsided into a background chatter of mutters and grumbles, punctuated by periodic squeaks that sounded like a highly rhythmic, repetitive rap.

"I always like to use Grandma Jane's old rotary hand-crank eggbeater." Mrs. Birkett opened a drawer and took it out. "It's quicker than a whisk and quieter than an electric mixer. And it makes me think of her." She took a couple of bowls out of the cupboard and put them on the table.

Searching for something to talk about — something other than Chelsea's kidnapping or vanilla murders — I remembered the reason I was here.

"Yesterday at the shop, you mentioned that you've rented your cottage," I said, "and that something about the arrangement is worrying you. Do you want to tell me about it?"

"Thank you, yes." She took an egg out of

the carton and broke it expertly, draining the egg white into one bowl and dropping the unbroken yolk into the other. "I wonder if you remember Shelley Harmon. She and a friend lived in my cottage a few years ago."

"I *do* remember her," I replied. "As a matter of fact, I was thinking of her just a few moments ago. Shelley worked for Ruby and me at the shops, so we knew her pretty well — and liked her, too. I've always thought that the university made a mistake, not releasing the details about her death. It seems to have been an accident, but the way the university authorities handled it left too much to the imagination."

"I couldn't agree more," Mrs. Birkett said. "Shelley was a lovely girl who did quite a few little chores for me in return for part of the rent — weeding the garden, washing windows, helping with the grocery shopping. I felt I knew her well, and Beth Craig, too, her roommate. Beth was one of the students in the van when it went off the road and down a steep hill." She paused, adding emphatically, "And it wasn't an accident."

"Really?" I remembered Beth, a tall, blond, athletic girl, who had come into the shop several times when Shelley was working there. "Did she tell you what happened?

There were lots of rumors floating around, but nothing very substantive. I heard several versions — all the way from a wreck that was caused by a rogue monkey to a shoot-out with drug smugglers."

"Beth said the van was fired on." Mrs. Birkett reached for another egg.

I stared at her. "Fired on? Drug smugglers, then?"

She shook her head. "Vanilla thieves."

I was shocked, but not surprised, not really. The price of vanilla had gone through the roof since Cyclone Enawo had hit Madagascar, and it took a lot less work to steal vanilla than to grow it. Theft was an increasing hazard for vanilla farmers, who sometimes lost their whole year's harvest to thieves before it was cured — often before it had even fully ripened. But surely a rented van full of American college kids couldn't have been mistaken for a truck with a load of vanilla beans. So there must have been something else, something —

"How in the world did it happen?" I asked.

"Beth said there had already been several robberies on the road." Deftly, Mrs. Birkett broke the egg and separated it. "The local people told Dr. Fairlee he ought to take a different road, especially because they were following a truck loaded with bags of ripe

378

vanilla pods — an easy target. He insisted that everything would be all right, but he was wrong."

"He *insisted*?"

"Beth said that even their guide tried to get him to change his mind. The thieves were dressed like soldiers and armed — with assault rifles. They had set up a barricade so they could stop and plunder any vehicles that were loaded with vanilla beans. The guide told Dr. Fairlee to wait — that the robbers would take what they wanted off the truck and then let them pass. But he panicked and turned around. The thieves fired into the rear of the van as he drove away, and he veered off the road and hit a tree." Her mouth tightened. "Shelley died of a gunshot wound. She was shot in the back."

Oh, God. So that's how it happened. I sucked in my breath. "You've heard, I suppose. About Dr. Fairlee, I mean?"

"That he killed himself?" There was something between sadness and a wry understanding in her voice. "Yes. I heard it on television yesterday evening. And I wondered, you know."

"Wondered what?"

"Whether it had anything to do with Shelley. His suicide, I mean."

I opened my mouth to correct her but decided against it. The police hadn't released the news about his murder yet. She would know soon enough. So I went back to the subject. "Was Beth injured in the wreck?"

"She had a concussion." Mrs. Birkett broke another egg, the white neatly into one bowl, the yolk just as neatly into the other. "I was quite worried about her for a while. But she recovered. She transferred to the University of Texas at the end of the spring semester. She said it was just too painful for her to live here without her friend. They had been together for several years."

"I guess I'm not surprised," I said.

"Neither was I." Mrs. Birkett rinsed her hands at the sink and dried them on a towel. "Actually, I heard from Beth just a couple of weeks ago. I thought she might have gotten over Shelley's death by now, but she hasn't. She's upset with the university for not doing a more thorough investigation — and especially for not releasing the facts. And she's still furious with Dr. Fairlee. She says that if he'd paid attention to the warnings instead of brushing them off, Shelley would be alive right now. She thinks he ought to have been charged. Negligent homicide, or something." She looked at me.

"You've had experience with this kind of thing. What do you think?"

I straightened in my chair. What did I think? To tell the truth, while Mrs. Birkett was talking, I had been wondering if Beth might have been angry enough at Carl Fairlee to kill him, in revenge for her friend's death. I didn't think so, or maybe I didn't *want* to think so. But I knew I would have to mention this conversation to Sheila, as a possible area of investigation. In my former incarnation as a criminal lawyer, I had come to understand that revenge is as powerful a motive for murder as sex and money.

But Mrs. Birkett wouldn't want to hear my speculations about Beth. "What do I think?" I repeated. "I think that making a charge against Dr. Fairlee would have been politically difficult for the Mexican police. And in the absence of a criminal charge by the local authorities, the university could hardly take a unilateral punitive action. What's more, if they admitted any kind of liability on Dr. Fairlee's part, they were opening themselves to a suit." I paused. "In fact, I heard that Shelley's mother was so distraught and angry that she'd hired a lawyer and was planning to sue both Dr. Fairlee and CTSU for wrongful death."

"I heard that, too," Mrs. Birkett said. "In fact, Beth told me that Mrs. Taylor — Shelley's mother — had gotten in touch with her several times. Apparently, she had talked to the Mexican authorities, to the students in the van with Shelley, and even to their guide on that trip, Señor Aguado. She said she was trying to find out as much as she could about the accident because she was planning to sue Dr. Fairlee for putting them into a dangerous situation."

"Easier to claim than to prove," I said. "And in the end, I guess Shelley's mother and her attorney decided they didn't have a strong enough case. There's a two-year statute of limitations for wrongful death. The time has run out and I haven't heard that they've filed."

"Illogical," Spock said, breaking off his private rap. He scooted along his perch from one end to the other, clicking his beak. "Illogical, zoological, biological."

Mrs. Birkett sighed. "There's more, I'm afraid — something I find very uncomfortable to talk about. I suppose I'm terribly old-fashioned."

"Old-fashioned?"

She took a breath. "Beth says that Dr. Fairlee should also have been charged with sexual misconduct."

Uh-oh. But I wasn't surprised by this, either. I had heard from Maggie about her ex and his students. "Was it Beth?" I asked. "Or Shelley?" Or both? I wouldn't put it past him.

"It was Shelley. Beth said he was 'hitting on her' all during the trip." She gave a small smile. "I had to ask her what that meant, and I was truly saddened — and shocked, too, I'm afraid — by what she told me. Shelley wasn't having anything to do with it, Beth said, but Dr. Fairlee wouldn't take no for an answer." She pulled down her mouth. "This is so hard for me to understand. In my day, you know, professors were gentlemen. They didn't behave like that."

Or if they did, I thought, nobody knew, because the women were afraid that if they told, nobody would believe them. That was long before #MeToo and public accusations in social media. And before colleges and universities became wary of lawsuits by young women like Shelley against lecherous professors like Carl Fairlee.

But I was puzzled, and perhaps just a little impatient with this detour the conversation had taken. "Are we on a different subject? We're talking about Shelley's death, and Beth, and I'm wondering what this might have to do with your current renter."

"Engage!" Spock squawked, and flung himself onto his trapeze, where he swung violently back and forth. "Engage! Engage!"

Mrs. Birkett seemed to be turning something over in her mind, feeling its weight, seeing it from different angles. "It's odd, you know," she said at last, reaching for a third egg. "Just very odd."

"What's odd?" I asked. "In what way?"

Mrs. Birkett wiped her hands on her blue apron. "Well, when my student renters moved out at the end of the spring semester, I ran an ad in the *Enterprise.* I usually rent the cottage just for June, July, and August, to girls who are here for summer school. So I was a bit surprised when I got a call from a middle-aged lady, a nurse who is filling a temporary position in the ER, over at the hospital. She said she planned to work in Pecan Springs only through the end of the year." She took a fourth egg out and closed the carton. "She didn't like apartments, and she had driven by the cottage and thought it looked very comfy — 'homey' was her word. She said her job was terribly stressful and she would be working odd shifts, so she wanted to live away from people, someplace where it was quiet and she didn't have to cope with a lot of neighbors. She especially liked the idea of living at the end of a street, at the edge of a woods. When I met her, I liked her." Glancing at me, she said, "You've met her too, China."

"I have?"

"Yes. When I told her I planned to attend your vanilla workshop, she was very interested. She asked if she could go with me. In fact, she was sitting right beside me at the workshop. She's the one who asked about vanilla's medicinal uses. Her name is Karen Taylor."

"Fascinating," Spock said.

"Oh, sure," I said, remembering. "As a matter of fact, I saw Karen yesterday, too. She came to the tea room for lunch. She said that her house has a greenhouse window in the kitchen —"

"It does," Mrs. Birkett said, and separated the last egg into the two dishes.

"— and that she was interested in getting a vanilla plant. So I sent her out to Sonora." I cocked my head. "Why is this 'odd,' Mrs. Birkett?"

"Because," the old lady said, "Karen Taylor is Shelley Harmon's mother." She finished separating the egg, picked up all the shells, and tossed them into the trash bin under the sink.

"Shelley's . . . *mother*?" I looked up sharply, as startled as if I'd been slapped.

"But why in the world —" I broke off, trying to make sense of this, then tried again. "I mean, I guess I can understand why Shelley's mom might want to stay in the cottage, for sentimental reasons —"

I stopped again. Actually, I didn't understand this at all. What was going on here? I settled for two rather lame questions. "Did she *tell* you that? When did you find out?"

Mrs. Birkett added a couple of tablespoons of sugar to the egg yolks, and began to beat them with the rotary beater. Spock cackled and started to make a whirring clatter that sounded remarkably like the beater.

Mrs. Birkett raised her voice. "No, she didn't tell me. I had to figure it out for myself."

I frowned. "So how *did* you find out?"

"By accident." She turned the beater handle rapidly for several moments, then stopped to add a couple of dollops of cream and a teaspoon of vanilla extract. "The water heater in the cottage had been leaking, and I ordered a replacement. Karen was at work the day the plumber brought the new heater, so I went next door to show him where it had to go. The heater is in a closet off the hallway, and Karen's bedroom door was open." She set the bowl of egg yolks aside and went to the sink to rinse off the beater. Over her shoulder, she said, "On the dresser, there was an altar to Shelley."

Another surprise. "An . . . altar?"

She came back to the table, put the clean beater into the bowl of egg whites, and began beating them, hard. Over the whirr of the beater and Spock's imitation of it, she said, "Well, I don't know what else to call it. A shrine, maybe? There were a half-dozen photos of Shelley — some taken when she was just a little girl, others as she grew older. There were a couple of small stuffed animals, a little doll and some child's jewelry, several candles, an incense burner." She stopped beating, turned the bowl and scraped it, then started beating again.

"Sounds like she deliberately kept it from you," I said thoughtfully. "That she is Shelley's mother. I wonder why."

"I wondered, too," Mrs. Birkett said. "That evening when she got off work, I went next door and told her what I had seen. At first she accused me of snooping, but when I pointed out that the rental agreement allows me to come in at any time to make repairs, she backed off. That's when she said, yes, she was Shelley's mom. She was afraid I'd think it wasn't a good idea, moving into the house where her daughter had lived, and that I maybe wouldn't rent to her.

She was hoping that living in the cottage might make her feel better — bring her some closure, maybe."

"I suppose that makes a certain kind of sense," I said slowly. "Still . . ."

"I know," Mrs. Birkett said, frowning. "It does, and it doesn't. Shelley has been dead for several years. Why now? And why —" She lifted the egg beater and the whites stood up in stiff, glossy peaks. "There's more, you see."

"More?"

She began folding the pale, creamy egg yolks into the stiffly beaten whites, blending them in carefully. "Well, something about Karen made me very . . . uncomfortable. I don't know what — her intensity, or perhaps a certain . . . imbalance. I'm sorry. I ought to be able to find a better way to describe it. But maybe if I tell you . . ." She turned to the stove, dropped butter into an omelet pan, and turned on the gas flame.

"Tell me . . . what?" I prompted, now very curious.

"You're going to think I'm terribly snoopy."

"Probably." I chuckled. "You're not going to tell me that you went poking around in Karen's house, are you? Looking through her dresser drawers? Reading her mail?"

388

"No, not that." She swirled the melting butter in the pan. "But I *did* start keeping a closer eye on her. So when I saw —" The butter was turning brown and sizzling softly. She picked up the bowl of blended eggs and cream and tipped it into the skillet.

I couldn't help myself. "When you saw . . ."

She set the empty bowl down. "When I saw her going into the storm cellar several times, late one night." She wrapped a potholder around the handle of the pan and picked it up, tilting and turning it so that the egg mixture evenly covered the bottom. "I began to wonder."

I blinked. "Storm . . . cellar?"

"That's what folks called it when I was a girl. I think they call it a storm shelter these days. Anyway, years ago, a tornado tore through Pecan Springs. It did quite a bit of damage and killed several people. Grandma Jane decided that she needed a place to go if a tornado was coming, so she hired a man to build it for her. They put it in the back-yard of the cottage, out by the fence. It's made of cement blocks, about six feet by six feet inside, half-buried in the ground, with dirt piled over the top. Grandma planted a honeysuckle on it, which has gotten quite large by now, so the cellar is pretty well covered up. And I planted some nandina bushes in front of the door, for a screen. If you didn't know it was there, you might not even notice it."

With a spatula, she began lifting the cooked portions of the omelet, tilting the pan so that the uncooked eggs could flow out toward the edges. Taking a breath, she went on with her story.

"To start with, the cellar had a wooden door. But it rotted out a few years ago, and I had it replaced with a metal door with a swivel handle. It's so heavy that I can barely lift it, but that doesn't matter because I haven't had to use it for years."

Leaving the omelet where it was for a moment, she reached for the platter of bacon keeping warm on the back of the stove. She put it on the table, along with a plate containing two plump, warm cinnamon rolls laced with vanilla icing.

"I always point it out when somebody rents the cottage," she went on. "I show them where it is, in case of a storm. But none of them have ever had to use it, either. Until —"

She picked up the skillet, shook it several times to loosen the eggs, then folded the omelet and slid it out of the skillet into a warm dish. It was puffy and a lovely golden brown. She cut it in half, put half on my plate and half on hers, and added sprigs of mint for a garnish.

"Help yourself to the strawberries," she instructed. "And the bacon and cinnamon buns."

"Where's mine?" Spock asked imperatively. "I want mine, mine, mine!"

"Later," Mrs. Birkett told him. To me, she said, "Are you ready for more coffee, China? How about orange juice?"

"I can help myself when I'm ready," I said. "Come and sit down." She took a chair on the other side of the table. There was a moment's silence while we spooned strawberries over our omelets and began to eat.

"This is delicious," I murmured appreciatively. "The vanilla is a perfect addition!" But I was anxious to hear the rest of her story, so I reminded her of what she had said. "None of your tenants have ever used the storm cellar until . . . ?"

"Until Karen Taylor," she said, picking up her fork. "I was gone for a couple of days last week, visiting my sister in Fredericksburg. It was late in the evening when I got back, just before dark. I had just come into the house and I hadn't yet turned on the lights, so I'm sure Karen didn't know I'd gotten home. I came straight back here to the kitchen, to check on Mr. Spock." She ate a bite of omelet, closed her eyes, and said, "This *is* really good, isn't it? The strawberries could maybe use another splash of Cointreau, though. Just a teensy bit more orange, do you think?"

"No, I don't," I said firmly. "It's perfect just as it is. So you came back here to the kitchen and —"

"And I happened to glance out the window. Karen was walking across the back yard to the storm cellar, carrying an arm-load of bedding. Blankets, a pillow. It looked like she was planning to *sleep* out there."

I frowned. "Were there any storm warm-ings?"

Mrs. Birkett shook her head. "No, the weather was perfect. She took the bedding down into the cellar, then went back to the cottage. I was curious, so I kept watching. A few moments later, she made another trip, this time carrying a cardboard box. By the time she made her third trip, it was so dark that she had to use a flashlight, so I couldn't see what she was carrying." She looked down at my plate, then up at me. "How is the cinnamon bun?"

"Couldn't be better," I said, and picked up a slice of bacon. It was dry and crunchy, just-right finger food. "So is the bacon. So is the omelet and the orange juice and the coffee." Without pausing, I added, "So. You were curious. Did you go out to see what she was up to?"

"I'm afraid I did." She hunched her shoulders, half-apologetically. "She had the Sunday morning shift at the hospital. I waited until I heard her leave for work and went out for a look. But I couldn't get in. She's installed a padlock on the cellar door."

"A padlock?"

"Highly illogical," Spock said disapprovingly. He gave a long, low wolf whistle. "Astrological, psychological, pathological."

"It's not a very big padlock," she said. "I thought of breaking it open. And then I thought maybe she had hidden the key someplace close by — under a rock, maybe. But if she did, I couldn't find it."

"And the cellar is in the cottage yard?"

"Yes, but the rental agreement says that we share it." She finished her omelet and reached for her coffee. "Should I ask her to take the lock off? I don't feel comfortable telling her that I saw her taking the bedding and other things into the cellar, though. She might think I'm just a nosy old woman who deliberately spies on her tenants. On the other hand —" She made a face. "On the other hand, I *am* a nosy old woman, and

I'm not very happy about that lock. If there's a storm, I want to be able to get into the shelter."

"Of course you do," I said. "And there are other issues. What if she's keeping guns down there? Or explosives?" At the look on her face, I said, "I know, I know. She probably isn't hiding guns." I reached for a coffee refill and offered her one, which she declined.

"Well, here's the thing," I said. "According to Texas law, a landlord has to change or re-key the locks on exterior doors when a new tenant moves in, and has to repair or replace any defective lock. But unless the rental agreement states otherwise, the law specifically says that tenants are *not* allowed to remove, change, replace, or re-key any locks without the landlord's permission. And Texas judges aren't very sympathetic to tenants who lock out the landlord. I think you should give her a written notice saying that she has to remove that padlock immediately."

"Set phasers to stun," Spock ordered, bobbing his head. "Engage!"

"Oh. I didn't know about that law," she said, looking relieved. "That's wonderful. To tell the truth, China, I've gotten myself into such a state that I'll be glad when

394

December comes and Karen moves out. She's a temp at the hospital, which means that she often works the night shift. Her garage is right next to my bedroom window, and that little green bug of hers is terribly noisy. When she comes and goes in the middle of the night, she wakes me up, and it's hard for me to —"

"Engage!" Spock commanded. "Make it so."

"Wait." I held up my hand. "What did you say?"

Mrs. Birkett frowned. "I said I usually can't get back to sleep. I have to get up and get a glass of milk and —"

"No, not that. You said something like 'that little green bug of hers'?"

"We are the Borg," Spock said in a threatening tone. "Resistance is futile."

"Oh, yes. She has a Beetle, you know. Those little things are really cute, and I'm sure she gets terrific gas mileage. But it makes a kind of whistling noise which is really loud when she presses the accelerator. I asked her about it, and she said she backed into a tree and pinched the end of the muffler, or something like that. She promised to get it fixed, but so far —"

"It's *green*?"

"Yes. It's rather cute. I'll bet it's the only

one in town." She picked up her coffee cup. "In fact, you can see it, if you want to. She must have worked a night shift at the hospital, because she got home around three a.m. She's probably still sleeping. If you want to see it, just go outside and look through the garage window —"

I took a deep breath. "Do you have a crowbar or a claw hammer handy?"

She blinked at me. "A hammer, in the toolbox under the sink. But why —"

I stood up, went to the sink, and found what I was looking for. When Mrs. Birkett pushed back her chair, I shook my head.

"Stay put," I said gruffly. "No arguments. I'm going out there." I didn't know what might happen, and I didn't want to have to worry about her.

"Boldly go," said Spock, with a loud cackle.

Mrs. Birkett's eyes widened as I went to the door. "China, what in the world —"

"I'm just going to do a little breaking and entering," I said. "I have your permission?"

"I don't understand this one bit," she said with a frown. "But I suppose, if you think —"

"Warp speed," Spock called, as I went out the door. "Engage!"

I found the storm shelter in the far corner

of the cottage yard, behind a dense screen of nandina bushes and under a tangle of honeysuckle. Karen Taylor's padlock had a long shackle, making it more vulnerable to attack. I stuck the hammer's claw into the shackle, gave a quick, sharp yank, and the lock sprang open.

I lifted the heavy metal door, and morning sunlight cascaded down the steep steps, brightening the darkness below. I heard a faint whimper.

"Chelsea?" I cried. "Chelsea?"

But I was already halfway down the steps — and reaching for my cell phone.

CHAPTER FIFTEEN

The problem with vanilla beans is that once they are ripe on the vine they are easy to pick, and hence to steal. They grow on supporting trees in forest plantations where it is difficult to guard every vine. In a subsistence economy where even $15 is worth having, desperate thieves are prepared to kill for vanilla.

Vanilla: Travels in Search of the Luscious Substance
Tim Ecott

Violent thefts of the highly valued crops have hit such a level that locals are calling for armed police guards. But many Madagascans are taking matters into their own hands. "We are constantly on the alert," says Dominique Rakotoson, producer and manager of an export company in Madagascar, who was robbed in 2017. "Many of us sleep in the middle of the plantations to monitor our crops. Last week, a man tried to steal plants in our area . . . he was stoned to death."

"People trust only the people's justice," explains Georges Geeraerts, president of the Group of Vanilla Exporters from Madagascar.

"Crisis in Madagascar As Price of
Vanilla Nears That of Gold"
http://www.france24.com/en/20180420-
magagascar-vanilla-price-trade-
crime-crop-weather

It took less than thirty seconds to tell Sheila that I had found Chelsea, alive; that the green VW she was looking for was parked in a garage at the end of Crockett; and that Karen Taylor, the woman who had kidnapped the child, was most likely still asleep in the cottage she rented from Mrs. Birkett.

I could hear Sheila's quick intake of breath. "On my way," she said, and clicked off.

Chelsea, still in her pink pajamas, was huddled under a blanket on the floor of the storm shelter, bewildered and a little woozy from the effects of the drug. "Hi, sweetheart," I whispered, not wanting to make her more frightened. "It's Ms. Bayles. Caitie's mom. How about we get you out of here, huh?"

"Oh, please!" she cried, holding her arms out. "Please!"

I caught her up, wrapped the blanket around her slight body, and ran with her to Mrs. Birkett's kitchen.

"What in the world —" Mrs. Birkett cried when I pushed through the door. "Who is this child? Where did you find her? How did she —"

"This is Dr. Fairlee's daughter, Chelsea." I sat down in a chair with the little girl on my lap, holding her close, feeling her shivering against me. "Karen Taylor abducted her from her bedroom last night." I patted Chelsea's face, watching her eyes open and focus on me. "She was in the storm shelter."

"The shelter?" Mrs. Birkett gasped. "Karen *abducted* her? But why —"

"Long story," I said, smoothing the hair back from the little girl's face. "I've called the police. They're on their way right now. EMS, too. They may want to take Chelsea to the hospital for a checkup."

"I'm a doctor, not a mechanic," Spock said reprovingly.

"Where's my mom?" Chelsea whispered. Her face was dirty and streaked with tears. "I was so scared when I woke up in the dark and I wasn't in my bed!"

I dropped a kiss on her forehead. "Your mom's at home, waiting for you. Tell you what, sweetie. Let's call her right now and let her know you're safe. She's been so worried. I know she'll be happy to hear your voice."

I got Maggie on the phone and gave it to Chelsea. "Mom," she said. "Mom, I'm okay. Ms. Bayles found me, and I'm with her right now. Please come and get me as soon as you can. I want to go home!"

When I got the phone back, I said, "She's been very brave, Mags, and I think she's really okay. But EMS is coming to check her out, just to be on the safe side. If there are cops at your house still, maybe one of them can bring you? We're on Crockett Street, at the end." I gave her Mrs. Birkett's house number.

"Oh, China, I can't thank you enough for rescuing her." Maggie grabbed a deep breath. "I'll be there in ten minutes. No, make that five! I'm out of here as soon as I find my shoes!"

"I canna change the laws of physics," Spock observed wisely.

"He talks!" Chelsea's eyes widened and she turned to look at the parrot. "Did you hear that? He sounds just like a person!"

"Fascinating," Spock replied, and did a

couple of 360-degree windmill spins on his perch.

"Funny bird," Chelsea said, and her smile warmed my heart.

"Funny bird," Spock agreed and, obviously pleased with himself, did several more windmills.

I put Chelsea on Mrs. Birkett's lap and got her a glass of orange juice to sip. Then I looked out the kitchen window, checking the cottage windows facing Mrs. Birkett's house. As far as I could tell, there was no sign of movement inside, and no lights burning. Karen had probably been up most of the night. Maybe she was asleep.

There was a loud knock at the front door and I went to answer it, leading the uniformed policewoman into the kitchen. "Are we all okay here, folks?" she asked, glancing around.

"We're great," I said, and gestured to Chelsea on Mrs. Birkett's lap. "This is our girl."

"Wonderful," the officer said with a smile. To Chelsea, she said, "You feeling okay, honey? Are you hurt anywhere?"

Chelsea shook her head. "I'm just waiting for my mom to come and get me."

The officer spoke into the mike on her shoulder. "Child appears uninjured, condition good. All secure here."

"Make it so," Spock said, and did another windmill.

I went out on the front porch. Sheila and Detective Miller had arrived — silently, with no sirens or lights — and were standing beside the car, out of sight of the cottage. The cul-de-sac was already barricaded by a couple of police cars. More were pulling up the end of the block, and cops were spilling out. The neighbors were beginning to realize that something unusual was happening. Across the street, a man had come out on a porch, and I could see others watching from their living room windows.

I waved at Sheila and caught her eye. I saw her pull her cell phone out of her pocket and a moment later, my cell rang. "Do you know if the suspect is awake and moving around inside that house?" she asked without preamble. "Any idea whether she's armed?"

"If she's up and about, there's no sign of it," I said. "I just checked the windows, and they're all dark. Don't know if she's armed." If she had killed Fairlee, as now seemed likely, she had left that gun at the crime scene. Did she have another?

"Thanks. There's a back door? Side doors?"

"A back door." I had seen it when I ran to the storm shelter. "No door on this side. I don't know about the other side, but I doubt it."

"Good. I'm sending a couple of guys around the back. Miller is going in the front, with somebody else."

"Not *you,* I hope," I said, thinking about the baby.

Sheila muttered something under her breath. At that moment, an EMS ambulance pulled up and a couple of med techs got out. Sheila signaled to them and pointed to the porch where I was standing. They hurried in my direction, one of them carrying a satchel.

"Chelsea's in the kitchen." I held the front door open for them. With a smile, I added, "I don't think you'll need to bring the gurney." I was about to follow them inside when I saw Maggie, jumping out of another police car and flying up the front path. She was barefoot.

"Couldn't locate your shoes?" I asked.

"Doesn't matter," she cried breathlessly. "Where is she? Where's my baby?"

"In the kitchen," I said, and opened the front door again. Spock was shouting, "We are the Borg! Resistance is futile!"

Maggie hesitated. "Never mind Spock," I

said hurriedly. "He's just a big-mouth parrot." I was about to follow her into the house when I was stopped again.

"China! China Bayles!" I turned to see Jessica Nelson, sprinting up the path to the porch, her reporter's notebook in her hand.

"Those red heels are gorgeous," I said as she dashed up the steps, "but how you can run in them is beyond me."

"China!" she said breathlessly. "Is it true that *you* found the little girl? Where was she? How did you find her? Who took her? Why? Is she okay? I want to talk to her. The chief gave me full access."

"Hey, whoa," I said, holding up my hand. "She's with her mom and an officer and the EMS techs. And Mrs. Birkett." From the kitchen came a loud, excited "Stand by for our transmission!"

"And the parrot," I added. "His name is Spock."

"She canna take nae more, Captain!" Spock cried, in a perfect imitation of Scotty. "She's goin' ta blow!"

"Parrot?" Jessica blinked. "What parrot?"

"Actually, I don't think you'd better try to interview the parrot right now," I said. "The kitchen is a crowd scene. But maybe I can tell you about him. What would you like to know?"

"Screw the damn parrot," Jessica snapped. "I want to know about the girl. And the kidnapper. I am interested in the *story.*"

"He's a pretty smart parrot," I said. "His name is Spock. He's a Trekkie. And he made Chelsea smile, which is pretty good story material. I suggest —"

At that moment, over Jessica's shoulder, I saw two officers armed with long guns moving swiftly toward the cottage, then splitting up to take opposite ways around to the back. At the same time, Detective Miller and another male officer, wearing body armor and carrying handguns, were headed for the front stoop. The cottage was set back from the street, so the front door was clearly visible from our vantage point on the porch.

"Looks like they're getting ready to go in," I said, and Jessica whirled around to watch.

If this were a scene in a James Patterson shoot-'em-up thriller, the front door of the cottage would have slammed open right about now. The villain would have rushed out, wild-eyed and disheveled, a gun in each hand, maniacally blasting at anybody who stood in her way. In another moment, she would have been dead. Suicide by cop.

If that's what you were expecting, I'm afraid you're going to be disappointed. This isn't a Patterson thriller. What happened was . . . well, more like real life than a novel.

Detective Miller shouted "Police! Open up!" and knocked loudly at the front door. When there was no immediate answer, he shouted and banged hard on the door with the flat of his hand. After a moment, he raised his hand to do it once more.

But the door opened. Karen Taylor stood there in blue striped pajamas and furry green slippers.

"Yes?" she said, knuckling the sleep out of her eyes.

"Karen Taylor?" Miller asked.

"Yes." She peered past him at the official vehicles crowding the street.

"Ma'am, you are under arrest for the kidnapping of Chelsea Fairlee." He turned her around and handcuffed her. "You have the right to remain silent. Anything you say can and will be used against you in a court of law. You have the right to an attorney. If you cannot afford an attorney, one will be provided for you. Do you understand?"

"Yes," she said, and her shoulders slumped.

In the kitchen, Spock had the last word. "Beam us up, Scotty. No intelligent life here."

It took several hours to wrap everything up,

dictate my statement to Detective Miller at the police station, and sit for an interview with Jessica Nelson, filling in some of the background details for the story she was writing for the next day's edition of the *Enterprise.* As it turned out, she knew some things I didn't about Carl Fairlee's orchid-laundering scheme, which was part of an investigation she'd been pursuing for several months. By the time we finished, both of us had a pretty comprehensive idea of what had gone down.

But it was nearly one-thirty in the afternoon before I finally got to the shop, where Ruby, bouncing from one foot to the other, met me with a barrage of excited questions.

"Is the little girl going to be okay? Why was she kidnapped? Who did it? Did you catch him? What was it all about, China?"

"Hey," I said. "I'm pretty wrung out after all the excitement and I haven't had any lunch yet. I'm starving."

So Ruby put Laurel in charge of both our shops, took me into the deserted tea room, and made me sit down at a table while she brought me a cup of Cass' tortilla soup, a croissant stuffed with chicken salad, and a big glass of hibiscus iced tea.

As I attacked my soup, Ruby took a seat across from me and poured a glass of tea for herself. Flipping her fringed magenta silk scarf over her shoulder, she said, "I was opening for business this morning when I saw the cop cars and the ambulance going past. I ran out to see what was going on, but of course, I had no way of knowing it was *you*. Or that you were rescuing a little girl and capturing a diabolical criminal. But an hour or so later, one of Mrs. Birkett's neighbors came in and told us what happened. She got the whole story from Mrs. Birkett, who said you were a *hero*."

"That's pretty silly," I replied, tipping the cup to get the last of the soup. "All I did was break open a padlock. And I didn't capture anybody. I called Sheila, and she and her cops did the rest." I licked the spoon and pushed the cup away.

Ruby tilted her head, frowning. "So you're not a hero after all? What happened? Is the little girl okay? Was there any shooting? Did anybody get hurt?"

I began on my croissant. Between mouthfuls, I said, "Chelsea is fine and back home with her mom. There wasn't any shooting, thankfully. The police went to the front door and knocked. The kidnapper opened the door and was arrested and hustled off to jail — in her pajamas. She's been charged with kidnapping and child endangerment.

409

The murder charge will be added later."

Ruby was taken aback. "*Murder?* You're saying that she's the one who —"

"Who killed Carl Fairlee." I finished my tea. "Remember Shelley Harmon, who used to work for us? And the woman who came to our vanilla workshop with Mrs. Birkett — the nurse?"

"Of course I remember Shelley. I think about her often, and wonder how she died." Ruby picked up the pitcher and refilled my glass. "What does Shelley have to do with any of this? And the nurse? How is she involved?"

"Well, it turns out that the nurse — Karen Taylor — is Shelley Harmon's mother. She was renting Mrs. Birkett's cottage, where Shelley used to live."

Ruby frowned. "But if she was Shelley's mother, why didn't she say so? Shelley was such a sweet girl — I would have loved to have known her mom."

"She had her reasons, apparently." I knew a few more details now, after Sheila's preliminary interrogation of Karen Taylor. "She had what amounted to a nervous collapse after her daughter — her only child — was killed. Shelley's father had recently died, and it was just too much for her to take. When she recovered enough to travel, she wanted to find out how Shelley had died. She flew to Veracruz to talk to the Mexican authorities and Señor Aguado, the guide on the field trip." I took another bite of my croissant. "Then she tracked down all of the students, including Beth Craig, Shelley's roommate. Everybody she talked to said that Dr. Fairlee was warned against taking an especially dangerous route up the mountain, but he refused to listen. They ran into a roadblock that had been set up by thieves to rob trucks hauling vanilla beans. Fairlee panicked and tried to drive away. Shelley was killed when the thieves fired on the van." I paused. "She was shot in the back."

Ruby's eyes were wide. "Oh, how awful," she breathed. "Her mother must have been simply crushed when she heard that!"

"Yes, and there's something else. Beth told Shelley's mother that Fairlee was hitting on her daughter during the trip. When they got home, Shelley was going to see that he was charged with sexual assault."

"Oh, dear," Ruby said, biting her lip.

"Yes. That may have added fuel to the fire. Shelley's mother originally planned to file a wrongful death lawsuit against Dr. Fairlee. But somewhere along the line, she seems to have decided to get her revenge in a different way. She began researching Fairlee online and found out — without a lot of difficulty, apparently — that he was in the business of buying and selling orchids." I finished my croissant and wiped my fingers on my napkin. "In fact, according to Jessica Nelson, black-market orchids were the mainstay of his illicit business."

"Wait a minute. You've lost me." Ruby was looking confused. "How did Jessica Nelson get involved in this?"

"As luck would have it, Jessie has been investigating black-market orchids for a story on what she calls the 'dark side of horticulture.' Apparently, international trade in illegal plants is a booming business these days — a global black market, actually. She had the goods on Fairlee. She had identified five or six of his suppliers and a source who could prove that he was raking in thousands of dollars a month. He was growing the plants in his greenhouse at the university."

"And Shelley's mother learned all this?"

"Yes. She prowled around online, got into a couple of discussion groups, and began asking discreet questions. She found out where he liked to show his orchids and emailed some of his customers, masquerading as an orchid fancier. She also researched

412

his family and discovered that he was divorced and that he had two kids, including a young daughter. She visited a gun show, where she picked up a stolen Glock, which came with a suppressor. Then she left El Paso, where she was living, and moved to Pecan Springs. She got a job at the hospital and rented the cottage where Shelley had lived — a cottage with a storm shelter in the backyard. She created an opportunity to meet Fairlee at an orchid show in Galveston. She had come up with a list of the exotic orchids he was looking for and she somehow managed to get one of them — the 'demon orchid,' it's called. She used it to strike up a friendship with him. And then something of a romance, according to one witness, who happened to see them sharing a kiss in Karen's little green Beetle."

"The VW? Oh, that's the car that was parked in Mrs. Birkett's garage!" Ruby exclaimed.

News travels fast. "Where did you hear that?"

"From Mrs. Birkett's neighbor — the one who told us what happened this morning. She said that the car has something wrong with the muffler. It's so noisy that it annoyed everybody on the block."

I nodded. "Anyway, Karen was apparently

413

using their friendship or romance, or whatever it was, as a way of getting close to him, to learn his habits and routines. She had decided to kill Fairlee, and she was looking for the best time and place. And she wanted a method she could get away with."

"She would make it look like suicide," Ruby said.

"Exactly. And she was smart about it, too. She decided do it on a Saturday or Sunday night, in his campus greenhouse, where he wouldn't be found until sometime on Monday. She was betting that campus security would lack the necessary forensic knowledge or experience to look beyond what appeared to be obvious. She also knew that the State of Texas doesn't require that suicide victims be autopsied." I finished my croissant, pushed the plate away, and reached for my napkin.

"She might have gotten away with it, too. But as it happened, the CTSU campus security director saw some things in the crime scene that made her suspicious. She picked up the phone and called her old boss, who is now a police chief. So the PSPD was in on the investigation from the get-go, which was definitely something Karen hadn't bargained for. Sheila insisted on an autopsy and fast-tracked it through the local hospital. It showed, indisputably, that Fairlee hadn't shot himself. And while only his prints were on the gun, there was a partial print on the suppressor — *her* print, as it turned out."

"Gosh. That sort of nails it, doesn't it?

"It does. And there's another piece of evidence connecting her to the crime. She left a latent fingerprint on the inside of the terrarium containing the demon orchid. The cops found it when they took the terrarium apart to check."

"Ah," Ruby said. "So there's proof that she gave him the orchid."

"Yes, which the prosecution will use to argue intent when the case goes to trial. Karen's defense won't be able to present this as a spur-of-the-moment crime of passion. Her fingerprints were required when she applied for her nursing license years ago, in El Paso. But the partial on the suppressor was too incomplete to be read by the AFIS system, and the second print — a latent — couldn't be immediately forwarded to AFIS. In fact, she was completely under the radar in the Fairlee investigation. She might have gotten away with it if she had simply packed up and left town after Fairlee's murder — if she hadn't abducted Chelsea. *That* was a mistake."

"It does seem pretty risky," Ruby said.

"It does. But it was part of her plan from the beginning. 'A daughter for a daughter' was the way she put it to Sheila this morning, after she was arrested. 'If I couldn't have mine, I would have his.' So she went into Chelsea's bedroom, injected her with a small dose of scopolamine — just enough to make her compliant — and put her in the storm shelter."

"Scopolamine?"

"A drug that's derived from plants in the nightshade family. It has a reputation for making its victims acquiescent. Even small doses are said to make people submissive. I've read that they become so docile that they've been known to help thieves rob their homes and even empty their bank accounts. Karen learned about it when she was in Mexico. And she had access to it at the hospital, where it's used in pain relief."

"But that's crazy!" Ruby exclaimed. "We're talking about a young girl! Did this woman intend to keep Chelsea doped up like a zombie for the rest of her life?" Her hand went to her mouth. "Or did she intend to kill her, too?"

"We don't know, Ruby. The kidnapping makes no sense at all. But neither does murder. Karen's lawyer will probably go for an insanity defense. And with her medical history — for instance, her collapse after Shelley's death — he might have a pretty good case."

"Well, I suppose," Ruby replied grudgingly. "But being crazy isn't the same thing as being insane."

I had to laugh at that. "You're right. But juries can have a hard time knowing the difference." I sipped my tea. "And as I say, she might have gotten away with it if Mrs. Birkett hadn't happened to invite me for breakfast and mention, almost by accident, that the woman renting her cottage was Shelley's mother. And that she had padlocked the storm shelter after she'd stocked it with blankets and a pillow. And that she drove a green Beetle. If Mrs. Birkett had been less observant, or if she had left out any one of those details, odds are that Chelsea wouldn't be back with her mom and Karen wouldn't be in custody."

"Well, I wouldn't say it was 'by accident,' " Ruby said firmly. "*I* would say that it was the Universe at work, making sure that a criminal was brought to justice. Mrs. Birkett was meant to ask you for breakfast, so she could tell you about Shelley's mother. You were meant to hear about the padlock and the green Beetle, so you could put two and two together and come up with the identity of a murderer and a kidnapper."

I frowned. "Ruby, if the Universe really wanted to get involved, wouldn't it have been better to interfere before a man was killed and his daughter kidnapped? After the fact is a little late."

"The Universe has its methods," Ruby replied in a knowing tone. "Dr. Fairlee sounds like a sexual predator who was responsible for the death of Karen Taylor's daughter. So from that point of view —"

"Let's not go there, Ruby," I said. "Blaming the victim pulls us into an endless loop. The law doesn't allow a person to appoint herself as judge, jury, and executioner. Shelley's mother —"

Ruby was paying no attention to me. "Shelley's mother was an instrument of karmic justice. What goes around, comes around, you know. We reap what we sow. Karma." She smiled. "Don't you get it, China? It's totally logical. *You* were the essential cog in the wheel of cosmic reckoning."

I rolled my eyes. "Ruby," I said, "that is totally *illogical.*"

At that moment, through the tea room's open door, we heard the softly amused tinkle of the shop-keeper's bell.

"There, you see?" Ruby laughed and picked up the pitcher. "Annie is expressing her opinion, too. Have some more tea, China. And do stop trying to be logical. Some mysteries just cannot be explained."

AUTHOR'S NOTE

The amount of all the vanilla beans in the
world is not sufficient to flavor everything
that everyone wants to flavor with vanilla.
                    Carol McBride,
US Vanilla Category Manager, Symrise
        (Symrise is a major producer of
              flavors and fragrances)

Vanilla has an image problem.

Somewhere in its recent history, the word
became a synonym for *bland* or *generic* or
plain. Unflavored, drab, typical. No flair, no
style, no panache. The most ordinary of
ordinary things.

Wait — what? No!

"Bland" is *not* vanilla, which — in terms
of fragrance and flavor — is one of the most
complex flavorings in the world, one of the
most expensive and in the greatest demand.
There is nothing bland about its history,
either.

Vanilla is native to the tropical jungles of the state of Veracruz, Mexico, where the long, green bean–shaped fruit was wild-gathered and dried by the Totonac people, who used it chiefly as a perfume and in medicines and magical charms. In the 1400s, the Totonac were subjugated by Aztecs from the highlands to the north and incorporated into the Aztec Empire. Enchanted by the fragrance and flavor of vanilla, the Aztecs demanded that their new subjects send an annual tribute of the fruit to their capital, Tenochtitlan, where they added it to their favorite drink, *xocolatl* or chocolate: cacao beans brewed with chile peppers and sugar.

But the Aztecs didn't have long to enjoy their vanilla. In 1519, Hernando Cortez invaded Mexico, and the Spanish *conquistadores* began shipping the cured pods back to Spain, along with the other spoils of conquest: chocolate, chili peppers, silver, and gold. For the next three hundred years, Spanish-ruled Mexico held a monopoly on the production of vanilla, supplying all of Europe with the new and wildly popular flavoring. Nobody could ever get enough.

Hoping to supplement Mexican production, the Spanish tried to grow the vine in their hothouses, but it rarely bloomed and when it did, it failed to produce the enticing fruit. Disappointed people all over Europe wondered why. The answer: not enough sex. Inside the orchid blossom is a flap of tissue called the rostellum, which separates the male anther from the female stigma. It takes a particular pollinator, of a particular shape and appetite, to push the flap aside and get the job done. These pollinators are native to Central America, and without them, the Spanish were out of luck.

The French, on the other hand, lucked out. Colonists who settled the tropical island of Réunion in the 1820s began trying to grow vanilla from imported cuttings, with the same disappointing results: blooms but no fruit. That is, until 1841, when a twelve-year-old slave boy named Edmond Albius picked up a bamboo sliver and used it to marry the male and female parts of the orchid blossom.

Voila! Vanilla!

This was the start of something big, for the climate was right and there were plenty of enslaved natives who could be taught Edmond's sexy little trick. The French plantations soon flourished, yielding ever increasing amounts of vanilla in an effort to satisfy the world's increasing appetite for this exotically fragrant flavoring. Vanilla plantations spread to other French colonies within about twenty-five degrees of the equator, the orchid's preferred habitat. Madagascar and Tahiti joined Mexico as dominant growers and producers. Vanilla was becoming big business.

But it was quickly clear that there wasn't ever going to be enough vanilla-bean vanilla to go around. The next big event in vanilla's history was the development of synthetic vanilla, a process that began in 1858 in Germany, with the isolation of the vanillin molecule, vanilla's chief active flavoring principle. In 1875, this discovery led to the production of vanillin from the sap of spruce trees. By the end of the century, vanillin was also being produced from clove oil; in the 1930s, from lignin, a by-product of the paper-making industry; and more recently, from rice bran and from a beech-wood derivative, guaiacol.

Synthetic vanilla, however, contains *only* vanillin. In contrast, vanilla produced from the vanilla bean contains more than 250 organic components, giving it a much richer flavor and bouquet — when it is properly cured. But production conditions are not well controlled in many developing countries, so it is unfortunately easy for poor-quality beans to flood the market. When that happens, synthetic vanillin may actually be preferable. And because it is so much cheaper, its production and sale far outstrips that of vanilla-bean vanilla. Sixteen thousand metric tons of synthetic vanillin are sold annually, compared to only 40 metric tons of the real thing. It's used in everything from (literally) soup to nuts.

So please don't turn up your nose at the synthetic stuff just because it's cheap. While natural vanilla enjoys a gourmet cachet, synthetic vanilla has its practical uses. In 2009, the magazine *Cook's Illustrated* conducted an extensive series of taste tests to see whether anybody could tell the difference between synthetic vanilla extract and "pure" vanilla extract (that is, vanilla-bean vanilla) in prepared foods. The bottom line: most people couldn't, especially in baked goods and highly flavored foods.

The taste testers concluded that vanilla-bean vanilla is a more flavorful choice in cold and creamy desserts and where the taste and fragrance of vanilla is intended to dominate. Synthetic vanilla is a satisfactory choice for foods with competing flavors (like chocolate or spices) or foods baked at high temperatures. (Flavor and fragrance begin to degrade around 280–300 degrees Fahrenheit.) Professional pastry chefs reported that they used the cheaper synthetic for oven baking and saved their vanilla-bean extract for confections made with moderate or no heat.

In my pantry, you will find a small (six-month) supply of vanilla beans, tightly wrapped in plastic wrap and stored in a lidded glass jar. These are pricey, so I use them carefully, where I'll get the most taste and fragrance from them. You'll also find several different kinds of home-crafted vanilla-bean products that I make and use for cooking and baking: vanilla extract, vanilla sugar and salt, vanilla paste, and vanilla syrup. (For recipes for these pantry items, see "Wonderful Things to Do with Vanilla Beans," below.) You will also find several bottles of synthetic vanilla, of different brands. These change from time to time, as I experiment with what's available.

If you want to learn more about vanilla, here are two books you'll want to read: Tim Ecott's *Vanilla: Travels in Search of the Luscious Substance,* and *Vanilla: The Cultural History of the World's Favorite Flavor and Fragrance,* by Patricia Rain. Rain also maintains an informative website, with the latest updates on vanilla availability: **www .vanillaqueen.com.** You can find the report of the *Cook's Illustrated* taste test online at **www.cooksillustrated.com/taste_tests/455-vanilla-extract.**

And if you're hungry for interesting, unique vanilla recipes, take a look at *Vanilla Table: The Essence of Exquisite Cooking from the World's Best Chefs,* by Natasha MacAller; *Vanilla: Cooking with One of the World's Finest Ingredients,* by Janet Sawyer; or Patricia Rain's *The Vanilla Chef Cookbook.*

And now that you've read and thought about all this, I hope you'll never again take *plain vanilla* for granted!

Susan Wittig Albert
Bertram, Texas

WONDERFUL THINGS TO DO WITH THE ICE CREAM ORCHID

VANILLA EXTRACT
3–5 vanilla beans
8 ounces vodka, rum, or brandy

Split the beans and chop into chunks. Put them into a lidded jar and add your choice of alcohol. (Vodka is neutral. My personal preference: brandy.) Screw on the lid, put it on a dark shelf, and give it a good shake from time to time. Use when its flavor suits you. Add more beans and bean scraps and top off the jar with alcohol for an infinite supply.

VANILLA SUGAR
2 cups granulated sugar (extra-fine, if you
   have it, or confectioners' sugar)
Vanilla bean, split lengthwise, or bean
   scraps

Put the sugar in a lidded jar. Bury the bean

in the sugar. Cover and shake. Store at room temperature.

VANILLA SALT

1/4 cup salt
1 vanilla bean

You might want to use a gourmet salt for this: a good sea salt, Maldon salt, or Fleur de Sel (which is slightly moist). Split the bean and scrape the seeds into the salt. Mix well. Store in a tightly lidded glass jar on a dark shelf. An excellent finishing salt for seafood, mild-flavored vegetables, eggs. Add the bean to your vanilla extract or vanilla sugar jar. (You don't know about Maldon salt? Read this *Bon Appetit* post: http://www
.bonappetit.com/story/history-of-maldon
-salt.)

VANILLA PASTE

6 whole vanilla beans
1 tablespoon vanilla extract
1/2 cup honey, agave nectar, or simple
  syrup

Cut the vanilla beans into 1-inch pieces. Purée the beans, extract, and honey (or agave nectar or simple syrup) in a food processor. Strain through a sieve, pressing to extract all of the syrupy fluid. Store in a tightly lidded glass jar on a dark shelf. In recipes, substitute one-to-one for vanilla extract or 1 tablespoon of paste for 1 whole bean. Add the strained solids to your vanilla extract jar.

To make simple syrup. Measure 1/2 cup water and 1/2 cup sugar into a small saucepan over medium-high heat. Stir to dissolve the sugar and bring the liquid to a boil for a minute. Cool. Use 1/2 cup for this recipe.

VANILLA POWDER
4 whole vanilla beans

Preheat oven to 350° F. Slice vanilla beans lengthwise (do not scrape out the seeds) and place on a baking sheet lined with parchment paper or foil. Roast for 4–5 minutes in a fan or convection oven, a minute longer without the fan. The beans may still be soft but will harden when cool. Cool completely. Slice each bean into 1-inch chunks. Place in a coffee or spice grinder and pulverize. Store in a tightly lidded glass jar on a dark shelf. In recipes, use 1/2 teaspoon powder for 1 teaspoon vanilla extract or paste.

VANILLA SYRUP

2 cups water
1 1/2 cups granulated sugar
1/2 cup packed light brown sugar
1 vanilla bean, split in half
2 teaspoons vanilla extract

In a medium saucepan over medium-high heat, mix water and sugar. Bring to a boil, reduce heat, and simmer until the sugar is completely dissolved. Remove from heat and add split vanilla bean and vanilla extract. Cool. Remove the vanilla bean and pour into a lidded glass jar. Refrigerate. Add bean to your vanilla extract or vanilla sugar jar.

VANILLA BUTTER

1 stick butter, softened
1 vanilla bean

Put the butter into a bowl and stir with a fork. Split the vanilla bean, scrape out the seeds, and add the seeds to the butter. Stir to mix well. Cover and refrigerate or freeze. If you wish, you may sweeten to taste. Add bean to your vanilla extract or vanilla sugar jar.

VANILLA WHIPPED CREAM
1 vanilla bean
1/2 pint heavy whipping cream
1 tablespoon vanilla sugar

Split the bean and scrape out the seeds. Pour the cold whipping cream into a cold bowl. Beat with an electric mixer on medium high or by hand with a whisk, adding the sugar and seeds slowly. Beat until soft peaks form. Refrigerate.

VANILLA VINEGAR
1 pint good-quality rice wine vinegar
1 vanilla bean

Cut the bean in half, lengthwise and crosswise. Put the pieces into a clean pint bottle and fill with vinegar. Cover and store on a dark shelf, shaking every few days. Best after 3–4 weeks, the longer the better. Use in dressings, vinaigrettes, fruit and vegetable salads, and sauces.

HOW TO STORE VANILLA BEANS
Wrap the beans tightly in plastic wrap and store in a lidded glass jar on a dark shelf. Or split the beans in the middle (crosswise) and place them upright in a jar containing about a half-inch of vodka (flavorless) or brandy or rum (complementary flavors).

Cover the jar tightly and refrigerate. After a couple of weeks, the alcohol will have wicked up into the bean, turning the seeds into a paste. Instead of splitting the bean and scraping the seeds out, you can simply squeeze them out, as if you were squeezing a toothpaste tube. Add bean to your vanilla extract or vanilla sugar jar.

HOW TO REHYDRATE DRIED VANILLA BEANS

Place the dried beans (broken or whole) in a shallow dish. Cover with hot (but not boiling) water. Cover the dish with plastic wrap. Rehydrate until the beans become plump and bendable.

ABOUT THE AUTHOR

Susan Wittig Albert is the *New York Times* bestselling author of more than one hundred books. Her work includes four mystery series: China Bayles, the Darling Dahlias, the Cottage Tales of Beatrix Potter, and the Robin Paige Victorian mysteries. She has published three award-winning historical novels, as well as young adult fiction, memoirs, and nonfictions. Susan currently serves as an editor of Story Circle Book Reviews and helps to coordinate SCN's online class program. She and her husband, Bill, live in the Texas Hill Country, where she writes, gardens, and raises a varying assortment of barnyard creatures.

LM